C0-DVV-827

The Hidden Fairing

Twentieth Century Scottish Women's Fiction
*Series Editor: Anne McManus Scriven,*
*Centre for Scottish Cultural Studies,*
*University of Strathclyde'*

# The Hidden Fairing

*N. Brysson Morrison*

with an Introduction
by Mary Seenan

Fairing : A present given at a Fair; a drubbing, desserts.
*Scots Dictionary*

Kennedy & Boyd

Kennedy & Boyd
an imprint of
Zeticula Ltd
Unit 13
196 Rose Street,
Edinburgh,
EH2 4AT
Scotland.

http://www.kennedyandboyd.co.uk
admin@kennedyandboyd.co.uk

First published in 1951
Copyright © Dr. Elizabeth Michie 2009
Introduction Copyright © Mary Seenan 2009

Cover photograph Copyright © G. Seenan 2009

ISBN 978-1-904999-77 5 Paperback

All rights reserved. No part of this publication may be
reproduced, stored in a retrieval system, or transmitted in any
form or by any means, electronic, mechanical, photocopying,
recording or otherwise, without the prior permission of the
publishers.

# Introduction

"Bartle," said the boy.
The name rose into the sphere of the monk's mind like a bird from some forgotten battleground.
"Bartle," he repeated thoughtfully, "Bartle," and felt for his pen.

When *The Hidden Fairing*[1] was first published, Nancy Brysson Morrison had already distinguished herself as a writer, with six novels and a life of Christ, in verse, to her credit. Born in Glasgow in 1903, she was the fifth child in a family of six, five of whom became published writers. She was educated at Park School in Glasgow, before spending the academic year 1919-1920 at Harvington College - previously called Heidelberg College - in London. Most of her life was spent in Scotland, where she lived at various locations in the Glasgow area, as well as at Kilmacolm and Edinburgh. She spent the last years of her life in London, where she died in 1986. Between 1930 and 1974 she produced ten novels, five biographies, three books with religious themes, and various short stories and articles. In addition, between 1939 and 1959, she also wrote romantic pot-boilers under the pseudonym Christine Strathern. Some of these were serialised in D.C. Thomson magazines such as *The People's Friend* and *The People's Journal,* and twenty seven of them were published in book form by Collins.

Following the publication of her first novel, *Breakers,* Morrison's work was praised by both writers and critics.[2] Compton Mackenzie said of *Breakers,* 'What I like about it is its atmosphere and narrative power. . . She writes like a poet.'[3] And later, in a review of *The Gowk Storm,* he reiterated this opinion saying, 'The quality of Miss Morrison's prose has something in it of Christina Rossetti's verse.'[4] The poetic nature of Morrison's prose also attracted praise from Edwin Muir. In a radio programme, broadcast on 1 December 1937, he said of her fifth novel *When the Wind Blows,* 'I find it difficult to give an idea of the rare poetic atmosphere of this novel. . . in mere poetic power she probably excels any other Scottish novelist writing today.'

In 1933 Morrison's third novel, *The Gowk Storm,* was a Book

Society Choice, and became a best-seller, thereby establishing her reputation among a wide readership.[5] Further recognition followed in 1950 when her sixth novel, *The Winnowing Years,* won the first Frederick Niven Award, a literary prize presented for the most outstanding contribution to literature by a Scottish writer published in 1949.[6] This was followed by publication of *The Hidden Fairing* which became a Book Society Recommendation and was later dramatised for radio.[7] In *The Hidden Fairing* Morrison returned to the clachan of Barnfingal and presented an alternative version of the story of the Highland dominie, Bartle MacDonald, the enigmatic character who had played a brief but significant role in *The Gowk Storm.*

Following the practice adopted in some of her earlier novels, Morrison prefaces *The Hidden Fairing* with a definition of the Scots word 'fairing'. This definition, given as '[a] present given at a Fair: a drubbing, just desserts', emphasises the word's double meaning, and I believe that this is intended to suggest that the book can also be interpreted in more than one way. Even her earlier working title for the book, *The Flowering Thorn,* with its dual association of pleasure and pain, carries similar connotations of both reward and punishment.[8] Such deliberate ambiguity is a recurrent feature of Morrison's fiction. Her prose frequently evinces a dialogic quality in which ideological complicity and subversion appear to overlay and undercut each other in such a fashion that neither can exist without the intrusion of oppositional echoes. Often this rich texture is achieved by the use of poetic imagery; at other times it is the result of the interplay of different perspectives constructed by the use of opposing ideologically-inscribed discourses. In the case of *The Hidden Fairing,* there is a particular focus on competing religious ideologies. The overall result is, I would suggest, an articulation of what Morrison saw as the complexity of Scottish experience during the period of social and cultural change in which she pursued her career as a novelist.

*The Hidden Fairing* charts the spiritual journey of Bartle MacDonald. It follows him from his childhood in a croft in the Highland clachan of Barnfingal, through his student years at Glasgow University and career as a village dominie, to his eventual transformation into the monk known as Father Bernard.

But Morrison's narrative is made more interesting than this brief summary would suggest by her handling of time. The use of a Prologue and Epilogue locates the beginning and end of the action in the period close to the time of publication – the years immediately following the Second World War. The main narrative, spanning a period of about fifty-five years, is presented as episodes in the monk's reverie, a reverie which actually only lasts for roughly the same number of minutes in 'real' time, as registered by the monastery clock. Furthermore, in the opening and closing Chapters we are confronted by the man who has become Father Bernard; in the rest of the novel we see Bartle MacDonald, the person he used to be.

As the narrative charts its circular course Bartle grows from being a likeable, if overly impressionable, little boy whose hero-worship of the wealthy Wain family from Glasgow, and his fascination with his grandmother's hidden past on the island of Wrack form his only imaginative outlets. Eventually both paths lead to the demise of Bartle, and the opportunities which seemed to be open to him, and the emergence of the cloistered Father Bernard. The Wain connection, while it opens doors for Bartle at Glasgow University, doors that enable him to shine as a mathematician, also leads to his sexual liaison with Maysie Wain. It is this episode which is regarded as his major moral lapse, and renders him liable to punishment. Maysie's haughty rejection of his love and offer of marriage turns him against the world of wealth and privilege she represents. His loyalty to Lady Wain prevents him from denying untrue accusations of paternity that actually should have been levelled at her son, Alfred, an altruistic but foolish action that ultimately deprives him of Effie MacLintock, the bride for whom he has waited. His grandmother's religious legacy also leaves an indelible, if initially unrecognised, mark on his spiritual nature. His decision to become a Roman Catholic may, at first sight, seem rash and out of place, but as one reviewer wrote: 'a second reading – which this unusual novel deserves – brings clue after clue into prominence'.[9]

When *The Hidden Fairing* was first published, C.P. Snow objected to the plot which he felt was too contrived, although he did approve of Morrison's characterisation. He said, '[She] approaches all her people with a tenacious fellow feeling, warm and yet utterly unforced or sentimental. Her truth telling in detail, in fact, is the quality which nearly lets her get away with the artificial structure.'[10] Morrison's portrayal of the young Bartle, in particular, won praise from Marion Lochhead. She wrote, 'Bartle is one of the truest and most attractive small boys in Scottish fiction (surpassed only by Neil Gunn's "Young Art") and his friendship with his Grandmother is a moving and lovely episode in his childhood.'[11]

Clearly, Morrison intended the reader to sympathise with the young Bartle, a fatherless child living in a harsh environment with a cold, resentful mother:

> Between Bartle and [Kirsty, his mother] there was a barrier of unfamiliarity although they had seen each other every day of his life. There was no taken for granted communion that customarily strings child to mother, no common ground they could share as equals. Even when he had been a baby she had not yearned over him, for she was not the yearning kind; and as he grew into a stocky little boy she treated him with a certain impatience because he was not older and could look after himself. [12]

Passages such as this encourage us to understand why the lack of any overt display of maternal affection might cause him to find a substitute, idealised mother-figure in the beneficent Lady Wain. As Father Bernard remembers his/Bartle's childhood, he recalls that his mother never made any fuss over him: 'Even the fact that it was his birthday made no difference to the days that swung by as evenly as the pendulum of the wag-at-the-wa' clock. His mother would pull down his darned jersey and ask him how old he was again'[13]. And this contrasts with the association he makes between Lady Wain and gifts: 'Lady Wain was the only person who ever gave him a present on his birthday, so that he associated presents not so much with birthdays but with Lady Wain'[14].

Sympathy is engendered, too, when he loses a finger in his attempt to free an injured vixen from a trap, and we are glad that this causes him to be rejected for military service in 1914. We are encouraged to approve of his friendship with Jamie Malcolm and his kindly treatment of Jamie's young sister, especially following Jamie's death in the trenches. We are led to approve, too, of his willingness to help Davie Thomson's wife although he knew his mother would disapprove, and we sympathise with his bewilderment with the noise and bustle of Glasgow, and the height of its tenement buildings. We might even see some merit in his refusal to tell the villagers that it was Alfred Wain, and not himself, who was the father of Rachel MacInnes's illegitimate child. Most of all, we understand his pain when he realises that he has lost Effie, and feel that his selfless act in helping Lady Wain, by protecting her son, who is likened to a fox, should have been rewarded to an even greater degree than his earlier sacrifice to save the vixen.

But from a very early stage, contradictory suggestions are allowed to creep into the characterisation. The emphasis on his second sight, which turns out to be useless as far as his own actions are concerned, marks him out as 'other', rather than someone with whom we can completely empathise. In fact, it has something of an alienating effect, a point convincingly made in the episode in which he carries on a wordless 'duel' with his teacher. Another potential reason for failing to achieve complete sympathy with Bartle's mindset stems from his idolisation of the Wain family. He labours under a false impression of their worth, and this prevents him from seeing the base reality that exists beneath the glowing exterior image he has created of them. And, to drive this fact home, the narrator interjects comments which emphasise the flawed nature of his perception:

> Sir Alfred was so busy turning everything he touched to gold in the city that he did not spend the weeks his family did at their country home. Bartle, his blunt chin wedged in his mug as he reflected upon them all, saw the brown spotted mountain trout flash into gold as Sir Alfred unhooked them from his line. [15]

Later, as Father Bernard, even he realises that his youthful enthusiasms have been misguided, and that 'the Big House probably appeared bigger at Barnfingal than it would have done anywhere else, [and that] the Wains, although well-to-do, had not the mythical wealth spun around them by the talk of the clachan'. [16]

Like Callum Lamont in Morrison's first novel, *Breakers,* Bartle is shown to have inherited characteristics from both sides of his family, characteristics that do not always sit comfortably together.

Indeed, his genetic makeup mirrors both the religious discontinuity between pre-Reformation and post-Reformation Scotland, and the divisions that still persist in the nation's religious character. From his Presbyterian mother he inherits a rationality which is translated into superior linguistic ability. Not only is he bilingual by the age of eight, but he masters Latin, studying it to degree level. His Protestant legacy is also represented by an extraordinary mathematical talent which wins him prizes at Glasgow University, and earns him the offer of a research post in what was then the prestigious new field of Atomic Physics. It could be suggested that it is also from his mother that he inherits the work ethic that enables him to resist the temptation to enjoy an active social life and devote all his attention to his studies.

In conjunction with these attributes, and in opposition to them, he inherits from his father's side of the family the Highland/Island 'gift' of the 'second sight', which, as well as enabling him to read his schoolmaster's thoughts, also foretells his friend's early death. He exhibits a strong fascination with his ancestral roots on the island of Wrack. As a little boy he is thrilled at the thought that the land of his ancestors had connections with the Vikings, for when his grandmother tells him about the discovery of the buried wreck '[s]omething tightened in Bartle like a fiddle string being strung.[17] And, although he does not at first grasp either the Marian implications of his grandmother's injunction: "'She's not my Lady but *our Lady*. Mind that, Bartle. Tell no one but mind it'"(my italics)[18], or her assertion that he is "' my son's son . . . the last of us'" [19], the full import of her words strikes him later. As a young man, on the eve of his depature to Glasgow University, he experiences a strange, visceral excitement when Mistress Stewart tells him of her suspicion that his grandmother was a Roman Catholic: 'He felt his heart becalmed with excitement, like a boat settling in the midst of a stormy sea, which contrary sensation had the effect of making him feel violently sick' [20]. Such a legacy is initially buried under the strictures of the Protestant environment in which he is reared, but, as the narrative unfolds, we see in his friendship with Father Owen and his conversion to Roman Catholicism the working out of Mistress Stewart's belief: "'[w]hat I aye say is, once a Roman Catholic, aye a Roman Catholic. As ye begin, so ye end. The wood ye die in is made of the same wood as the cradle that rocked ye'" [21]

Like many Scottish writers, Morrison's fiction often explores religious themes. In some novels, like *Breakers, The Gowk Storm* and *The Winnowing Years,* the action takes place in a manse, thereby providing the possibility of offering a critique of the social consequences of Calvinistic Presbyterianism. *When the Wind Blows* (1937) introduces Quakerism, and in both *Solitaire* (1932) and *The Strangers* (1935) the main characters, Mary, Queen of Scots and the Italian immigrant Bernardo Monti respectively, are Roman Catholics. To some readers, conversion to Roman Catholicism might seem a strange thematic focus for a Scottish Presbyterian novelist of Morrison's era to adopt. However, early notebooks, dating from around 1925, before the publication of her first novel, demonstrate that she had been interested in this subject for a long time.[22] It is my opinion that Morrison became interested in the fictional possibilities afforded by such a conversion when, as a young girl, she heard, from her aunts, details of its actual occurrence in the landed Perthshire family from whom they rented a cottage. In this instance, it was the father, the staunchly Presbyterian laird, who broke off relations with his son, and forbade his wife to have any contact with him. It was only on the father's death that the son was able to return home as a Catholic priest. In fact, the priest not only became Morrison's aunts' landlord, but he was also their neighbour for about the last thirty years of their lives.

Did this mean that Morrison, herself, was interested in Roman Catholicism as anything other than an imaginative possibility? On balance, I am inclined to think not. However, when we compare this later novel with *The Gowk Storm,* where the dominie is immediately dismissed from his post when the Elders discover that he is a Catholic, she does seem to be registering an ameliorating change in Protestant attitudes. The later Bartle MacDonald manages to keep his job at Faal. Now the blame for transferring him to Tornichon is laid at the door of the Roman Catholic Church; perhaps this reflects a Protestant antagonism towards the segregated education privileges awarded to the Catholic community. As with much of Morrison's fiction, we can never be quite sure.

Nor can we be absolutely sure about how we should interpret the novel's ending. One contemporaneous reviewer, who sensed the novel's determinist overtones, was of the opinion that '[t]he story is perhaps most reminiscent of Hardy in its central conception of an inexorable fate which uses love as the instrument of the hero's downfall'.[23] Bartle, on the other hand, believes that he has been the author of his own fate. He thinks that he has lost Effie as a punishment for his fall from grace with Maysie Wain:

> For now he knew why this calamity had befallen him. It had not fallen upon him so much as been brought about by himself. He was harvesting now the sin he had committed all those years ago with Maysie Wain. He had thought that lay behind him but he had been forced to learn that sooner or later what lies behind has to be faced: it could not be shut away as though it had never happened. [24]

But, in his attempt to put all that behind him, was he justified in making the life choices that he did? Should he, for example, have renounced the career for which his innate mathematical ability and expensive university education had made him eminently suitable? Or, perhaps more importantly, was he justified in abandoning the Protestant religion in which he had been reared, especially when he must have known how his mother would react? Consequently, is Father Bernard's 'fairing' a reward or a punishment? Is the arrival of his namesake, Bartle MacLintock, Effie's son, to be read as a reward for the older Bartle's loyalty to his moral principles? Or is the presence of the product of Effie's union with another man to be interpreted as a thorn in Father Bernard's flesh?

Having already noted that Morrison's portrayal of Bartle is complicated by his possession of both attractive and distancing characteristics, we can detect a somewhat similar ambiguity in her portrayal of Roman Catholicism. In the Prologue, the silence of the monastery and the monk's serenity are endowed with an 'otherworldy' quality in the poetic imagery of a 'flower hold[ing] light, luminous to the cup's brim'[25]. That he is a favourite among his pupils is not surprising when we are told:

> He was a big strong looking man, but this serenity robbed him of massiveness. Instead of rugged as some boulder on a mountainside, he was polished as veined marble or like quartz scintillating so brightly in the warm sunshine it looked nearer than it was. [26]

He is described using religious imagery when we are told that '[h]e was like the feast day on the calendar or the altar ablaze with candles in the chapel', creating an impression of light and warmth with spiritual overtones [27]. Father Bernard's compassion for the boy's unhappiness, and his attempt to provide him with religious comfort would seem to be laudable. We are also told of the joy he experiences in his new religion [28] However, not all of the novel's references to Roman Catholicism paint the religion in a favourable light. The Catholics of Wrack, if Grannie's stories are to be believed, were a cruel people, luring ships on to the rocks in order to salvage the flotsam from the wrecks. Their rituals are more suggestive of paganism than orthodox Catholicism. For instance, Grannie's attempt to ward off evil from the sickly infant by taking a knife and making crosses over the bed smacks of superstitious practices rather than a proper sacramental rite. This interpretation of Catholicism is repeated in Mistress Stewart's reminiscence of some of Grannie's strange habits:

> 'I mind one Lammastide she telt me that in the parts she came from they would be holding up the cup to each other and saying, "Lord, open the mouth of the grey fish, and haud Thy hand about the corn." Gey queer, outlandish they must have been . . . I sometimes thought they were worse than pagans in the parts she came from.' [29]

It is also found in Bartle's mother's disapproval of Grannie's 'crucifixes and beads and nonsense' and the 'wee hair bag with its bean and puckle of fern seeds' to which she believed Catholics prayed. In a vitriolic outburst, Kirsty condemns Grannie's feigned adoption of Protestantism as hypocrisy and asserts it as proof that Roman Catholics cannot to be trusted:

> 'I blame her for making a show she was taking the wine at communion when she was doing nothing of the sort. I blame her for crossing herself when our backs were turned, and being softer than butter to our faces. I blame her last of all for teaching ma son to forsake the true faith and turning him into a heretic.' [30]

How then are we to interpret Father Bernard's final revelation? Should we see Bartle MacLintock's presence as an earthly reward, bringing, as it does, the comfort that Effie now knows that she had not been involved in what she had subsequently been led to believe was an incestuous relationship? Or should we read it as retribution; seeing it as a constant reminder of the loving family relationship which he had been denied? And if we read it as the latter, is it punishment for his sexual impropriety with Maysie Wain, or for his abandonment of the person he used to be and rejection of his mother's Protestant religion to become a 'heretic'? Whilst the novel can be read as a spirtual odyssey, narrated against the backdrop of the conception of the world as a 'vale of tears', I think that, in the end, although Father Bernard advocates adherence to Christ's words 'not to count the cost', it is Calvin's angry God whose judgement he faces:

> But Father Bernard's thoughts were not far away: they were near as thunder to judgement-tied mountains. He was not thinking of Matthew but of his Master whose words Matthew had stored. And as he remembered them, 'Heaven and earth shall pass away, but my words shall not pass away,' *Father Bernard's eyes were wide open.* [31] (my italics)

It is impossible to reduce the italicised sentence, with which the book ends, to one single meaning. There is sufficient evidence to suggest that, as Bartle MacDonald, the dominie's goodness is rewarded with assurance of salvation. But there is also enough anti-Catholic sentiment to suggest that, as Father Bernard, he is conscious of God's wrath for his rejection of Protestantism. Both interpretations co-exist, and each subverts the other.

Like most of Morrison's fiction, *The Hidden Fairing* has long been out of print. It has, therefore, been omitted from many considerations of how twentieth century Scottish writers have dealt with the controversial topic of religion. Once more available, it exemplifies Morrison's willingness to consider possibilities other than her own Presbyterianism, and it also demonstrates how that openness is complicated by the recurrence of motifs that speak of the residual influence of her Calvinist heritage.

*Mary Seenan*
*Skelmorlie*
*2009*

1 Morrison, N. Brysson, (1951 rpt., 2009) *The Hidden Fairing*. Glasgow: Kennedy & Boyd.
2 Morrison, N. Brysson, (1930 rpt., 2009) *Breakers*. Glasgow: Kennedy & Boyd.
3 Quoted in letter from John Morrison, 24 September 1930, N. Brysson Morrison Collection, National Library of Scotland (hereafter given as NLS), MS27368, fol.34.
4 Mackenzie, Compton, 'Again a Woman Writes the Week's Best Book', *The Daily Mail*, 14 September 1933.
5 Morrison, N. Brysson, (1933 rpt., 1986) *The Gowk Storm*. Edinburgh: Canongate.
6 Morrison, N. Brysson, (1949) *The Winnowing Years*. London: Hogarth.
7 Broadcast on 6 March 1957 and repeated March 1958, B.B.C. Home Service.
8 'A Scotsman's Log', *The Scotsman*, 22 August 1950.
9 H.P.E., 'From the Lone Shieling', *Punch*, 7 February 1951.
10 Snow, C.P., 'Plot or No Plot', *The Sunday Times*, 14 January 1951.
11 Lochead, Marion, 'While Winter Lingers . . . Breath of Spring in Books', *The Bulletin and Scots Pictorial*, 1 February 1951.
12 Morrison, N.Brysson (1951 rpt., 2009) *The Hidden Fairing*.p.18
13 Ibid., p.5
14 Ibid.
15 Ibid., p.9
16 Ibid., p.6
17 Ibid., p.16
18 Ibid., p.15
19 Ibid., p...15
20 Ibid., p.66
21 Ibid.
22 See notebook for The Moonling, NLS, MS27287, vols 9-10
23 *Britain Today*. June 1951.
24 (1951 rpt., 2009) *The Hidden Fairing*, p. 179
25 Ibid., p.1
26 Ibid.
27 Ibid., p.2
28 Ibid., p.65
29 Ibid., p.65
30 Ibid., p.151
31 Ibid., p.183

# Contents

# Prologue

THE schoolroom in which the monk sat was large and airy. Through the broad, square windows poured the freckled sunshine of a Scots spring, flecking the wood of the desks and splashing the walls as brightly as maps.

The orderliness of the rows of desks revealed they had not yet been taken possession of for the term, and the stillness of the room was matched by the stillness in its one inmate. But because he was living and the schoolroom inanimate, its quiet was his silence. He held it as a flower holds light, luminous to the cup's brim.

He was a big, strong-looking man, but this serenity robbed him of massiveness. Instead of rugged as some boulder on a mountainside, he was polished as veined marble or like quartz scintillating so brightly in the warm sunshine it looked nearer than it was.

Footsteps clattering suddenly up the wide staircase sounded like an army, but he was attuned by this time to whole classes of footsteps and could tell these were made by two boys, probably small ones. They always made the most noise. They came charging down the gloriously empty corridor and drew up outside the half-opened door of the room where he sat. One boy had evidently grabbed the other to make him stop there, for there was an exclamation and an explosion of laughter hastily subdued. The husky whisper outside the door reached the man within more surely than if its owner had spoken in his natural voice.

"This is your classroom. Father Bernard's your form master. Mind you call him that and not 'sir'. He's all right. But mind not to speak to him until he speaks to you. There's nothing to be scared about," the whisper grew huskier in its urgency to be reassuring, "you don't need to be, with Father Bernard. I've told you he's all right. We all like him. Much the best."

The boy who entered behind Forbes was a newcomer, the boy Father Bernard had been told to expect. The child of Scots parents living abroad, he had been allowed to enter the school now, at the beginning of the summer term, rather than admitted at the customary autumn one. Beside Forbes, square and ruddy with good health, he looked small, knobby and pallid.

"Thank you, Father Bernard, I hope you had too," Forbes said dutifully in answer to his teacher's enquiry about his holidays. "This is the new boy—Father Gervase told me to bring him to you."

He stood, his hands behind his back, facing the monk, as one might stand in the sun. Father Bernard always gave Forbes this feeling of amplitude, as if in his presence he felt manhood about to descend upon his shoulders.

He was like the feast day on the calendar or the altar ablaze with candles in the chapel. It just seemed a pity, where Forbes was concerned, that there were so many other days on the calendar shouldering out the feast day, so many things to do they left no time at all to think of altars or candles.

But it was nice to know that Father Bernard was there, and he would be thinking of them—hard and long. As the boy looked at the monk's face, he corrected himself as he might have corrected a laboriously penned essay—no, sure and strong.

"Father Bernard," he said, breathless as he suddenly thought of all he had to do and the little time to do it in, "please, may I go now, as I've promised Lithgow and Grey to go and see the field."

Left by himself in an unfamiliar room with an unknown man, the new boy was too alarmed to raise his gaze from the floor. The monk was aware of his panic-stricken thoughts scuttling hither and thither like a many-legged spider whose place of refuge has been demolished: "I want my mother. I'll never get used to this place. They told me I would love it and I don't. I can't. I can't. I can't. I want to go home. These great trees outside and everything so big inside, I'll never know where to go. I'm lost. I'm lost. I'm lost. I can't find my way. So many boys, all bigger than me, and I'm all alone."

Somewhere outside, a clock began to strike.

"Listen," said the man he was not looking at, "that is the monastery clock. It is going to strike twelve. You will hear it in whichever part of the school you are. And when you hear it striking each day, do you know what you must think of? The twelve apostles, of whom our blessed Lord said, 'These are my friends.' There is a Gaelic proverb and as you are not likely to know the Gaelic, I will tell you what it says in English. It tells us prayer is the key of the day and the lock of the night. A disciple for every hour of the day and night to watch over us and stand guard for us and help us to fight our battles. All you have to do is think of them when you hear the clock strike—that will be the same as turning the key in the lock. Now can you tell me the name of any of the apostles?"

"I can tell you four," the boy said proudly. "Matthew, Mark, Luke and John."

"Matthew and John are the only two of these four to be numbered among the twelve," said the monk, "so we will not take up the hands of your clock thinking of Luke and Mark, great men though they were. We'll begin with Matthew." The boy had drawn nearer until he was almost touching, his dark eyes intent on the monk's face, his lips beginning to answer with a smile. "Each day you hear the clock strike one you'll think of Matthew and all the things you can remember about him. He was an outcast amongst his own people when our Lord said to him, 'Follow me,' so should you ever feel lonely amongst a crowd remember not to feel alone because you have Matthew beside you. The twenty-first of September is his feast day, and country folk used to say that St. Matthew shut up the bee. They meant by that saying that good St. Matthew knew after his feast day, when the chill dews begin to fall, it would become too cold for the bees, so he shuts them into an old tree-trunk or a hole in the earth to keep them safe for the winter. In pictures you will know it is St. Matthew if he is holding a bag of money, because the Master found him counting out money and taught him not to count the cost. Or he may have a pen in his hand, because he wrote when he was old what he remembered about his Master and we have his book to this day, safe as the bee in the tree-trunk, in the New Testament. Or he may be pictured as a winged man with a lance. A lance has the head of a spear and flies a little flag of its own. A man with wings can be at your side as quick as you can think of him. Now that is plenty for you to remember when the clock strikes one."

"Tell me about who I'm to think of when the clock says two," the boy said confidingly. His hand was on the monk's knee by this time. He had small hands even for a child, as delicate as a little girl's.

"You must creep afore ye gang," replied Father Bernard, smiling down into his upturned face. "The blessed St. Matthew will keep your clock ticking for many a long day yet, but when your hour comes depend on it I will tell you who to think of next. So that by the time you are grown up, when you leave school and are out of earshot of the monastery clock, you will have all twelve safely wound up in your watch for ever and on, secure against the thief time." He opened the desk and removed from it a note book. "It will be one o'clock before we know where we are!" he exclaimed, "and I haven't yet taken your name. I'll write it down in this book amongst all the others, and that will make you belong to us. First, tell me your Christian names."

"Bartle," said the boy.

The name rose into the sphere of the monk's mind like a bird from some forgotten battleground.

"Bartle," he repeated thoughtfully, "Bartle," and felt for his pen.

# Chapter One

HE remembered when he was that child's age. His mind slipped past the anniversaries of the feast of St. Bernard, on which he had received the habit of a monk and the name of that great Saint, to his birthdays. They lay so far behind the halo that his name days cast that he had some difficulty reaching them. Carefully, as though unaccustomed to figures, he counted back to when he was eight. Next week, on the twenty-first of September, he would be—what; Sixty-three, wasn't it? Fifty-five years ago then—what had he been like? How had the world appeared to him?

Fifty-five years ago he had not known he had been born on St. Matthew's feast day. The calendar in the cottage at the roadside had not been marked by festival or saint's days. Its year had been punctuated by weekly visits to the kirk between Barnfingal and Auchendee, when he had pushed his feet into squeaking boots and taken the penny for his collection from the window-sill where his mother had placed it. Even the fact that it was his birthday made no difference to the days that swung by as evenly as the pendulum of the wag-at-the-wa' clock. His mother would pull down his darned jersey and ask him how old he was again, and his grannie, when he moved near her at the fire, would intone, "Eight are thee? Eight? Yon's a grand age, a braw age to be." And that was all. She would sigh, like a wind amongst reeds, as though since she could not move the years clumped like mountains upon her, she would try to whistle through them.

Lady Wain was the only person who ever gave him a present on his birthday, so that he associated presents after that not so much with birthdays but with Lady Wain. She with her family came to the Big Hoose up the brae every summer. There was a Sir Alfred Wain but he never swam into Bartle's ken. It was his lady everyone knew. Her annual link with the cottage at the roadside was through his mother who aired the Big House and did the rough scrubbing each year before the servants came through from Glasgow to prepare it for the family.

Barnfingal was a clachan scattered up the hillside, its whitewashed cottages under their thatched roofs like pebbles from a distance. The schoolhouse was little more than a but and ben; and when the dominie wanted to give the boys the tawse, he took them outside where there was room for him to swing his arm. Gow Farm was the only two-storied building in the place but, edged by byre, bothy and stable, it made no pretensions to size. So that Bartle realized now that the Big House probably appeared, bigger at Barnfingal than it would have done anywhere else, just as he realized now that the Wains, although well-to-do, had not the mythical wealth spun round them by the talk of the clachan.

The Big House had no history attached to it, having been built to Sir Alfred's own design. He had something to do with railways and shipping and his country house had the uncomplicated lines of a short-cut, standing square and solid on ground reclaimed from moorland, entrenched with elaborate plumbing.

Bartle, trotting behind his mother on her way to her annual scourings, had no knowledge of the fairies upon which the Wain children had been reared. Certainly he would never have associated these pretty tales with the forgetful people or Other Folk of whom his grannie sometimes spoke. When therefore the gates clanged behind him and his mother, he did not think of himself as entering enchanted but quite different ground, ground that his grannie's forgetful folk had never overcast.

Here the rutted brae road spread into a broad avenue that swept to the house which had the dimensions of a castle to Bartle. Rhododendron bushes screened and high walls shut off the harshness of the countryside beyond them. The enclosed ground was not hummocked or gnarled with heather roots, but smoothed into green lawns and bright with garden paths.

His mother never left the cottage except when she wanted to reach somewhere, which meant that she always walked quickly to save as much time as possible on the way. Once inside the grounds, she tore towards the house. Plot, lawn and garden walk streamed past Bartle following her, like green-fringed ribbons unfurled for someone else's favour.

He had no right here. He knew his mother felt she had no right either. Always she would pause on their journey home at least once to mutter, "Did I lock yon door? Bartle, did ye see me turn the key in the lock?" Or, "Bartle, what about the kitchen window?

Are ye sure I snecked it?" As she seldom spoke and never asked his opinion, which he was not supposed to have, he knew she felt as he did about the Big House.

For a child to be left to his own devices meant as far as his mother was concerned for that child to get into mischief, and she had enough to do without having to worry what Bartle might be doing with himself. So that when she clattered back into the servants' quarters for broom, pail or brush, she expected to find him, and always did, standing satisfactorily exactly where she had left him, like a clock that had stopped.

But the clock began to tick whenever it was left by itself. In the silent house his mother's scrubbing operations could be heard rooms away which gave him a certain amount of freedom. Holding his hands, in case he touched something he shouldn't, and inadvertently set it working, Bartle had not only been all over the kitchens and servants' quarters but into the rooms the Family used. He had once even penetrated as far as the drawing-room. The windows were still shuttered but there was sufficient light to see that even the walls were draped with dust sheets. He lifted the edge of one to discover what it was hiding and dropped it hurriedly, as though guilty, when he saw it was some kind of yellow cloth.

Carts from Gow Farm sometimes rumbled past the cottage at the roadside, darkening the shadowed kitchen and hollowing it with sound. But they were the only vehicles to use the road, for the weekly coach went by on the other side of the loch, except for the Wain carriage. Then the bowls leapt on the dresser, the wooden table danced and the porridge spurtle jigged where it lay. Bartle's mother would stop whatever she was doing to listen and when silence descended once more would remark to his grannie, "They're here." While a fierce joyous excitement would take possession of Bartle and he would wish this moment could be prolonged for ever, when the Wain carriage passed with so much stir it sounded as though it were coming into the cottage. Perhaps one day it would—drive right through it and never notice what was flung from its wheels——

He never saw any of the Family but when he thought of them, and he always did when he sat drinking his milk before he went to bed, he was filled with that inner excitement. He would fix personalities to the names he heard lifted in the clachan, Miss Hetty and Miss Maysie, Master Alfred, the Lady herself, and Sir Alfred. Sir Alfred was so busy turning everything he touched to gold in the city that he did not spend the weeks his family did at their country home, but when he did he fished most of the time. Bartle, his blunt chin wedged in his mug as he reflected upon them all, saw the brown spotted mountain trout flash into gold as Sir Alfred unhooked them from his line. The sun always shone on their faces when he thought of them, they never went to bed but lived goldenly all through the night in a house that stood in a garden where it was always bright as day.

One afternoon when he went to the door to answer a knock he found one of Them without. He knew it must be the Lady herself because she was fully grown. He backed before her into the kitchen and she followed him, talking all the time to him in a low voice as though he were of note. He heard her voice but was too intoxicated to make out what she said. She must have brought the sun in with her for she lit the dark room as it was not lit even at high noon.

"Mrs. MacDonald," she exclaimed when she saw his mother, "I was passing in the wagonette so brought the keys with me. I know you'll keep them safe until you need them next year."

His mother cleared the big chair for her, turning uppermost the unfaded side of the limp patchwork cushion, and she seated herself to lean forward upon the tall ivory knob of her parasol while Bartle heard without listening to the sweetness of the words that poured from her lips. For her words were secondary to the thoughts he saw forming as undubitable as polished marbles on the floor of her mind.

How can they endure it, she was thinking, how can they live here—if it were not so clean it would be a hovel. Outside so picturesque with its thatched roof and garden netted to its whitewashed walls, and inside everything scrubbed to a bareness, as dark as though even light had been scoured away. That old bent woman opposite—her mind must be gone, she looks as though her mind were gone. How terrible to do nothing all day but sit in the same chair, and the only thing that happens to you to grow more twisted with rheumatism, like an old root——

So overcome was Bartle with the deluge of Lady Wain's pity that he did what he had never done before in his life, thrust himself forward that he might staunch, appease, stay the torrent of her thoughts, tell her that they had everything they could want and that grannie could see who was passing on the road from her chair.

"Bartle," his mother's scandalized voice reached him, "how dare ye rub against the Lady like yon? Awa' back with ye."

But Lady Wain would not hear of such a thing and murmuringly demurred, stroking his head that she might keep him close to her. He could feel the softness of her hand through the hair cut as close as his mother's shears could crop it.

"So this is your little boy, Mrs. MacDonald? I did not know that you had a little boy."

"He is eight the day."

Only Bartle knew that his grannie's voice startled Lady Wain. Her mind could not be quite gone then if she could make a rational remark. That somehow seemed to make it so much worse—to have the wits to watch your own disintegration.

"Is it?" she exclaimed delightedly to him. "Why, you are my Alfred's age then—he is eight too to-day. And have you had a happy birthday? And many presents? Yes, he is my eldest boy—he has two sisters who are older," she said as though in answer to him. "He is taller than you but you are stronger than he," and she cupped his head even more gently in her hand to make up to him that her Alfred should be taller than he. "What do they call you?" she asked.

"Bartle," his mother replied for him.

"He has the English," the old woman, her chin resting on her chest, said from her corner.

"Has he?" smiled Lady Wain. "You are clever, Bartle, to know two languages before you are eight."

"We had to talk the English ben the house before he went to school," said his mother, determined that what was merely accidental should not be attributed to his cleverness, "for his grannie doesna come from these parts, and her Gaelic is no the Gaelic they speak here."

"And where do you come from?" enquired Lady Wain, to make up to her for keeping her out of the conversation for so long.

"A far cry awa'," the old woman mumbled in a wandered way, as though the thread that tied her to where she came from was so stretched now she could not quite remember to what it was attached.

"Grannie comes from Wrack," said Bartle, pushing against their visitor in his eagerness to let her know how forfunate grannie was once to have lived on Wrack, where the spume from the sea was sometimes thrown against your window.

When his mother returned after accompanying Lady Wain to the door, they all listened until silence muffled the light wheels of the wagonette and the quick beat of the horse's hooves.

"Yon was grey she was gowned in," she commented to his grandmother.

"Ay, everything of the same colour except the flowers on her ponnet," contributed the old woman. She said 'thoo' and 'thee' for 'you' and 'ye and sometimes still her b's would lapse into p's.

"Yon was a hat she had on and no a bonnet," corrected his mother.

Bartle looked from one to the other, his lips compressed tightly together to keep himself from shouting them down that the visitor had worn grey—grey which was next door to black. They must have seen her clothes were golden as sunshine: even now she was gone her personality was diffused about the room in splinters and beams of light. When he passed her chair, he placed his hand on its wooden arm to discover if it would be lit by the radiance that still clung to where she had sat.

When he was drinking his milk that night, another knock came to the door. His mother answered it as she came from the byre built on to the gable-end of the cottage. In the silent kitchen the listening old woman and small boy heard an unknown man's voice speaking in tones so unlike to what they were accustomed he might as well have been talking a foreign language. His mother entered carrying a large shiny flat box.

"The Lady sent this down for his birthday," she said to grannie. "She wantit him to have it the night so employed one of her servants to fetch it down—what a fash to put herself to for but a bairn."

Bartle put out his two rough hands that emerged from the frayed cuffs of his jersey to touch it.

"New as the day's milk too," continued his mother. "Something one of her bairns had done with would have served just as weel."

Speechlessly Bartle, still holding the box, looked up into her face.

"Take aff the lid and see what's inside," she said encouragingly. "Ay, take it over to your grannie and let her see. It's too good by far for ye to play with, Bartle, but we'll put it up here where ye can see it," and she stretched her arm to place it on a high shelf.

The fabric of his life was so even, the weft of days shuttling into the woof of weeks, that when it was summer the blueness of the loch and the greenness of Gow Farm fields patterned his hour; and when snow capped the mountains and speckled the shores of the loch, with storm gusts rapping at the door like travellers without, winter composed his past, present and future. He only came upon a tuft in that fabric when all the strands of his life seemed to be gathered into some tremendous happening, such as Lady Wain's visit. The next knot that made his lingering thoughts pause was one evening that winter when his mother took her spinning-wheel round to old Mistress Stewart's to join in a ceilidh. Rarely was the kitchen left alone to grannie and him.

"Fetch it down," she said to him.

He stood on the chair to reach for the box from the high shelf and placed it on her knee, lifting the lid that they could both see inside.

"It's called Snakes and Ladders," he told her, tracing out the pictures with a square finger. "Ye throw the dice, grannie, and gang up the ladders and down the snakes."

"Is that so?" she enquired politely. "Well I never. And thee would never have had it, Bartle, had I not minded to tell the Lady it was thoor birthday. Put it away now pefore thoor mother comes pack and catches thee."

She was his equal when he was alone with her, but when her daughter-in-law was present she was merely the younger woman's echo.

"I'll sit by ye for a wee," he suggested, able because his mother was not yet 'pack' to dawdle beside her while he undressed before the fire where it was warm.

"Put on your mother's shawl then," she now said, but he demurred.

11

He resented the shawl as making him into a lassie. "Many a petter man than thee has worn that shawl," she commented, but did not press the point. "Thoor father spend his last days in it."

"Yon would be a lang year syne," Bartle prompted more than questioned. One had to be careful with grandmother. Once let her know information was wanted and she would remain mute as a fish; but throw out a few careful baits, being adroit enough not to let her see the hooks, and she would rise with a splash. Like most of the old, she liked to digress on the days before the tides of time washed her into a backwater.

"It was nine years and a pittoch," she said carefully. "Eh, but thoor mother was reel blythe in these days. Pefore she married thoor father—and mind thee," she put in hastily, "she was more set on him pefore they married than ever he was on her—she would come dancing down the road to milk our cow, and then she would whirl the pucket full of milk in the air and never a drop would be spik."

"And after she marrit him, he was no weel, was he, grannie?"

"Na, he got a sore hoast—it would have proken any mortal heart to hear him moaning and hoasting all the night long. I'll say that for her, she did her duty by him then and he was never cappernishious with her as he was with others—mebbe because she had a sharp tongue in her head. After his hoast went he did not want to leave his ped. Your mither was aye at him to get up. 'Birds dinna grow in the nest,' was what she would say, but he was feared to try his strength. 'I'll have to be the man for both of us,' she said then, and he would sit in ped with her shawl happed round his shoulders. He did not like her to leave him, thee would have thought she was his mother. Kirsty must heat up his gruel and Kirsty must hap up his pillows, and if Kirsty was not there to do it, he would turn his face to the wall and never open his mouth. She could never leave him for two minutes but he was wondering and fretting where she was."

"Was that so, grannie?"

"So it was. Then one morn she came in with her ponnet on. It was the day of the Dormay Fair and he got up in an awful way and cried out she was leaving him when he was dying to go to a fair and she was not to go. She turned on him then, for she was real passionate, and said she would go to the Fair if so she willed and no one would say her nay. At that he began to greet and she looked at him and said, 'It's not a man I have married but a bolster,' and out she went and panged the door pehind her. I mind it well, real well." His grandmother was shaking her head. "We could do nought with him after that, he would speak never a word or look at any food, and then about four in the afternoon he asked for his clothes and said he was going to the Fair and if he died on the way mebbe she would be sorry. He was distraught, poor man, for she was cold one minute and hot the next, enow to drive any man to his wit's end, and he was feared in case she was carrying on with any other pody. Then after four Kirsty came home. She had peen to Mhoreneck to see about a pig and had no peen near the Fair. Ay, but it was real like Kirsty not to say where she was going—real like Kirsty," and the old woman ruminated.

"Was that so?" Bar tie repeated non-committally, tremulous not to break his grannie's thread of talk so anxious was he for her to pursue it.

"And when I said to her," she went on, bitterness creeping into her voice," 'He's got up out of his ped to go and fetch thee from the Fair and buy thee a faring,' she said calm as could be, 'I never thought there was muckle wrong with him.' And hardly were the words out of her mouth when young Peter Thomson put his head round the door. 'Mistress MacDonald,' he said to her, 'they've lifted your man out of the loch.'"

"Oh," exclaimed Bartle, and he shut his eyes as though from shock. His grandmother had told him many things when they were alone together but never had she mentioned this before.

"Ay," she said, and she stared fixedly in front of her as though she were seeing the very sight she was recounting painted on her eyeballs, "and then old Peter Thomson and Malcolm MacPherson, the ferryman, prought him in on an old door dripping wet and dead as a stone, his eyes near pursting out of their sockets."

Bartle stared into the fire. It was not the picture of his dripping father he was trying to see but a picture of his mother whirling a bucket of milk round her head out of sheer exuberance of spirits. Try as he would he could not imagine her as young, even though in the effort he thought of her as smaller, and he could not visualize the mother he knew coming dancing down the road to milk a cow.

Two years ago, when he was six, his grandmother had told him his mother was thirty years of age. He remembered the information had depressed him. He had always thought of her as old, almost as old as grannie, but never anything like thirty.

"Thee were porn soon after that, sooner than thee should have peen. But Kirsty was aye strong enow to stand anything."

The kitchen was lit only by the fire and two resinous splinters of a Scots pine. On the low roof were thrown flickering, giant shadows of the hams hanging from the rafters and of the head of the old woman sitting at the fireside. They enlarged her already prominent, hooked nose to fantastic scythe-like proportions.

"It was thoo I was feared for. Thoo were wee as a skinned rabbit, coming pefore her time. But I saw to it no harm came to thee."

"Did ye now?" he enquired conversationally and when she did not reply, pressed, "Now how would that be, I wonder."

"When Kirsty was asleep, I took a knife and made crosses over the bed, over thee. I kent ill would go by thee after that."

He felt his heart beginning to knock against his side.

"How?" he asked, his voice thickening.

"How what?" she demanded.

"How did ye think ill would gang by me? What crosses, grannie?"

"I did not think, I knew. And I was right. Instead of puking into nought, thee thrived." She stirred in her chair. "Bartle."

"Ay, grannie?"

"Turn the cushion on thon chair good side up and give it a pit dust with your arm."

He obeyed, then reseated himself on his creepie, a hand on each bare knee as he surveyed the chair.

"Why did ye want me to do yon, grannie?"

"For her. Lest she's passing by and thought of coming ben."

His thoughts clouded. Was grannie beginning to wander? If she were, that meant the beginning of the end.

"Ye mean for Lady Wain?" he said ingratiatingly. "But, grannie, they're all awa' and will no be back until next summer." His voice trailed as though years separated him from next summer.

"I mean for the Lady but no Lady Wain. What way would she be passing at this hour of the night?"

Relief broke over him that she was not after all wandering.

"What way would your Lady be passing at this hour of the night?" he cajoled.

"She's not my Lady but our Lady. Mind that, Bartle. Tell no one but mind it."

Again he felt his heart knocking wildly at his side.

"What will mother say if she sees her?"

"Kirsty'll never see her. She'll not come ben when any of them are about. But she would not mind thee. Thee're my son's son—thee're the last of us." Her eyes were very bright through the darkness.

The old woman and the young child contemplated each other across the hearth.

"I tell ye what," he said, when he had licked as far down bis empty mug as his tongue could reach, "I'll get into your bed and give it a bit heat up for ye."

"Ay," she returned, "it will be warmer for thee ben here but thee must not bide too long."

She did not like to be left alone even in the summer evenings when it was light, then the silence preyed on her; but now she liked it still less when the wind dirled down the chimney and thirled at the door.

Bartle climbed into the big bed and lay watching the mammoth shadow grannie shuffling on the roof. It was always to the island of Wrack that he tried to steer the conversation when they were alone together—that strange island which scared him while it enthralled, as the swirling edthes of a whirlpool terrify but fascinate.

"Ye'll have seen many deid folk I'm for thinking, grannie, syne ye lived on an island with wrecks and all," he said at last, so would-be casually that his words were fraught with meaning.

"Ay," she answered, "and many a wreck there was that should never have peen," Already her voice had that harp in it which told him she was well under sail. "Many a time can I mind them tying a lantern to a bull's horns and hurrying it along the shore at night. Up and down would go the bull's head and up and down would go the lantern with it. Ships at sea, seeing the light tossing about like another ship, would think it safe and follow it and be wrecked on the rocks. I have seen them do the same thing with tying a lantern to a cask and setting it afloat. They got many a thing thon way—salvage belongs to him who finds. Thon kist at the window was washed ashore from a wreck such as one of them and my father took it. 'If I take it not, someone else will and I might as well have it as any other pody,' thinks he."

Bartle had heard it all before. When passing the rude, square seaman's chest he would place his hand on the top and the contact alone was sufficient to raise him to a peak of ecstasy. To think what it must have gone through. It had been tossed from port to port, had had strange masters who had put in it strange things. It had been wrecked, swallowed by the sea; marine weeds and fungi had clambered over it, round-eyed, scaly fish sailed through its open lid. Then it had been tumbled ashore by rough waves and been taken into one of the fishermen's houses. He saw them in a grey, bleak row facing the sea—all, as his grannie had told him, with old ship's heads in their gardens. And now, most unaccountable of all, it was in Croft Fionn under the window————

"There was a drowned man peside it," his grandmother's voice broke in upon his thoughts; "he was the captain of the boat and he would have peen a very handsome man had the partans not eaten off his nose. I mind they found five guinea pieces on his pody and after that none of the farm hands would take their fee in gold for many a long Ne'er-day for fear they would get that plood money and the curse of it."

"There were wrecks before your time, were there no, grannie?" Bartle asked craftily.

"Their have aye peen wrecks," she made answer. "I mind two landmarks in the sand as a bairn. Some said they were the wreck of a Viking ship and some said they were not. Then one winter there was a great storm. I mind hearkening to it in ma ped and thinking the world would blow over. And after it was by, they found some of the wreck was washed away but more was uncovered. And they found queer things peside it—outlandish coins and prooches and suchlike."

"And wha would they belong to, are ye for thinking?" he asked.

"The Norse."

Something tightened in Bartle like a fiddlestring being strung.

"Say it again, grannie."

16

"Say what again?

"Wha did ye say the brooches would belong to?"

"The Norse. And it was after thon storm that ma prother and me were going along the shore and we found the pody of a drowned woman lying on the sands."

"Were ye feart?" asked Bartle, his eyes wide.

"She had twa apples in her pouch,"remembered his grandmother. "We rubbed them on my petticoat and they did not taste so salt."

# Chapter Two

HIS mother always looked the same to Bartle, he could not remember in the years to come any change in her. Her face was brown as a gypsy's, her black hair streaked with grey, her eyes were melancholy, her under-lip hung out, and always her head was to one side. She wore men's boots which usually had clods of earth sticking to them, and her hands, tanned as though stained with tea, were large and coarse skinned with broken nails. Yet she always had to take the cockerels to the roadman to have their necks drawn, and after having seen a duck devouring tadpole jelly she could never eat a duck's egg. Between Bartle and her there was a barrier of unfamiliarity although they had seen each other every day of his life. There was no taken for granted communion that customarily strings child to mother, no common ground they could share as equals. Even when he had been a baby she had not yearned over him, for she was not the yearning kind; and as he grew into a stocky little boy she treated him with a certain impatience because he was not older and could look after himself. Early she taught him to dress and undress himself. Now he peeled potatoes, cooked the porridge, washed and dried the dishes, collected eggs from under the hens, made up their hash and fed them with it. "Mistress MacDonald's man," the roadman called him, when he passed on his short sturdy legs driving before him the cow to the common herd or home to the Croft Fionn byre. But to his mother he was always younger and smaller than she wanted him. She made no attempt to imagine herself his size but waited for that time when he would have made up on her, when she need no longer look back for him or trouble to hurry him on the way.

His grandmother had no need to imagine herself his height, for they met on a common ground where size was no diminishment and age no reinforcement, where the communion between them was an unspoken language that accepted the fantastic with the blandness of fact, and fact with all the wonder of the fantastic.

Snow obliterated every landmark, folding from sight field, dyke and brae, filling hollows, rounding hill tops, submerging gardens, swallowing the school playground. Drifts, soundless as dreams, formed themselves through the night, until the whole world took the form of a static sea, wave undulating upon wave as far as the eye could see.

"Mind and ask the dominie now and he'll let ye take your piece in the school before the fire," his mother said to him next morning as he prepared to set off to school. "The snow is too deep by far for ye to come trapesing home for your dinner. Have ye got your sums now? Ye would forget your head, Bartle MacDonald, if I was no here to mind ye of it. They'll be ben the kitchen—I saw your jotter lying on the dresser. Now mind, none of your short cuts but gang round by the road."

He turned at the corner of the brae to wave to her although he knew she never waited. Now the speckled shut door of Croft Fionn gave him a curious feeling of unfamiliarity as he saw its darkness wreathed round with snow.

The schoolhouse was not five minutes' run from his home but that morning it took him about half an hour to plough through the drifts, an eventuality his mother had foreseen by turning him out of the house earlier than usual. He saw no one on the way and the sense of unfamiliarity increased, while his difficulty underfoot began to turn this gleaming white world into something alien. He felt walled in, banked out with snow that was not powdery and soft and resistless as it looked, but implacable as a slammed door and obdurate as rock, yet sucking at his footsteps as though it had so many mouths.

He did not hear the dominie ringing the handbell and when eventually he reached the small building, he listened at the door to hear if he were late but no sound came from within. Pushing it open, he entered the room to find it empty.

He hung his coat on a nail, then made his way, his footsteps echoing hollowly on the floor, to one of the chipped, scratched benches. There he blew on his hands, cleaned his slate, placed his 'piece' in its paper poke on the ledge underneath the desk, opened his jotter and waited.

Silence sat upon this place like unease. No squeaking of skte pencils, no subdued chattering, or hum of conning, no shuffling of feet, or cracking of fingers to claim the dominie's attention. He felt like one returned to an emptied world after sleeping a hundred years.

Uncomfortably the realization dawned on him that he was to be the only scholar that day, for he was the only one who lived within quarter of a mile of the schoolhouse. The snow was too deep for the MacPhees or the MacTaggarts or Jamie Malcolm to venture out.

Footsteps sounded along the passage from the house adjoining and he knew in the emptiness after they paused that someone was looking into the schoolroom through the door behind him.

"Well, Bartle," came the rasp of the dominie's voice, "so you are to be my only scholar." He received the distinct impression that his master regretted the record of absentees had been broken. "I looked in to see if by chance any of you might have won through."

He had walked to his desk at the end of the room, beside the blackboard, a heavily built man, the hair on his square head beginning to grizzle. Although his hair was cut short, it was so thick that despite its shortness it could be seen that it unmistakably curled. What had not begun to grey was still black as a bird's back, so that he had a startlingly piebald effect on his scholars when they saw him for the first time. "The black and white man" they called him to each other on their way home, and they never outgrew their first impression of him, one with the distrust of fear about it, as though he were a foreigner to them.

"Look over your history," he ordered Bartle, and opened his own desk to take out a book.

The boy was very conscious of the dominie's presence, the dominie quite unconscious of the boy's until an appreciable time later when his cold eye lit upon him.

'I havena been put on to the Latin yet," Bartle said ingratiatingly, watching him.

He became aware of the full weight of the other's glance concentrated upon him.

"I didn't say anything about Latin to you," he remarked.

"Na?" Bartle faltered.

"Na. But I was about to tell you to get your Latin book and we would construe some prose."

"Ay, so I kent, but I havena learnt the Latin yet," reiterated Bartle, as though doubling back on his traces and relieved to find himself home again.

20

The dominie had taken his watch out of his pocket to see the time. He now swung it to and fro on its chain with his finger, still studying Bartle.

"And how do you know what I am about to say?" he demanded.

"I didna ken I kent," blurted Bartle, feeling caught.

"No? Most informative." His sarcasm had the effect of terrifying the child, as though his words were traps to catch him in, or trip him up with. "Since Bartle knows what I am about to say, it is really unnecessary for me to say it." He lengthened the chain to swing his watch higher and caught it into the palm of his hand. "And does Bartle ken but doesna ken he kens with everyone or is it just a favoured few he tries it on with?"

"I'm na trying anything on, dominie," the boy assured him, beginning to blubber. He was unused to crying and the sobs shook his whole body as though he did not know what to do with them.

"At this rate," continued that inexorable voice, "you should be dux of the school before you are very much older and changing places with your dominie. How old are you by the way?"

"Eight year and four month," wept Bartle, and it was only when he felt the tears like chuckie-stones tumble down his face that he put up his cuff to wipe them off.

"Well, we'll start you on the Latin since you have got such a handsome start in other directions. Latin, Bartle, is a dead language which means that no nation speaks it to-day. It was the language of the Romans and is closely related to the Gaelic and a stepping-stone to French. We will take the verb 'to love' first. It is aye the verb that is taken first in Latin—the Romans apparently found it easier to say than we do. Bring me your slate and I will write it down for you, or mebbe you know it before I can tell you? No? Well then— 'amo,' I love or I am loving. Note that in Latin you do not use pronouns with the verbs as in English, the pronouns are expressed by the personal suffixes. O is the sign of the first person singular, present indicative. 'Scio' I know, 'rego' I rule, 'audio' I hear—we get our words audience, auditorium from that——"

His voice laboured on and Bartle stood beside him, watching him writing down examples on the slate, while he thought of Hadrian's Wall stretching across Scotland and the battle of Mons

Graupius where the Caledonians, 'men of exceptional stature with red hair and the bravest fighters of all the Britons,' had grappled with the Romans and been defeated.

"Now learn the present indicative of the verb 'amo'," said the schoolmaster. "I have written it down for you, it is quite simple— to anyone who knows as much as you do," he added with false encouragement as he caught the boy's dazed stare.

Bartle went back to his seat where he sat until twelve o'clock with his elbows on the desk and his head in his hands learning his new verb. It gave him something of a turn to think of himself, a living person, being able to say I love in the language of men whose mouths had long since been stopped for ever.

The dominie stretched his muscular chest and yawned.

"Well, Bartle," he said, slapping shut his book, "you'll be going home for your dinner now." He looked at the window against which the snow had banked, darkening the interior. "No need for you to come along in the afternoon, for it will be dark before you can turn."

"My mother gave me a piece awa' with me," said Battle, "and tellt me I was to eat it ben the schoolroom."

"She did, did she?" replied dominie Shaw, and his pupil could feel he was distinctly annoyed. "Mistress MacDonald is apparently another person who knows, but in quite a different way from her son! Well, well, Bartle, we will bid each other farewell until after dinner then."

Left by himself, Bartle went over to the hearth and sat down on some logs. He cogitatingly took his 'piece,' a large triangular scone, out of its paper, which he placed on his knees to catch any crumbs. The poke had been used more than once and now was transparent as clouded glass. The black-currant jam with which his scone was spread had soaked into it and dyed it purple but Bartle was sorry when the last bite was eaten. He licked his finger-tips to pick up the crumbs and ate them too; then realizing the paper would not stand another journey, he blew it up, flattening it with one knuckle. After that he sat with a hand up each one of his sleeves, saying over and over to himself, rocking to and fro as though in rhythm, amo, amas, amat, amamus, amatis, am*ant*.

His body jerked forward and his eyes wide, he fell to wondering again about the Romans before they had all died, when the world had shaken with the tramp of their feet. Agricola's forts A.D. 81, Hadrian's Wall A.D. 120, repaired by Severus A.D. 209, Antonine's Wall (called by the vulgar Grime's Dyke) A.D.140, Roman Roads branching out to every airt as straight as the spokes of a wheel——

He remembered them all, the few bare facts presented by his history book. And Mons Graupius, the place that no one could trace 'owing to the similitude of Tacitus's description to many of the Highland glens.' He remembered thinking as he had read it that it might have been the very glen where now stood Croft Fionn and the familiar schoolhouse that the red-haired Caledonians, with their too small shields and blunt swords, had met the helmeted Romans. It might have been, it might have been, there was nothing to say it was not——

To amuse himself in the afternoon, dominie Shaw attempted to communicate to his solitary scholar without speaking to him, but Bartle, holding his slate in both hands and eyeing him mistrustfully, knew what he was up to and refused to play his game. "Come away, my wee doo," the dominie signalled to him, "and show us your slate." "Ye'll ask me before I budge one step," Bartle replied in his wordless battle; "ye'll no make me greet a second time." "So you're not coming'" the dominie enquired without opening his mouth, his eyes bright with spleen, "Bartle is surely dour this afternoon." "As dour as Grime's Dyke," Bartle dared back, whereupon the dominie laughed aloud. His laugh was as shattering to the boy as though every prison gate in the world were clashing down upon him.

"Take your boots aff in the lobby," his mother told him when he came home after four o'clock. "Weel," she asked as he entered the kitchen in his stocking soles, "and wha was at the school?"

"Only me," replied Bartle. After a pause in which no one spoke he said, "I'm learning Latin now."

"Muckle good that will do thee," commented his grandmother.

The snow lay for long that year. Perhaps that was why when spring did come, and in that Highland district springs were always as tardy as they were short, Bartle was made conscious of it for the first time. Across the loch, every burn that veined Fingal's sides leapt and gushed in spate; the trees in Mar Woods were sticky with buds and pinioned leaves; newly born lambs, white as snow beside the old grey of their dams, toppled to their feet; a mare licked her foal where it lay in a weak patch of sunlight in one of Gow Farm's fields; every cottage door was loud with the clucking of hens outside it and the sharp, infinitesimal cheeping of their brood; while in the Croft Fionn pig-sty the enormous pink-skinned sow lay grunting contentedly amongst her squealing litter.

It was always very quiet in the Croft Fionn kitchen. The clumsy tick of the wag-at-the-wa' clock, the whirr of his mother's wheel, the flickering of the flames, were such accustomed sounds they had become part of the silence. His grandmother always sat very still. She never moved from her chair at the fire now, except to be helped to the box-bed. Bartle could dimly remember a time when she had been able to walk about the kitchen and as she had done so she had been wont to hum to herself under her breath, a low, unconscious monotonous crooning, but when she was confined to a chair even that sound had ceased. At first she used to knit, but she had grown easily muddled and knitted back instead of forward. "Eh, but I'm a foolish old pody," she would say when she watched Kirsty unpicking her work at night and putting it right for her. Then one day the stocking had fallen from her hands to the floor and Kirsty had always forgotten to give it to her again.

"Davie Thomson's taking a wife to himself this Whit-tide."

Bartle, sitting at the wooden table doing his lessons, heard his mother's voice jar the silence as she stood at the fireplace turning the clothes on the piece of string stretched across the mantelpiece. Davie Thomson, he knew, was the roadman: it always struck him as curious that a grown man with a beard should be called Davie.

"Is that so, Kirsty?" His grannie's voice sounded both wheedling and conciliatory to the boy. "Deed now? Of course he's getting on."

"We're all getting on," his mother cried fiercely. "All older, no younger. Even him."

A stillness chilled the boy at the table as he realized that by "even him" his mother meant not Davie Thomson but him, her son Bartle.

"And is it a Barnfingal lass?" enquired his grannie's deprecatory voice. "Sheena Turner mebbe?"

"Sheena Turner!" exclaimed his mother, as though the other's words were clouts that she would fain tear to pieces. "Why Sheena Turner of all folk? What's come over ye to jump at the notion of its being her?"

"Mebbe just because Sheena Turner's the one unmarried lass in the place who's suitable," placated his grandmother.

"Sheena Turner's no lass. Twenty-five on her last birthday. Let me tell ye that if she hasna found a man for herself before she's twenty-five, and even her best friends ken it's no for the want of trying, she'll no find one after. Certain no a man like to Davie Thomson."

"But she's young compared to Davie Thomson, wha must be near to forty," vindicated grannie.

Bartle was confused by the conversation with its strong undercurrents, but even he knew that this was the last thing of which to remind his mother at that moment.

"What has age to do with a man?" she demanded, her voice still loud as though she were disputing.

"If it's no Sheena Turner, wha may it be then?" wavered his grandmother.

"A town lass."

In the pause that followed both the old woman and the small boy knew that whatever she said would be wrong but that say something she must.

"Is that so, Kirsty? Well now. And how do thee think a town lass'll manage seeing to Davie's house?"

"Better than the Sheena Turner ye're so set on because even a town lass couldna be worse." She apparently was having difficulty with the unknotting of some tape on a piece of clothing for she tugged at it violently.

"Mebbe," grannie agreed peaceably, "but still a town lass—I doubt me that's a mistake, Kirsty."

"Mistake or no mistake it's what's going to happen."

"Ay, but it's a mistake," continued his grandmother, harping on the one string that she realized instinctively was having a mollifying effect, "a great mistake. What does a town lass know about peasts and hens and suchlike."

"Davie's been by his lee lone self a long while now syne his mother died. Even a town lass will be company for him." The very conviction of his mother's voice was crying out to heaven for contradiction.

"Na, na," hastened his grannie, "instead of company, it's going to be nought but aggravation. And she'll pe a young feckless pody into the pargain, I'm thinking."

"She's thirty-three."

The import of his mother's words was lost upon her son. He only knew that he felt as though her walls were breached from without as well as within and were tumbling down on top of them all.

"Do you say so, Kirsty?" His grannie's voice fairly galloped to fill up any pause. "Well I never. Well, thirty-three or no thirty-three, he'll find a town lass real feckless and handless about his place, and Davie Thomson's used to seeing a woman managing well. There was his mother, thee mind. Mistress Thomson was aye one to keep a well redd house. And thee, Kirsty. He must see thee managing thoor man's croft as though thee were himself."

"And my man's mother and my man's bairn," she cried back at her.

"He's thoor pairn as well as my son's pairn, Kirsty."

The child at the table hardly heard his grandmother's words, as when ears and sight are filled with the tumult of the ocean, the immovable rocks upon which it breaks are never noticed.

"Ay, he's my bairn as weel. Who's saying he's no? And a bairn gangs with his mother. But even if a man puts up with another man's bairn about his house, he can no be expectit to take in another man's mother. Ye must see that. Ye must ken that. But ye'll never say it. Ye would think it would kill ye to say it."

"I go with Bartle, Kirsty." His grandmother's voice was as weak and persistent as the creaking of her chair. "I'm his grannie. He's double mine now I have no son."

"Bartle gangs with me. I'm his mother. He's mine as muckle as he was your son's. Ye've just said so yourself. And I've got to bide ben this house as though I was tied to it because of ye, while down the road——"

She could go no further and the stillness was filled with the uneasy creaking of his grandmother's chair, but the words his mother could not utter had such force to her son that he seemed to see them stampede like things, to tear down the road and stand back, like a barricade, outside the roadman's cottage.

So strong was this impression that after that, when Bartle passed, driving the cow before him, he always felt he was going through something. Sometimes the roadman himself stood there and he would say when he saw Bartle, as he was wont to say, "Mistress

MacDonald's man." But now his voice seemed to taunt the child, as though each word were the crack of a whip, and he would pass with never a look or a word, as if no one stood in the dark doorway of the low browed cottage.

Rain fell suddenly, sounding like the swish of a broom. The Wains returned to their country house, and with their advent the whole world shone and sparkled, waste moorland bloomed with myriad flowers and throbbed with bees, every bird broke into song and dragon-flies glinted like needles. Each day span by light as a cobweb to Bartle because it enmeshed them to Barnfingal. At any moment, at any hour, he might see one of them, or hear them on the road outside.

But they did not clatter past on their ponies or dash by in their carriage. Their voices never sounded on the still summer distance like the voices of a people from another clime. Bartle knew why. Everyone in Barnfingal knew why. The youngest child, a boy little more than a baby, had sickened soon after the family had arrived at their country house.

Dr. Geddes from Dormay passed the cottage at the roadside on his brown mare, on his way up the brae. He did not return all that day, grannie said. As he lay in bed at night, Bartle heard ruin on his way home, his horse picking its footsteps through the dark with the surety of anvil strokes.

"They've sent for a specialist from Glasgow," his mother said to his grandmother some days later. "He's to be here the night."

"All for a bairn, all for a bairn," mumbled grannie, still in the box bed. She always sounded less distinct when she was lying on her back than when she was sitting in her chair.

"The specialist'll no be able to help Master Charlie, mother," mourned Bartle.

"What are ye talking about?" demanded his exasperated mother.

"I've seen him lying in a black box with tassels to it, and his face all covered up."

In the grim silence that met his words, he became conscious not only that something was far wrong, but that he was the cause of it.

"Bartle MacDonald," his mother pronounced at last, "what's come over ye, I'd like to ken. Ye've seen no such thing, as weel ye must ken."

27

"He means he's dreamt it," grannie said leniently from the bed.

In the charged atmosphere mounting between mother and son, neither heard her.

"And if his face was all covered up," Kirsty was asking the chidden boy looking at her over the thick edge of his spoon, "how did ye ken it was him;"

"I kent," he muttered, indistinct as his grandmother when she was lying on her back. "I didna need to see because I kent."

"We'll have none of your lies here," retorted his mother. "Ye stop that stuff and nonsense, do ye hear me, Bartle? Awa' to the school now. If you'd be Mr. Ken All about your lessons instead of making up lies it would be more to the point, so it would."

Bartle was still at school that afternoon when Lady Wain called at Croft Fionn on her way back from the post office. She wanted to ask Mrs. MacDonald about the spare keys for the Big House, but as she did not listen to the answer, Kirsty knew she had called merely to give herself something to do.

"He is so much better, so much better," she replied in answer to the other's question with the loquacity of one labouring under stress. "Ah, my beloved Charlie—your baby, your youngest, the one who comes after all the others—he seems more to you because he is so much smaller. Naturally you are more anxious for him than you are for any of the others, but Dr. Geddes says he has every chance of winning through now. I left him sleeping so peacefully. It is the first time since he fell ill that I have felt reassured enough to leave him."

"Ma grandson was dreaming of thoor lad last night."

The ardour on Lady Wain's face blinked between tears and smiles. Now she turned its brightness to the forgotten old crone sitting where the fireside shadows shifted to and fro across her stationary form, so that sometimes she did not seem to be there.

"Did he?" the visitor enquired wonderingly. "Your little boy, Mrs. MacDonald, he is not here this afternoon; I missed him. Of course, at school. And what did he dream about my Charlie?" she asked, turning back to the shadows.

"That he saw him weel and strong as he has ever been," Kirsty interposed before her mother-in-law could say a world.

The tremulousness on Lady Wain's face strengthened into radiance.

"Ah, bless him, bless him for that," she cried. "As well and strong as he has ever been! Life has indeed crowned me with every blessing, my cornucopia is brimming over.

Why should a child's dream have infallibility rather than a doctor's diagnosis? Perhaps because a child is nearer heaven. God bless him for dreaming it, and you for telling me." She was speaking to the old woman now as she rose to her feet, her skirts lisping and rustling.

Charlie was going to be restored to her. Ah, how much was seen to be superfluous and redundant in one's life when extremity laid bare the only thing that mattered, flesh and blood.

The school was scailing as the wagonette bowled along the loch road. When she saw the children close to, she always thought what strong-boned, healthy children they looked. But to-day when she noticed them playing in the school yard, with the immensity of loch behind them, frowned upon by great boulders of mountain, in a green glen carved out by a glacier in some distant ice age, she had the feeling of how frail and tenuous was the hold of flesh and blood on its rocklike world.

A small sturdy boy was coming along the road, kicking a stone before him with his bare foot. He looked up at the sound of the wagonette and stood, as though bereft of movement, at the road's edge, amongst the ditch weeds and wayside flowers, waiting for it to pass.

She told the driver to draw up and had slipped down. from the vehicle before he had time to dismount to help her, half kneeling in the grasses beside the boy.

"You're Bartle, aren't you?" she said, her voice low as she spoke only to him. "Bartle MacDonald. I remember you so well from last year." Her fingers felt in her purse for a guinea piece she knew was there. Surely a small token in return for all the joy he had given her, for such lightening of heart. "You dreamt of my little boy, didn't you, Bartle?"

He was not looking at her but scowled past her, drawn into himself until he bristled like a small well defended rampart. They were all so shy, these Highland children, even when they knew English, as she knew he did.

"What did you dream, Bartle?" she coaxed, pressing his arms lovingly to his sides.

For the first time in his life he had a headache. He felt pulled in every direction at the same time, and wished he could go where he was pulled to stop it all, but he knew nothing would dislodge him. That was why his head was sore.

"I'm no for telling ye," he said, his voice rough.

Her mind froze. Of course, she had not noticed that at the time—his mother had spoken too quickly before the old woman could get in first.

"But you must tell me, Bartle. They've told me already, you know. I was at your cottage."

No wonder his head was sore, it might have had a mountain on top of it.

"Then ye'll ken without me telling ye."

She knew as she rose to her feet that he knew 'they' had done nothing of the kind. She felt very tall as she stood over him, yet as she looked down she had the curious feeling that he was more permanent than she, a rock so small the glacier had been unable to shoulder it aside or sweep it along with it.

"Tell me what you dreamt, Bartle."

His voice was so thickened she had to listen attentively to make out what he said.

"He's no getting better."

Her breath spiralled in her body, leaving it hollowed.

"Isn't he, Bartle? Tell me how you know."

"I saw him in a black box with tassels to it, and his face all covered up."

The mountain had eased somewhat on top of his head but he felt now as though his heart were being squeezed.

The guinea piece in her hand stabbed her as if it had a point.

"That's for you, Bartle," she managed to say, her words sounding unreal to herself, and she held it out to him. "I want you to have it, dear."

Even their pennies were golden—He backed from her.

"My mother wouldna let me take it," he told her huskily.

"No? Even for a keepsake? Well, perhaps she wouldn't." She slipped it back into her bag. "Goodbye, Bartle. These things are in God's hands, you know, not ours."

She climbed into the wagonette and closed her eyes. She must try to remember that: Charlie was in God's hands, not the specialist's nor the doctor's, but in God's. And she had behaved as though his life lay in that country child's slow Ay or Na!

When she opened her eyes again, the wagonette had climbed the brae on to the moor. Mosses splashed it in patches brilliant as sunshine, and she noticed the turf on the old drove-road across the hills was as bright as the grass that grows on graves.

# Chapter Three

THE harvest was poor that year, the grain shaken out it of it by the wind. But as always, bright birds flew round the small newly-made haystack at the edge of the Croft Fionn field. Kirsty had planted nasturtiums to border the potato patch, and their strong yellow colourings looked prettier and less strong and yellow used on so large a scale. Davie, the roadman, used to lean on the dyke when he passed to say, "Your flowers are reel bonny, Kirsty," and "Wha but ye would grow flowers to brighten a potato patch?" But Davie could not have been passing so often now, for although the nasturtiums put up as brave a show as ever he never was there to remark on them.

This year's leaves layered Mar Woods, brilliant or ghostly, with veins branching across paper-like surfaces, spotted and blistered, lying on top of the mould of past seasons. Bartle and Jamie Malcolm stood foot deep in it in some places. The ground, where it could be seen, was veined too, dried and hairy as a root. Light fell darkly between the trees so that Bartle felt that entering the woods was like entering a bottle which the light never really reached. It was airless, as if the upper branches of the trees had sucked not only the sunshine but any air into themselves before either could penetrate their lower reaches. The only things that appeared to flower here were toadstools, sporing and spawning in the twilight, without roots so that at the slightest touch they crumbled as they scaled the barks of trees. The whole place was filled with the stillness of decay, where the cracking of a twig sounded like the report of a gun and the rustle of the leaves they disturbed like someone following them, who stopped when they stopped.

'I'm getting out of here," said Jamie.

He was Bartle's best friend, for although a little older they sat side by side on the same whittled bench in school, keeping close together in masculine comradeship because the scholars who were immediately older and younger than they all happened to be girls.

Jamie lived at Brae Farm with his uncle, two sisters and his elder brother Dugie who had been taken away from school the moment he was thirteen because he was needed on the farm. Dominie

Shaw had wanted Dugie to try for a bursary and go to college but his uncle Rob had forbidden it. "Latin and Greek dinna help tatties to grow," he had said when the dominie approached him on the subject.

Bartle always felt sorry for Jamie, because his uncle was morose Rob Malcolm. And Rob Malcolm was not unlike his square, grey house, which hardly an inhabitant of Barnfingal had been known to enter, standing bleak and inhospitable in a dreary glen scoured bare by the winds, far from any other homestead.

Sociability was not encouraged either at Brae Farm or Croft Fionn, where a boy was expected to be too old for play once he was old enough to go to the school. The only time therefore they saw anything of each other except when they were at their lessons was immediately afterwards. Then Bartle would accompany Jamie for a part of the way home or Jamie would accompany Bartle, as on this afternoon, on some short comprehensive expedition.

"I'm coming with you," Bartle now agreed hurriedly.

The person following them charged like an army at their heels as they began to run helter skelter through the leaves. Suddenly a metallic clank sent their blood curdling. They stopped, and the army behind them stopped dead to a man.

"What was yon noise, Jamie?" asked Bartle.

"I kicked something," diddered Jamie, "I dinna ken what." He felt he would stand stock still for a thousand years if that would prevent the clang repeating itself.

"Look at yon," Bartle pointed, his voice huskening.

They stood as though rooted to the spot and looked at yon: a semi-circle, like some witch's spell, of dead mice, rats and birds. Then they saw a pair of eyes glaring at them from the ground. They were charged with such malignity that they appeared to be by themselves, like elements, and it was a second or two before Bartle realized they belonged to a vixen who was hardly distinguishable from the leaves all round her.

"Do you see what's happened, Jamie?" he whispered. "Her mate's brought her food but the clanking of the chains has made him so feartie he's no taken it near enow to her."

"I'm getting out of here," Jamie repeated with decision.

"Na, Jamie," said Bartle, "we'll need to get her out. Can ye no see she's trapped?"

"It's where she ought to be," retorted Jamie, his voice harsh with fear. "I'd rather see the likes of her in a trap than out of it any day. Dinna do it, Bartle, I tell ye dinna do it." He hopped from one leg to another in his extremity. "It's a vixen, no even a fox. And she's as good as dead now anyway."

The trap had the vixen by the thick part of her hind leg; it was a hard ugly thing for Bartle's puny fingers to attempt to move, particularly when he had no idea how to set about it. All he wanted was to raise the claws and set her free. He seized a piece of wood to attempt to insert it as a lever, but she did not understand he was beginning to succeed. She turned on him her ferocious face as emaciated as a starving cat's. He had to push her matted leg for all he was worth to prove to her that she was free. He never knew whether his finger got caught in the trap or whether it was that she bit it.

Someone behind him was ejaculating in Gaelic and the next moment he felt himself gripped in strong arms. Because the pain in his finger was excruciating and he did not want to make up his mind about anything, he went to sleep. Or that was what he thought. Then when he woke up things would not, could not be so bad. Only when he woke up it was to see the dark frowning face of Jamie's uncle bending over him, and Bartle wondered what could be much worse than that.

"That'll teach the pair of ye to gang springing the traps I set," the man's voice rumbled grimly in his ear.

"Jamie didna do anything, Mr. Malcolm," Bartle said loyally. "I wantit her out. And I've just hurt ma finger, that's all"

"Ye've no got a finger to hurt," Jamie's uncle informed him.

It was true. When he looked down at his gory right hand, Bartle saw three instead of four fingers. It gave him the oddest sensation, to see a gap where something of himself had been. Just as he was often to marvel in the days to come that he sometimes still felt his finger aching although there was no longer anything there to ache.

Even on such a day as that, Jamie and he managed to exchange marbles before parting. This had become something in the nature of a rite, for there was one, a glass bulger exotically whorled, which was the wonder of them both and which changed hands each time they met. The pocket it left always felt empty as a drum.

"I'll be seeing ye the morn's morn," Jamie would say exultantly, his hand tightly closed.

"Ay," Bartle would agree dourly. "Take care of King Bull now, Jamie."

In spring they collected birds' eggs, Jamie contributing the big blotched eggs of moor birds and Bartle the smaller speckled ones from bush or tree. They kept them in a cardboard box which they hid behind some stones in the dyke on the road to Brae Farm.

The only person who knew of their secret was Annie, Jamie's small sister, and she had to know as she tagged on to Jamie after school to be taken home the lonely uphill road, which was the only time her brother and Bartle could visit their hoard. When Bartle was there, he shared the trial of Annie equally with Jamie, and one or other would give her a hand once they were out of sight of the last cottage. Bartle did not object much to Annie knowing about their eggs because by the time they were put into the cardboard box they were merely empty shells, light as feathers. It was when the lobe of a plover's egg before it had been pricked filled the cap of his palm that he felt he held the universe in his hand. "What's this one, Jamie?" he would ask insistently, while his gaze stroked it with love as he thought of the eagle it might enclose.

\* \* \* \*

The moment he pushed open the house door when he ran home, he could tell if his mother were not inside. One afternoon he heard his grannie calling him whenever she heard his bare feet in the lobby, for she had been listening intently for the first sounds of his homecoming.

"Come away, Partle. Thoor mother's away to see Katie Stewart. Eh, but thee have peen a long time coming from the school the day."

"If I'd kent ye were by your lone self, grannie," he said, swinging the kettle on to the swee, "I would have run all the way back from the school to ye, so I would." It struck them both as a great waste that they should not be sharing all the time together on the few occasions that his mother went visiting.

"Has it pegun to esk?" she asked.

"Na yet, grannie."

"It will before the night draws in," she assured him. "I ken from the way the wind's cluttering the leaves."

He knew that 'esk' meant to rain a little. It was one of the words they used where grannie came from, like 'wain' for hope and 'foles' for the small bannocks his mother made when she held a ceilidh, as she was going to do to-night. But Kirsty did not like Bartle to use any of grannie's words and corrected them when she heard either say 'acre-a-bunk' for plain rye-grass or 'smorra' for what everyone else in Barnfingal knew as clover.

"Grannie," Bartle asked ponderingly as he put a cup of tea as strong as he could brew it into both her hands that began to shake whenever they held something, "what way does mother no like ye or me to speak like they speak in Wrack?"

She was very old and her mind had made many a circuitous detour in the past to avoid what was distasteful so that by now it was impossible for her to retrace her steps by a straightforward route.

"What's that?" she demanded loudly, as though she had not heard correctly, which he knew by now was her method of not answering. "Give me another spoonful of sugar, Partle. Kirsty never minds I take twa spoonfuls."

He had given her two but now ladled in a third, taking none in his own that his mother would not notice any shortage.

"Where did ye meet grandfather again?" he asked invitingly, altering his course of enquiry.

"At Raxdale, when I was at the curing and your grandfather had come north to see about some island sheep for his laird."

"Raxdale's on the mainland, is it no, grannie?" he enquired chattily.

"Ay."

"And ye never went back to Wrack after that?"

"How could I when I came to Barnfingal and have been here ever syne?"

"How indeed," he agreed consequentially. "And ye and grandfather would be marrit at Raxdale I'm thinking."

"Ay. The vow was put on us there by the minister. I came to Barnfingal a married woman."

It was as though she felt if she merely answered his questions she would satisfy him enough to lead him away from any danger point, like an animal believing that if it remains still enough it will be overlooked.

"And what sort of place is Raxdale?" he answered.

"The stirriest place thee ever saw," she answered with sudden garrulity, as if she had succeded in leading him astray. "When the boats were not putting out, they were coming in, with us lasses at the barrels from morn to night, and the men shouting to us when they passed. Thon harbour was as full of life as a net with fish."

It was of Wrack then his mother, and therefore his grannie when she was about, did not like to be reminded. He wondered why.

"And did grandfather get island sheep for his laird?" he prodded.

"Ay, we fetched some back with us. But they did not do well in these parts. The laird thought they would be real hardy, but they must have missed the sea and the salt over everything, for they all sickened and died aff."

"And did ye miss the sea, grannie?"

"Thee forget to miss what has long syne gone past thee."

"But when ye came to Barnfingal at first," he suggested discursively, "it would all seem different from Wrack, did it no?"

"Real different. The folk and the houses, the way they made their fires, the very stones on the road, even the minister———"

"The minister?" he asked wonderingly. "What way was he different, grannie?"

"What's that?" she repeated, as though she were deaf. "Ay, and everything so green, it made my stomach turn."

"It's no green on Wrack then, grannie?"

"Not green at all. All the colour has been pleached out of everything over yonder long syne." At that moment his mother entered, her hair blown about by the wind and her cheeks glowing with the cold air, like russet apples suddenly touched to life. With her presence the island of Wrack, which had rocked ecstatically near when he and grannie were alone together, disappeared again behind the horizon into the regions of lang syne.

"We will need to be quick, Bartle," she said. "Ye clean up the dishes and I'll set the table for the night. I couldna get awa'," she exclaimed, unusually loquacious, to the grandmother as she busied herself about the kitchen. "Three times was I up to get out of the door and three times did I sit down again. Margaret MacLauchlan wha marrit on John Stewart—Bartle, ye will crack them dishes if ye pour boiling water on them—is biding with Mistress Stewart the now. She's coming the night. A fine set up body she has grown into and weel spoken too. Na, Bartle, use the other towel. Is yon the time!" she exclaimed, looking at the clock, "and me with naething ready!"

"Hoots," comforted her mother-in-law, "thee're dressed and all. Who's all coming the night?"

"Margaret MacLauchlan, Teenie Robertson, Katie Tyson and Sheena Turner," replied the younger woman, her mouth full of hairpins as she undid her long hair to wind it more firmly into a knot at the back of her head. It always surprised Bartle, when his mother's hair was down, to see the tail was quite unstreaked with grey.

"And no Mistress Stewart?" asked the grandmother, disappointment hollowing her voice.

"She's so bad with the rheumatics she canna put her foot outside her own door," Kirsty replied unconcernedly.

In the days past the grandmother had been in her element when a ceilidh was held at Croft Fionn for then old Mrs. Tyson, Katie Stewart and Mary Thomson would sit together with their spinning-wheels and ask one another if they minded when—
— But now Lizzie Tyson had whirled the wheel and twirled the distaff for the last time, and her place had been taken by Katie Tyson, who talked of quite different things to Kirsty. They had never known the people who had lived in the now ruined cottages scattered like tombstones through the clachan. Gentle Mary Thomson, the youngest of the four nodding old women, had made her last journey past the cottage at the roadside. And now Katie Stewart, the sole link, was too bad with the rheumatics to move from her house. Katie might as well be in her grave like the others, thought the grandmother as she creaked in her chair at the fireside and told herself that she had lived too long.

"Will I put the foles here, mern?" asked Bartle, waiting attentively to hear what she would answer as he hovered at the already crowded table with a plate in his hand.

"Bannocks, Bartle," his mother corrected him instantly. "Na one will ken what ye're talking about if ye call them by yon outlandish name. Ay, set them down beside the cruppocks—careful now."

"But foles are no the same as bannocks, are they now?" Bartle asked obstinately, not looking at her as he gingerly lowered the platter. "Bannocks are any size but foles are wee thick ones. I like your foles better'n any bannock, mern."

"Ye ask for a wee bannock then and dinna let me hear ye call them anything else," Kirsty said shortly, shaking out a half-dry cloth before folding it from sight. "Now dicht your face and come and I'll do your hair. It's cutting it I should be instead of combing—aweel, it will keep until Saturday now. Run and put the comb by, and if I let ye bide up till the half hour, ye'll undress smart, will ye no?"

He promised he would, and they sat and waited for the unusual guests in the quiet room where the clock knocked off the moments until they heard voices. Kirsty went and threw open the door. A blast of cold air whistled round the kitchen. There came the crunch of footsteps and voices greeting her, then they entered with their spinning-wheels and said, "Good even, Mistress MacDonald, and is it no a cold night?"

Three of them had come together and Margaret MacLauchlan entered alone five minutes later when they had all settled round the fireside. Hail clung to her dark hair and so tall was she that she had to bend her head to avoid the rafters, while her loud, free laugh made the china ring.

"I mind thee as a pairn," the grannie told her.

"Is he no as like to Bartle MacDonald as like can be," exclaimed Margaret MacLauchlan. "He gave me such a start standing there— for a moment I thought it was him."

Six pairs of eyes were riveted on Bartle with a fixity that confused him and made him wonder where to look.

"We call him Bartle too," said his mother.

"He's learning Latin now," said his grandmother.

"Just the way his hair used to fall over his brow and all," pursued Margaret MacLauchlan.

"He doesna stand like his father used to," commented Teenie Robertson, whose staring globular eyes seemed to Bartle to protrude still further on unseen stalks.

"He stands like a soldier," said Margaret MacLauchlan. "Are ye going to be a soldier, Bartle?"

Bartle had never been told what he was going to be so he replied, "I dinna ken."

"The deer are coming over the Gow hill—ye should gang out and see them, laddie," proposed Margaret MacLauchlan.

"Ay, run away with ye," said his mother, "but put something over your shoulders." Then as he shut the door he heard her say, "He thinks he willna catch cold, ye ken, if he's just outside the door!"

A moon shone fitfully between the clouds flying across it and in those glimpses of partial brightness the world below seemed not to be of substance but of liquid. When Bartle first looked at the rounded Gow hill, he could see nothing moving, but as the moon slid from behind the clouds he saw a dark procession trooping over the hill.

"Like a regiment of soldiers," he said and hugged himself close.

The cold air cut round him like a knife and lifted the hair that, when his mother forgot to crop it close, fell over his brow in the same way his father's had done. It was one of those moments, distinct and apart, which no one but he knew about, that brought with its exultant content the fear that it might never come again.

At the half hour, his mother told him, "Now take something aff the table and awa' to your bed, Bartle." As he let down the catch of his bedroom door, he heard her say, "He likes twa wee bannocks better'n one big one!" But although he went to bed, he could not sleep for his excitement listening to the whirring of the spinning-wheels and the unfamiliar talk threading through from behind the wooden partition that served as a wall. They all raised their voices when they spoke because of grannie, who did not like to miss anything.

"—If ever there was a bachelor, I would have said it was Davie Thomson," he heard Margaret MacLauchlan say.

"Mebbe Davie Thomson was a bachelor as some women are widows," came his mother's tart voice, "because they canna help themselves."

"Mebbe Davie Thomson was a bachelor for so long because the lass he wantit turned him down," suggested Sheena Turner. She was the one unmarried woman present, which made her perhaps sound strident as if she felt she had to assert herself to get a hearing.

40

"I ken of no lass wha would turn Davie Thomson down," his mother took her up sharply.

"The town lass apparently couldna say No to him," came Margaret MacLauchlan's pleasant deep tones.

"She's no lass," buzzed Sheena Turner's waspish voice, "she'll be thirty-four her next birthday."

"That's old enow to have your first wean," remarked Teenie Robertson.

"I dinna ken apout that," came his grandmother's drone. "I was older than that when I had Partle, for I was married twelve years before he came. But I aye knew I would have a pairn, for I was married when the moon was growing, just as I knew David Thomson's wife would for so was she. It's only if thee marry when the moon is waning that the marriage ped is parren."

"Is that so, Mistress MacDonald?" Teenie Robertson asked politely.

"And is Rob Malcolm no thinking of putting a wife in Brae?" enquired Margaret MacLauchlan.

Bartle sat bolt upright in bed to listen to what was said about Rob Malcolm, because he was Jamie's uncle and Jamie was his best friend.

"Sheena can answer ye that better'n any of us, eh Sheena?" said his mother.

"I'm thinking there's a gey distance between what Rob Malcolm's thinking and what he's putting," Sheena replied at last, and from the change in her voice Bartle knew her lips were pursed.

"All the distance that a wee word like Na makes?" Katie Tyson suggested helpfully.

"Mebbe it didna get the length of Ay or Na," conjectured Teenie Robertson.

"Mebbe it did so," Sheena retorted with spirit. "He askit me up to have a look at Brae and all."

The whirring wheels had paused.

"Na?" "Awa' with ye!" "Do ye say so, Sheena?" "And did ye gang?"

"Ye're no likely to gang," came Katie Tyson's thoughtful voice, "when the only time ye ever see a Brae servant lass is on her way to the farm and, a month later, on the road back, her bag in her hand."

"Of course I went. What was to hinder me? I'm no servant lass—I kent the door I went in by would have to ope to let me out."

"Aweel, Sheena, ye were aye one to gang your ain gait."

"Thee maun be apout the only pody in Parnfingal wha has ever put a foot inside of Prae."

"And what was it like, Sheena?"

"The bairns all washed clean as though it was the Sabbath. She's a smart lassie, yon Bessie Malcolm—the floor all sanded and no a spurtle out of place."

A wheel was started and Bartle lost the next few words.

"Ay, she's fifteen, Mistress MacDonald," came Sheena's voice.

"That's plenty old enow to handle a house," put in someone.

"Bessie's reel fair—she's like to her mother there," remarked his mother. "All the Malcolms were black as robbers."

"And did ye no think of becoming mistress of Brae, Sheena?" queried Margaret MacLauchlan.

"Mebbe it was the bairns that put ye aff," suggested Teenie Robertson.

"The bairns did no such thing. They would have been company at a lonesome place like Brae. I would no have been their step-mother but their step-aunt. Na, I could swallow the bairns with small trouble. Mebbe it was their uncle I found more difficult to put over, when I kent if he had had his way all four bairns would have been his."

"They say that Annie is."

"Dinna blaspheme the dead, Teenie."

Next door, a solitary child was sitting upright in the big box-bed, his eyes round with incomprehension.

"We all ken it's true. Bess Malcolm's conscience must have been as heavy as her husband when she watched him the in her arms. She was no old for child-bearing like Davie Thomson's wife. It was no bringing forth her fourth wean that did for her but a sore conscience. And mind how Rob Malcolm burit her."

Several voices, suddenly sunk and hushed, spoke now.

"It wasna right at all," he heard his mother say.

"Not consecrated ground or anything," chided his grandmother.

"Just at the end of the house," said Katie Tyson, "and carved on the gable-end above, 'Here lies Elizabeth Middler, spouse of Dugald Malcolm'."

"What way do ye think he did yon?" asked Margaret MacLauchlan.

"Weel," put in Teenie Robertson, "they say Rob did yon that she could no settle where she belonged, beside her husband in the kirk-yard."

"I wouldna sleep in yon house," Sheena Turner's voice broke in, "if I was paid a sackful of gold."

"Na. Ye're right there, Sheena."

"They were aye queer stock, yon Malcolms."

"Talking of grave-stones they're saying the Wains'll no be back next year as the Lady will no be able to bide being minded of the place where she lost her wean."

Bartle suddenly put the blankets over his bed-roughened head. It wasn't true, it wasn't true. They would be back. They must come back. He couldn't bear it if they didn't come back. No wonder Teenie Robertson was known as Hoodie because she was forever flapping ill omen over everything. Oh God above, make them come back that heaven might again touch earth, amen and amen over and over again.

His mother heard from Lady Wain in early summer and Bartle accompanied her as usual to air the Big House. That meant that they were coming back, every blessed one of them except of course poor Master Charlie.

Waves of feeling transported Bartle to heights of bliss, all the giddier because of the abyss into which Teenie's inadvertent words had thrust him. Any day now the carriage, like a victorious army streaming with banners, would thunder past Croft Fionn.

There it was now. He felt intoxicated with happiness as he heard the grating of the wheels, the beat of the horses' hooves, the pressure of air against the low window. Once more he was caught up with them, as though he were inside a giant clock that had begun to strike, where the rumble of the present and the clang of the past were trumpeted aside by the volley of the future.

It was enough to know that they were there. He never sought to see them, even at a distance. If such happiness came his way, he marvelled at the miracle; but it would have been like taking that miracle to pieces if he had presumed to spy upon them.

So that one afternoon, after saying goodbye to Jamie and shaking off Annie, when he came across one of them on the moor, he could only stand and stare, drinking deep of so brimming over a moment.

He was a boy, more slightly built than Bartle but taller. This must be Master Alfred then, the eldest son of the Wain family. The sunlight gilded his head and his hair sprang round it bright as a halo. Why, this was not only the eldest son of the Wain family—he was straight out of Bartle's history book. Undoubtedly he was a Caledonian—"men of exceptional stature with red hair and the bravest fighters of all the Britons." Fascinated, Bartle took a step closer to him.

"Who are you?" The words rang out in the clear air as imperiously as a king's.

"Ma name's Bartle MacDonald. I bide in Croft Fionn at the roadside."

"The word is my not 'ma'." He mimicked Bartle's accent and in so doing exaggerated the 'ma' into 'maw'. "And after this say 'live' not 'bide' when you're talking to me."

As he would have accepted the least sway of an emperor's sceptre, so Bartle accepted this boy's every word as law.

"Ye and me," he said ingratiatingly but still keeping a seemly distance, "have the same birthday."

"Oh!" exclaimed the eldest son of the Wain family, as though suddenly struck by something. "So that's who you are! I know all about you—to my cost. You're the son of poor Mrs. MacDonald who works so hard." Was it possible that it was the Lady he was mimicking now? "And what's more—you've got something that really belongs to me! You've got my Snakes and Ladders! Yes, you have!"

"It's mine now. Your mother gave me it."

"It's nothing of the kind. It's mine. I want it back. It was one of my presents and my mother took it from me to give to you."

"She askit ye for it, ye had so muckle. And she paid ye weel for it into the bargain."

"How do you know that?" demanded the astounded Master Alfred.

44

"I know because I ken," Bartle replied reluctantly.

Just as I ken now you're not brave at all, he wanted to shout at him to keep himself from crying, just as I ken now the only weapon you would ever use is your tongue, just as I ken now you would run away to save your own skin——

"And what does ken mean when it's at home?"

"It means the same as know at home or abroad."

Master Alfred looked taken aback by this sudden stiffening of front. He attempted to cover up his momentary discomfiture with a display of fire.

"You speak so commonly you might be talking a foreign language," he said loftily. "I can't make out what you're saying."

"Ye ken right weel what I'm saying."

"You'll listen to what I'm saying for a change," retorted Master Alfred, changing his tactics from the defensive to the offensive. "That Snakes and Ladders is mine. I want it back. You go home straight and bring it out to me—this very minute. Do you hear?"

"Ay, I'm hearing ye."

"Then do as I tell you."

"I will no. The Snakes and Ladders is mine. If ye want it, come and fetch it."

Come on, his heart cried in agony across the patch of moorland separating them, bash me on the neb for daring to speak to the likes of you like yon. You're bigger than me and I swear I'll no lift a finger to you—as long as you show me you really are worthy to be her son——

"I'll do nothing of the kind," replied Master Alfred when at last he had made up his mind. He might be taller than Bartle MacDonald but Bartle MacDonald was undoubtedly heavier than he, with bigger fists— "And let me tell you I wouldn't touch your Snakes and Ladders with a ten foot barge pole after it has been in your dirty cottage all this time——"

He turned his back and walked away across the heather in an excess of dignity. But Bartle saw now, instead of the Wain splendour, only what that splendour had once surrounded. He felt he could never forgive the diminishing figure for separating what should have been as indivisible as the sunbeam and the sun, the blessing and the blessed.

For he knew now it was just an accident that Alfred Wain was her son and had red hair. He knew now for certain he was no Caledonian, for the Caledonians had fought to the death behind too small shields and with blunt swords.

# Chapter Four

IN the long winter evenings his mother would sit knitting on the settle or spinning at her wheel, while his grandmother blinked her over-bright eyes at the fire and Bartle sat at the table, his slate leaning against its edge, his pencil squeaking across it.

"What are ye doing, Bartle?" his mother would query when it was time for him to go to bed and she rose to pour out his milk.

And always he gave the same reply, "Ma Latin."

"Hoots, do thee no ken it by now;" his grandmother would ask while his mother remarked,

"I notice ye dinna spend near so muckle time on your spellings as on your Latin!"

The window was not only small and low but screened with growing things, so that the light that did penetrate during the day mottled the ceiling and spotted the walls like a trout's skin. Kirsty kept a shallow pan full of water from the well across the road on the dresser and its reflection glimmered ceaselessly on the roof, like a spring or burn.

It was company for grannie when someone passed on the high-road outside but very rarely did anyone knock at the door, unless perhaps some 'poor gangrel body'— a pedlar, selling buttons and tapes, a tinker rattling amongst his stock-in-trade like a marble in a kettle, a troop of wild ragged gypsies, or once a year the old pig-wife who, putting down her heavy burden of china, would have a gossip with Kirsty.

Bartle was so attuned to his grandmother that sometimes he felt himself rocked by the tide on which she now ebbed and flowed. So different were her days to his that when this happened it was as though he felt not like himself but as she must feel as she sat in her chair or lay in the box-bed.

It was not unpleasant, being grannie. Night lightened into day behind the curtains, patterning the room, until darkness swallowed the fire smoored on the hearth. If the continuity of her hours was even, the smallest break in them, such as her meals or her grandson running home from school, assumed enormous proportions, while the least deviation from the daily round caused unbounded excitement. She lived off the last happening until the next took place and because the very length of her years had coiled the thread on which they hung, her earlier recollections were often closer to her than those of yesterday, so that in her old age she still fed off her youth.

Summer and winter had now flattened for her against the window-pane, she was removed as though in the shell of her body from all extremes of heat and cold. When therefore she heard what the weather was like outside, it was remembered warmth, a remembered breeze, that stroked or freshened her old lined face. After the wildness of her island home, where even in summer a wind blew across pink bents and stirred the haddock-sands, the green glen where she now lived held for her all the uneasiness of cessation. Here the Highland winds trooped and foraged from afar, they did not breed as on Wrack, where they were as much a part of the island as a clapper is to the bell.

She had none of the thrust and impact now that her grandson had when he went to school, of feeling the slap of the wind against his knees, holding out his hand to watch the hail stot off it, covering each year that passed a little more ground with lengthening stride.

Every detail of a certain day stood out in his memory as though engraved. It was in early spring and his mother and he were looking over the edge of the pig-sty where the sow lay with her newly born litter. Bartle was very excited as he gazed down at her above his hands gripping the uneven sty door.

"Twa, three, four, five—I think there's six, mern, but they willna bide still. Look, mern, look, do ye see yon wee one. Yon must be the baby."

"Ay, yon's the cricklet," replied his mother in her flat voice, "there's aye one born wee'r than the others." Suddenly Bartle lifted his head and sniffed. "I smell something burning in the kitchen," he said. His mother hurried into the cottage while Bartle still stood on tip-toe to peer over the sty door at the sow, an island of inactivity surrounded by the restlessness of her squealing offspring.

"It was the porridge," she remarked when she returned. "Move awa', Bartle, I must fill the trough now."

"I have a very quick nose," he said with childish pride.

48

"It's a wonder it has no run aff your face then," she replied dryly. "Run and gather the eggs now and then come ben for your tea."

As he passed the kitchen window, he heard his mother and grandmother talking, but when he entered their voices suddenly ceased. Once or twice in the last few days the same thing had happened; and the night before, when he had been lying in bed, he had heard them talking in the next room long after ten o'clock. He did not know what was the subject of their discussions although once when he had interrupted them, his mother had asked him, how old he was again, exactly as though it were his birthday.

That evening, after he had brought home the cow, he found his grandmother alone in the kitchen. He asked where his mother was but the old woman was in one of her uncommunicative moods and would make no reply, sitting with pursed lips as though afraid if she opened them she would give away something she had determined to keep to herself.

As he was shutting up the hens for the night, voices floated to his ears. Glancing towards the schoolhouse he saw, walking across the playground, his mother with the dominie. Startled, he watched them pause at the gate; then, after some minutes of conversation, saw him open it for her to pass through. But before she had reached Croft Fionn, Bartle had climbed into the loft and was out of sight.

"I was down seeing the dominie the night," she remarked as he was taking his supper, and at her words the mug of milk he held jolted as though it were holding his hand, instead of the other way about.

"Your grannie and me were thinking of putting ye through the college," she said.

Milk splashed from the mug on to his knee and he bent his head and dumbly licked it up.

"I was saying to dominie Shaw it would pay us in the end," she went on.

There was a pause which his small rough voice broke.

"I could try for a bursary, mem, like Danny MacPhee did."

"Na," she replied, but she looked pleased, "we will send ye, laddie."

"Ay, ay," agreed his grannie, speaking for the first time and knotting her hands together in her excitement, "leave the bursaries to them wha canna afford to pay."

That night the moment he was in bed, he put the blankets over his head and lay still as a stone, as though he thought the darker it was and the quieter he remained, the better chance this stupendous happening would have of making up on him. By the time he fell asleep he was worn out with excitement.

Next morning he went early to school, looking round at each person who entered to see if it were Jamie. He had King Bull all ready to thrust at him before he was asked for it; he wished he had a pocketful of King Bulls to give Jamie.

And that morning Jamie missed just being late, ducking in before the dominie without a minute to spare while the ubiquitous Annie, who knew by now to disassociate herself from her brother except when they were alone, trailed in as Mr. Shaw was making his way to the front.

Jamie bumped down beside Bartle and grabbed King Bull from him below the desk, while he opened his history anywhere to give a prepared impression. But the dominie was a terrible one for not being deceived. After giving out the lessons for the first hour, he came and stood before the two boys. Jamie pretended to be so engrossed in his history that for the life of him he did not see him, while Bartle's glance explored no higher than the teacher's watch-chain with its dangling fob.

"So you are going to the university, Bartle?" dominie Shaw remarked peaceably enough and the boy's gaze was encouraged to climb a little further. "Bide behind the others on Tuesdays and Thursdays and I'll give you some extra schooling—you'll need it." By this time Bartle had reached the fortification of his massive chin. "It's a pity that more'n you haven't a mother behind them, pushing them on from the back." Bartle lowered his gaze to the dangling fob. "You know I wanted Dugie to try for a bursary, Jamie," the dominie was saying now, "and your uncle would not hear of it. If I thought Dugie would be worth taking trouble over, I think the same and more of you. You're quicker and brighter than he. But your uncle will not hear of you either, although I've been at him twice when I've seen him with the carts.

After school that day Jamie pelted up the brae with Bartle beside him. At the top, where the stony road became the cart track to Brae, they climbed a bank and a low dyke into the field on the

50

other side. They always felt secure and alone here, for there was an appreciable drop into the field which meant they were shielded from any passer-by who happened to use the brae. It was on this side of the dyke that they hid their store of eggs and where Annie, let out of school earlier because of her more tender years, waited for Jamie to take her home. She was there to-day, but her brother and Bartle were usually too engrossed in their own ploys to pay her much attention, and certainly had none to spare this afternoon.

"I hate him. I hate him. I hate him," said Jamie, his voice rising with each denouncement.

"Ay, he's a bad black man, your uncle," roared Bartle. "He'll come to no good, ye'll see. Ye keep King Bull for keeps, Jamie. We could have gone thegither. The dominie likes ye and he doesna like me, and he would have got ye on fine."

"I hate him. I hate him. I hate him," repeated Jamie, baleful with his thoughts.

"I hate him too," cried Annie, and, since only Bartle was present, she clung weeping to her brother to comfort him. "Ye could have gone with Bartle, Jamie. I would have missed ye sore, but I would rather have missed ye than ye didna gang." Her grief was such that it forced both Bartle and Jamie to heed.

"Now, Annie, ye stop that greeting," said Jamie, catching hold of the hem of her dress to scrub her eyes with it. "Ye ken Uncle Rob will cuff me if he sees I've made ye greet."

"Ye'd never make me greet, Jamie," sobbed Annie, her eyes like fountains. "It's him being bad to ye that's making me greet. Ye can no gang with Bartle now. I hate him."

"Now, now, Annie," counselled Jamie, "dinna take on like yon. Ye ken Uncle Rob's reel set on ye, and ye're no to hate him but love him weel." Annie's tears became so vociferous at this that Jamie temporised, "Aweel, look as though ye love him."

"Is her Uncle Rob set on her?" enquired Bartle, staring fascinated at the weeping Annie.

"Ay, reel set and she's more scared of him than any of us," confided Jamie.

"Why do ye think your Uncle Rob's set on her?" asked Bartle.

"I dinna ken," vouchsafed Jamie, looking at Annie in a worried brotherly way. "Mebbe it's because she's the smallest of us all. Do ye think that's why?"

"Ay, Annie's the cricklet. Mebbe, Jamie, mebbe. But your Uncle Rob's no the one to like something just because it's wee, is he now?" A half forgotten memory was struggling towards consciousness. "Jamie?"

"Ye dinna think your Uncle Rob's set on Annie because she's his, do ye?"

"Annie's no more his than any of us," considered Jamie. "He's just our uncle. He's no our father. I'd dee if he was our father."

"So would I," wept Annie. "He's just our uncle, that's all"

"Ay, but dinna ye tell him I said so," warned Jamie.

"We'll give ye an egg to keep, Annie, just for yourself," proposed Bartle. "Will we no, Jamie?" He dug a loose stone from the dyke with his finger-nails and brought out the cardboard box. "Now which would ye like, Annie? Take your pick. Big or wee—just ye say and it's yours."

Considering the length of time Annie took to make up her mind, it was something of a reaction when she pointed to the smallest in the box, a tiny egg, as blue as an eye, Bartle had taken from a mossy nest in the hawthorn bush near the roadman's.

Jamie carried it for her to keep it safe until they reached home and Bartle watched her jogging beside her brother until both were out of sight. Then he picked up the cardboard box, which had begun to wobble through dampness, inserted it once more into its hole in the dyke and replaced the stone he had removed.

He must have been a year or two older when the next incident took place, but looking back upon life it was the landmarks he saw and not the miles between. A creepie served him now instead of a chair when he reached for the Snakes and Ladders to show his grannie.

Davie Thomson's wife always spoke to him if she saw him pass their cottage, and Bartle quite enjoyed seeing her, for she was different from the other women in the scattered crofts and had for him still the attraction of the newcomer. She wore shoes not boots and changed out of her working clothes into a blouse and skirt every day of her life, instead of waiting for Sunday.

He never told his mother that he had seen or spoken to her unless she happened to ask, and then he would be plied with questions: which of her two blouses had she been wearing, what had she said to him, how had he made reply, and had the bairn been about? No matter how varied were the answers to these questions, Kirsty never ceased to marvel at the time some folk had on their hands.

He was passing the roadman's cottage one evening on his way to the march gate for the cow, when Davie Thomson's wife came to the doorway and invited him ben. Her words might have been a little more clipped but she spoke very much the same as they did in Barnfingal, for the "town" from which she come was a small market place not thirty miles distance. Tonight Bartle knew she had been listening for him: he also knew that his mother would not like him to cross that threshold, but he was glad he could not think out an excuse in so short a time.

The roadman's cottage was a replica of Croft Fionn, with the same rough whitewashed walls and thatched roof outside and the fire in exactly the same place inside,but to Bartle everything looked very different. No string across the mantelshelf on which clothes hung to dry, no big black pot with the hen's hash on the hob, no hams hanging from the rafters, their shadows involved on the roof with the shadow of an old woman's head. The box-bed was hidden behind drawn curtains that were sprigged with flowers, so that the room was not pitted with darkness like the Croft Fionn kitchen even at midday. As though embodying the difference between her own house and that of the one along the road was, instead of an old grannie in a chair at the fire, a fair-haired little girl, in a light coloured frock, sitting on the floor stringing beads.

"Now, Daisy," said her mother, "here's Bartle. Ye like Bartle, do ye no—ye watch him pass when he gangs for the cow. It's like this, Bartle," she said to him in the false voice a grown-up assumes when she does not want a child to hear what she is saying, "Daisy's starting the school the morrow and I wondered if ye would take her with ye and bring her home for her dinner. It wouldna take ye so muckle out of your way and I would have her at the door all ready for ye in the morn, but she's wee enow for the road by herself. That's reel good of ye then —I'll see ye'll no be the loser. Ay, Daisy, ye show Bartle your satchel and your pencil-box—her father bought it for her in the town."

There certainly was not another pencil-box like it on Loch Tarrolside, a feminine looking affair with a flower piece painted on a lid that slid off under the flat of your hand to reveal different coloured pencils and an eraser, each lying snugly in its own compartment. Daisy pushed the lid on and off several times that she and Bartle could see inside.

He was unhappy about what he had been asked to do, not so much because of being seen taking the roadman's daughter to school but because he knew that it would annoy his mother. He wondered then if he should tell her, but he knew she would find out sooner or later and wisely came to the conclusion that he should be the person she should find out from and the sooner the better. Even so, he found he could not bring himself to break the news to her until the next morning when, before starting out for school, he heard his voice croaking harshly as it tried to say with great casualness,

"I'm awa' for Daisy then."

"Wha's Daisy?" his mother not unreasonably asked.

"Davie Thomson's wife's bairn," blurted out Bartle, and even in the extremity of the moment he did think that was a long, roundabout way to describe so small and short a person.

His mother was staring at him, her black brows drawn.

"And what has Davie Thomson's wife's bairn to do with ye?" she demanded ominously.

"Naething at all," he hastened to assure her, "except that her mother askit me last night, on my way for the cow, if I would take her along the road with me each morn syne she starts the school the day." If his luck held, she might not find out he had been inside the house.

"She did, did she?" she boded. "Weel, ye listen to me, Bartle MacDonald, ye'll do no such thing—this morn or any morn. Wha does she think ye are—her servant lassie to take her bairn to school?"

"It's only because I gang the same road, mern. And I'll have to gang for her the day, so I will, for I said I would. I canna gang back on my word."

"Ye'll gang back on more than your word if I find ye at your promising tricks again without asking me. Ay, ye gang for her the day," she said, looking grim, "and I'll see her mother on her way home from the van the night."

54

Daisy came running towards him the moment he rounded the bend, her new satchel, empty but for the pencil-box, slapping at her legs. He gave her his left hand so that she would not be frightened if she felt he had a finger off, and told her to wave back to her mother before they turned the corner.

Outside Croft Fionn Kirsty was stretching her washing to dry over the bushes. She looked round as they passed but did not speak. Daisy may have sensed something or it might have been merely the inveterate curiosity of childhood that made her demand, "Wha's yon?"

"Yon's my mother," Bartle explained firmly.

After that Daisy kept her breath for walking but Bartle knew she was glad that yon was his and not her mother.

Donald, the vanman, came once a week from Dormay and stopped at the foot of the brae, beside the bridge, where the crofters' wives congregated from miles around to buy provisions, which they carried home in pillowslips. Kirsty seldom patronised Donald and, if she had to, sent Bartle; in her opinion it was a sign of thriftlessness and bad management to have to go often to the van. As for those who paid him a weekly visit, like Davie Thomson's wife, the only explanation Kirsty could find for them was that they had more money and time than sense, and wanted to gossip.

Tonight she stood in the doorway, waiting for the other woman to pass her. Davie Thomson's wife did not carry her pillowslip, like the other Barnfingal women did theirs, over her shoulder but in her hands. As Kirsty eyed its bulging contours, she commented to herself, "Ye must have run out of an awful lot."

Bartle could hear everything his mother said as he sat in the too quiet kitchen: she was word perfect.

"Good even to ye, Mistress Thomson. Bartle was telling me ye wantit him to take your Daisy to the school. But ye'll have to employ someone else to do that, I'm thinking, or make the time to take her yourself, for Bartle's going to the college, and I canna have his schooling held back by any bairn, yours or any other body's. It's a pity it's a lass ye have and no a lad wha could gang by himself. Good-night to ye."

She clattered back across the narrow stone passage into the kitchen.

"Thee did prawly, Kirsty," said his grandmother. "The likes of her! Who does she think she is?"

* * * *

Jamie was removed from school when he was thirteen, long before Bartle, which made Bartle feel like a lassie, particularly now he was the oldest scholar and had worked his way from the crowded front benches to a solitary seat at the back. He missed Jamie badly and the odd times they did meet in no way made up for the certainty of their almost daily contacts. Also the dominie liked him no better on closer acquaintanceship. "Well, well," he would say as he seated his heavy body beside the boy, "let us see how our lad of parts is progressing," and he would consider the sums, theorems and problems Bartle had worked through, like some black hen brooding strange eggs.

His last day at school, therefore, was all the more welcome to Bartle when it did arrive because it had taken so long on the way. It happened to be a Thursday, one of the two days during the week he waited behind the others for extra tuition. Across a sea of empty benches the master and his pupil surveyed each other, like opponents watching for the other to make the first move.

"Well," remarked the dominie at last, taking snuff, "so this is the lad of parts' last day at school, is it?" He spoke genially which was in itself, Bartle knew now, a danger signal, as he closed the horn snuff-box with a practised finger. "And how do you think you are going to manage at the university?" he demanded, bringing a checked handkerchief the size of a duster from a back pocket and stertorously blowing his nose. "You may not be quite so lucky there, may you?" He was looking at him over the handkerclikef with inflamed eyes. "You may not get into the professor's mind as easily as you have done into mine, and pick up all his apples merely by shaking his tree."

"I do nothing of the sort," Bartle repudiated indignantly. "And I can prove it to ye. Ye were wrong this morn when ye were setting out yon algebra for me. I kent ye were wrong but put it right as I worked it out. Ye can see it for yourself on my slate. I'm better than ye because I'm better than ye, and no because I cheat ye."

56

When he removed his handkerchief to stuff it back into his pocket, the schoolmaster's face with its too strong features was revealed to be as impassive as stone, as though even the bitterness upon it had fossilized.

"I too must have gifts," he remarked with elephantine lightness. "The gift of prophecy. Mebbe you will mind that when you were eight and a half, I prophesied this very moment to you. That you would exchange places with your dominie. Mind?"

"I wasna eight and a half," Bartle replied with deep affront, to show he was not disarmed, and he rose noisily to his feet. "I was eight and four month. I have to thank ye for all the extra fash ye have taken over me."

"No fash at all I can assure you," the dominie answered with polite if laboured formality. "Mebbe if there had been more fash I would have felt I had more of a hand in you—It's the extra that counts, MacDonald."

Until he went to Glasgow, Bartle took over the duties of herd, for which he received a few pennies a week and his food free, each crofter taking it in turn to be responsible for his meals. Jobs were scarce enough in Barnfingal to be looked upon as something like perquisites, such as that of the "beaters" Mr. Wain engaged when taking a shooting party out on the moor. Bartle received that of herd for the few weeks before he left because his mother was a widow.

The bull and the majority of the twenty-five cows belonged to Gow Farm while the rest were owned individually by the crofters and even bore the same surname. "Has Bessie MacLean come down yet?" Hamish MacLean would ask of Davie Thomson who was driving Myrtle Thomson before him. Each morning the herd collected the cows at the march gate and brought them back every evening to where the crofters, gathered in a small gossiping knot, waited for him.

Sometimes Bartle left the cows grazing near to Barnfingal while he strode into the strange, forsaken country behind the hills where nothing met his gaze but more hills, their sides scarred with screes and grey with rock. Between them stretched dreary wastes where ashen-stemmed, prickly thistles, like skeletons, reached to his elbows and added the final note of desolation. Long-woolled sheep and ferocious rams with glassy brown eyes, rabbits in their hundreds, warning one another of his approach with thumping hind legs, bounding hares, peopled this country, while small, noteless brown birds flitted from stone to stone. In the hollow of some of the hills lay small lochans which were stocked with strange-gilled fish whose like were to be found nowhere else in Britain and which the northern diver had brought on its feet as spawn from Iceland.

In the evening, as the sun declined, he would sit on top of the hill on whose side the cows were pasturing and wait until it was time to take them back. Mountain tops circled round him: mist wreathed Ben Gorm, the steep ridge known as the Droms, towering Ben Yar, the haunted Aillse Tor, pointed Sgur, and across the loch grim, discountenancing Fingal. Ben Yar, castellated like a giant's dwelling, hid the actual sunset but the radiance from it threw unearthly effects on the mountains opposite. Then western Ben Yar would grow dark and shadowed, while eastern Sgur, fell and menacing during the day, would be suffused with light.

The herd of peacefully grazing cows was like a banner proclaiming its keeper's whereabouts, and more than once Jamie visited him. He would lie on his back amongst the heather beside Bartle while the drowsy drone of wild bees filled the air, the mountain scents of heather and thyme, myrtle and birk in their nostrils, and return once again to the subject that now seemed to engross his mind, a subject that struck Bartle as odd for Jamie to be so curious about in a world that held so much else—lasses.

"Yon Rachel MacInnes," he would enquire, nibbling hard at a piece of grass, "what do ye think of her, Bartle?"

"Ye mean MacInnes, the mole-catcher's second daughter?" enquired Bartle, consciously thinking of Rachel for the first time.

"Ay, her."

"She's older than us," contributed Bartle, as though that precluded Rachel from further discussion.

"Older than ye," corrected Jamie, "but there's scarce a year between her and me."

Bartle stripped a willow branch of its bark and frowned as, for Jamie's sake, he assembled Rachel MacInnes together from the various times he had seen her lately at the kirk. Her face was as profileless as though painted on a vase, her features all slope. As she was what is called in the country blind fair, he pronounced,

"I think she's like a white horse."

"Ay," Jamie agreed guardedly, "I ken what ye mean. She's no natural looking. Mebbe that's why ye have to keep looking at her——just to find out how she's different from any other body. And mebbe that's why other lasses seem sort of ordinary beside her."

"Mebbe," said Bartle, whittling away at his stick.

"Mind," continued Jamie, pulling another grass to nibble, "I dinna hold with the likes of her—one minute ye're good enow for her and the next ye're no. She'll no try on her fancy-dancy airs twice with me."

"What has Rachel MacInnes to put on airs for?" Bartle enquired as flatly as his mother.

"Because she's one of the kitchen-maids at the Big House."

"Oh," said Bartle, interested in Rachel MacInnes for the first time as he thought how wonderful it must be to live under the same roof as Them, to see all, or even one of Them every day of your life.

"Ay," Jamie went on savagely, "and because the Lady has promised to take her back with them to Glasgow when the family gangs. Ye'd think she was going on a visit from the way she talks, instead of as a servant."

"Rachel MacInnes has no the brains of a button," Bartle assured him. "Dinna ye heed her, Jamie."

"Wha's heeding here" Jamie demanded with some truculence. "And it's no brains I'm after," he added darkly.

Bartle did not tell him that he had the Lady's town address, 4 Victoria Quadrant, safe in his pocket and that he had been told to call on a certain day when he was in Glasgow and ask for her. He always avoided both the university and Glasgow when he was with Jamie because Jamie was not going with him, as he should have done.

But poor Jamie could not keep away from either subject the next time he sought out Bartle, for this was the last time they would meet before his departure. Annie accompanied her brother to say good-bye.

"Ye'll no be for knowing us when ye come back," began Jamie, very much on the defensive. "And then one day ye'll no come back."

"Why should I no be for knowing ye?" Bartle replied carefully.

"Because we're no Glasgow bred and have no gone to the university."

"If I'm no for knowing ye when I come back, Jamie," said Bartle, "I'll be no worth the knowing."

"Ay, Jamie," cried Annie, "what did I tell ye? Bartle'll aye ken us, will ye no, Bartle?" Her eyes always looked wet, as though she had just finished or was on the verge of crying, and now with the strength of her feelings the ready tears sprang from them. She wore a pinafore she had washed and starched herself and which was as clean as a newly born lamb and so starched it crackled with her slightest movement.

"Weel," said Jamie, mollified in spite of himself, "all I have to say is I may no be getting to Glasgow," he tugged at an earthfast boulder with both hands, "and we all ken I'm no going to the college, but I'll get awa'—One day I'll get awa'."

"Ay, that ye will," said Bartle. "I ken ye will, Jamie."

"Ye're sure, Bartle?" pleaded Jamie.

"I'm dead sure, Jamie. One day ye'll get awa' and no come back. Annie will too."

They sat on the green hillside and looked at each other. Inside the stiff tabard of her pinafore, Annie kept so still that it did not even crackle.

# Chapter Five

IT was on his next day, his last, that he received a visitor other than Jamie. She came behind him so quietly where he sat on the hillside that he did not even hear her and only knew he was not alone when her skirts touched his shoulder. His gaze followed them until it reached the face of Rachel MacInnes.

"And how's yourself?" she asked him. "Ye must have a reel good conscience for I didna even startle ye!" and she bumped herself down so close beside him that he had to move over.

No sooner had he done so then he realized that was the last thing she wanted him to do, just as he knew she had meant to startle him.

"And how's yourself?" he bantered back, turning where he sat to face her.

"Ye're going to Glasgow and so am I," she said to that.

"Ay, so we are," he agreed, as though the realization had just dawned on him.

"So I thought the pair of us should get better acquainted, as I'll have to have a lad to walk out with on my nights out, and wha better than a lad I ken?"

He leant sideways on his elbow to survey her good-naturedly.

"Until ye get to ken a Glasgow lad ye mean," he said.

Her fairness was such that it emphasized the slightest change of colouring.

"I mean no such thing," she repudiated with over much warmth. "That is," she looked at him through her eyelashes but being so fair she might as well have had none, "if the lad I ken makes himself agreeable to me,"

"It's no one lad ye want making himself agreeable to ye, it's lads," he returned.

All sideways glances, when she did look at you direct, her face seemed to slope in all directions.

"And wha do ye think ye are talking to me like yon?" she demanded, affronted. "I'd never heed the lads if I could get the lad I want," she continued, changing her tune as if she had received a different key. "And what's to hinder me being your lass and ye being my lad?"

"Naething except ye," he conceded.

She tossed her head and as far as he was concerned might as well have whinnied.

"Ye'd need to take some trouble," she assured him, "for I'm no just for the asking."

He knew not only that she would not need to be asked twice but would not even wait for the asking, but did not say so. He might as well have done so, however, for her face that had gone pink before suddenly flamed.

"It's grand for ye the Lady taking ye to Glasgow with them," he said, to lead the conversation out of corners into the open.

"Ay, they keep a big household or I would no have gone a step."

He had no objection to her putting on airs with him but he felt he could not bide it when she affected them about the Wains.

"Na?" he drawled misbelievingly. "Aweel, in such a big household ye'll have no lack for company, or need to look outside the door for it."

"The company I want is the company I can choose,'she retorted, "and I'm no choosing a fellow servant to walk out with."

"Mebbe ye should wait and see before ye make up your mind," he counselled.

"I'll thank ye to let me make up my own mind, Bartle MacDonald," she said hotly. Something about him frustrated her: it was as though when she was with him she had no mind of her own or rather, what was worse, as though he knew exactly what was in it. "What a carry-on in the winter in their Glasgow house by all accounts!" she exclaimed, as if she felt the more she spoke the less chance would he have of studying her. "When they're no giving a ball, they're going to one."

"Ye mean Miss Hetty and Miss Maysie?" he questioned, feeling something tighten across his chest when he even mentioned their names.

"Ay, them. And Master Alfred. He's a perfect divert if ever there was one, and no mistake. He's worth twa of them."

"Twa of wha?" he questioned coldly.

"Yon fine Miss Hetty and yon Miss Maysie—Miss Maysie's so proud it's a wonder her head doesna catch cold stuck in the air."

He gazed at her broodingly.

"And what's wrong with the Lady in your opinion?" he demanded.

"Her? If I have to have a mistress I'd sooner have her than anybody. But wha's saying anything's wrong?" she enquired suspiciously.

"If ye'd said a word against her, I'd soon have warmed your ears."

He was surprised as she at the intensity with which he spoke. Her mouth dropped open as she looked at him, but she felt impressed by his masculinity and was drawn to him for that most primitive of all reasons.

"I'm no against anybody," she said, "and ye least of all. I like ye better than Jamie Malcolm. Ye're bigger and brawer. Jamie's awful wee. Ye look older than he does into the bargain."

"Do I?" he countered with the wariness of the stalked. "Aweel, my looks must belie me. I'm younger than he is. Younger than ye are. Ay, than the pair of ye."

She was not listening but lay back on the short grass starred with minute flower heads to smile to him with her slack mouth.

"We're all alone," she invited, "with na one to see us. What's to hinder us getting acquaint now—properly acquaint I mean?"

He stared at her blankly to pretend he did not know what she meant.

"We can ken each other no better here," he said. "Ye'll have to wait for Glasgow for that when ye have your nights out."

"Na, na, Bartle, ye ken what I mean," she said encouragingly. "There will no be a chance there like to this. Folk'll be all round us then, and I'll have to be back by ten.'

"I'll have to take the cows home the night long before that," he said.

"But we've plenty of time the now. Here we are—the pair of us. Just ye and me. What's to hinder us?"

Stolid with deliberation he stared at her, as though to stare her down.

"Doing what?" he enquired.

She sat up, her fair hair parting where she had lain on it, her voice when she did speak raised and discordant.

"So ye think I'll think ye dinna ken what I mean?"she demanded.

"I ken ye ken fine. What sums did the dominie teach ye when ye stayed on at the school?" she jibed. "That a couple could never make one? Me saying I liked ye better than Jamie Malcolm. He may be wee'r than ye but let me tell ye he could make twa of ye. And dinna ye dare come near me in Glasgow unless ye want to find a door in your face. I would as soon walk out with you as I would walk out with a pew in the kirk. Ay, and ye would get me as far——"

As he had not seen her coming so he did not watch her go. Only looked at where she had lain to notice that the turf was so close cropped by sheep her body had left no impression upon it.

"Ye'd better gang the night and say good-bye to Mistress Stewart syne ye'll be awa' the morrow," his mother said when he returned home that evening.

"Ay, so thee had," agreed his grandmother. "Tell her I was spiering for her—she's growing old, poor pody."

Mistress Stewart lived in the cottage at the mill. Her husband was dead and one of her middle-aged sons miller now. The cottage, sunk below the level of the road, was built beside the mill on the banks of the burn which, broad and violent as a river, plunged at that point below the bridge. It filled the cottage with tumult, like the sea a shell; and, once inside, the opening of a door made the waters sound as though they were coming in upon you. Or did to a visitor such as Bartle, but those who lived there were not conscious of them even as an accompaniment. Although when the family, far scattered now, heard the sudden sound of water, even if it simply splashed from a tap into a sink, the years were spanned in an instant and childhood burst upon them like a river in spate.

It was Donald the vanman's night tonight, and her daughter-in-law had joined the women waiting for him on the bridge, so that Mrs. Stewart was alone when Bartle entered. She was younger than grannie and much cosier looking, with her comfortable figure buttoned roundly into a black dress that although rusted and darned still retained something of its Sabbath grace, while thrown across her shoulders was a capacious grey shawl. Perhaps it was this shawl of grow-grey wool he had never seen her without that made her always remind Bartle of a sheep, roaming about contentedly and oblivious of the bracken and twigs that stuck to her long wool. The bracken and twigs were her memories, and they were quite

64

different from grannie's. Mistress Stewart's memories hung on to her, whereas grannie clung round hers until the pressure of the years had polished and ground them into the very core of her being.

"So ye are aff the morn," Mrs. Stewart said to him, "weel, weel," and he felt like another twig caught on her wool. "And how is your grannie?" she pursued without waiting for his answer. "Poor body, she's growing old. She never liked when the nights began to creep in, even when she was young. Now, is it no a grand thing Morag's at the van and I have ye to maself? That clock's standing, so dinna heed it. Ach ay, I mind when John MacDonald brought her home with him. Your grannie I mean, when she was a lass. We were all lads and lasses then. Went awa' single he did, and came back a marrit man. Such a clash as it stirred up. It was all over the lochside before the hens went to their roost that night. I saw her the next morning on my way to the pier. Dark as a gypsy she was, just as everyone had tellt me. They were marrit all right, for she showed me her marriage lines when I had her to maself at Croft Fionn. She took to me and I took to her, but there was aye something foreign about her. All glint and glisk she was, aye at the top of her lilt although she might never be saying a word. Aye keeping holidays too. 'It's Johnmas,' she once said to me when I askit why she had more out on the table than would be eaten. And when I askit what Johnmas was, she tried to make out she had just said June. I mind one Lammastide she tellt me that in the parts she came from they would be holding up the cup to each other and saying, 'Lord, open the mouth of the grey fish, and haud Thy hand about the corn.' Gey queer, outlandish folk they must have been ben the parts she came from, if you ask me. Her door was aff the sneck more with me than most, but if I tried to spier from her this or that, she would no say a thing. Ay, reel pagans they sounded in the parts she came from. Do ye ken what I have often thought to maself?" She smoothed her lap as though to keep him waiting for what she had often thought. "I'll tell ye, Bartle, although I never mentioned it to any other body, for I liked her weel enow. I sometimes thought they were worse than pagans in the parts she came from."

"What could be worse than pagans, Mistress Stewart?" asked Bartle, gazing at her with widened eyes.

"Roman Catholics of course," she returned, flattered at the sensation she knew her words were causing. "They're a sight worse than any pagans, Bartle my lad, as ye must ken." She was looking at him conjecturally.

He felt his heart becalmed with excitement, like a boat settling in the midst of a stormy sea, which contrary sensation had the effect of making him feel violently sick.

"Na, na, Mistress Stewart," he said, making an effort to repudiate her with some force that he might carry a conviction he did not feel, "na, na. A minister married her and grandfather. I ken that. She tellt me so herself."

"Ay, she was reel carried about that. She thought that was why I wantit to see her marriage lines. I ken she believed that turned her into a Protestant but what I aye say is, once a Roman Catholic, aye a Roman Catholic. As ye begin, so ye end. The coffin ye die in is made of the same wood as the cradle that rocked ye."

"I dinna think grannie was a Roman Catholic—ever," Bartle said weakly. "Na, Mistress Stewart, I ken she was no. Mr. Napier comes to see her now she can no gang to the kirk," he fenced. "He was ben the day before last, and put up a prayer for her and all."

"No all the prayers put up for her in heaven or on earth will turn her into a Protestant," pronounced Mrs. Stewart. "Think back, Bartle lad, and have ye never had a suspicion she was no like other folk?"

"Never," he lied.

"Mebbe ye might hear your mother telling her to wheesht when she said something without heed?" Mrs. Stewart continued hopefully.

"Na, never."

"Aweel, mebbe your mother did it behind your back," she said, disappointed. "She was aye reel close was Kirsty. There was never any clash heard about what happened ben Croft Fionn, no because there was no clash to hear but because Kirsty was there to see it went no further than the door. Ay, but ye're more like to your father to look at than your mother, Bartle. I would have thought ye'd have been opener with your friends, but as the mother swaddles so the bairn remains even when he grows to be a man."

Bartle was glad that Morag Stewart returned at that moment, her pillowslip bumpy with what she had bought, because that meant conversation became general instead of particular. He noticed old Mrs. Stewart was very polite to her daughter-in-law as she enquired from her all whom she had met on the bridge. Something in her attitude reminded him of grannie's to his mother, ingratiating, almost subservient. The older women were relegated to a back seat at the fireside when they found a younger woman had filled their place as mistress, and their thoughts turned back to the days when they had waited for the vanman on the bridge and had a man to prepare for and full sway over the tea-caddy.

"How are ye travelling to Glasgow, Bartle?" enquired Morag. "By the coach or the new rail-road?"

There was nothing particularly new about the railway which had reached Dormay by the end of the century, but those in the district would still think of it as new even when they were old.

Bartle said the rail-road, in as subdued a voice as he could, that they might not think he was in any way puffed up.

"Ay," nodded Morag, "yon's the way the Family travel. It's quicker, and there are no changes."

"There are no changes," repeated Bartle.

"Ye'll have heard the Lady's taking Rachel MacInnes back with them to be in the kitchen," said Morag.

"Ay, so they say," agreed Bartle.

"Ye'll be seeing something of her syne the pair of ye are to be in Glasgow I'm thinking," suggested Morag.

"Mebbe," Bartle said guardedly.

He was to start off very early next day to give him plenty of time to walk the nine miles to Dormay, but early as it was, his grannie was in her chair at the fireside that she might partake as much as possible in her grandson's departure.

"Ye'd better awa' now, Bartle," said his mother when he was about to wash his porridge plate. "The sooner ye're aff the sooner ye'll be at the train. Say goodbye to your grannie, and be on your way."

"Thee're awa', lad," said his grannie, trying to speak casually when he came close to her. "Eh, eh, awa' thee gang then."

Her eyes were small but, bright with excitement at such a moment, they glittered, lighting the oldness of her face as embers might the greyness of a dead fire. He knew when he turned back at the door to look at her that he was beyond her orbit and she could no longer see him, but she was still staring in his direction, one humped hand plucking at her lap, as though she could. He knew once he was outside, she would keep the same, repeating her words to him as though he were still there.

His mother walked with him to the turn of the brae before the roadman's, then gave him his bag, told him to mind his things and wished him well. He swung past David Thomson's cottage, his footsteps echoing as though there were more than one of him. No one but he was stirring in this world washed bright as a pebble and beginning to waken for his benefit alone.

The firs that bordered a field on the other side of the loch were like the points of a crown in the morning light. He had seen that field move uphill grey with deer. White clouds like polar bears circled the sky that arched far above the corn-coloured earth beneath. When he passed the Mar Woods he smelt their acrid smell, as though they still smelt of last year's leaves.

The post office was housed in a but and ben no different from any other cottage in the district, except for the telegraph wires leading to its thatched roof. Everyone connected the post office with the Wains: they felt that if it had not been for Sir Alfred pulling wires with those purposeful hands that turned everything to gold, Barnfingal would have been without this modern blessing which left its inhabitants singularly unaffected. The only one who benefited was Kenny, the post master, who was allowing his croft to go to seed to save him the trouble of attending to it.

Once he had climbed the post office hill, Bartle was beyond the confines of his boyhood. He had walked into Dormay several times in the past to shop for his mother or do some other business with which she did not wish to gratify the inquisitive Kenny, but past the post office he was beyond the country whose every contour he knew by heart.

He knew he was not going to return that day by the steep brae he had just climbed, and he felt for the first time outside the egg that up till now had enclosed him. He was leaving his shell behind him, he was striding out by himself.

In Dormay, autumn was coming down the summer village street with a rustle of leaves pricked on by the wind. Bartle went straight to the station, and after ascertaining that the waiting train was the right one, climbed into it. The hours before it started were interminable: the cycle of a lifetime seemed to hang in tedium before revolving to be superseded by another exactly the same.

But whenever the train began to move excitement packed itself into every moment for him and clutched him by the throat. "This is the way the Family travels," he thought to himself until the very wheels were saying it, "you're going the same road they go." And as he saw mountain, dyke, field and river flung behind him into oblivion, he thought of the Wains taking this flying haphazard unlikely world as much for granted as he took the stationary road outside the cottage at home. He saw each of their lives streak like a comet that left a blaze of stars in its wake.

That he might think of them to his fill, he avoided entering into conversation with his fellow travellers, trying to quieten his thoughts as the train neared its destination towards the close of day by dwelling on what they would be likely to think in such circumstances. "We're going home now," they would think, "our holidays are over," and he smiled to himself to think of any Wain ever thinking anything was over for them.

The carriage emptied at one of the stations and a wee skelf of a man put in his head to tell him, "Sitting'll no take ye any further—this is Glesca." He was into the carriage before Bartle could get out, whisking up a piece of newspaper, hanging on to the racks to see if anything had been left, on his knees to look below the seats, his actions so quick that to Bartle they had something of the animal in them.

When he descended, the clangour of the station assaulted his ears like threats. He had never heard such din, which had the effect of bewildering and stupefying him.

"Are ye Mr. MacDonald?"

He all but denied his own name, so unfamiliar did it sound on this stranger's tongue. He was a boy of about his own age with a face as round as a ball and a dent in each cheek even when he was not smiling, as though the ball were punctured.

"My name's Sam Heggie," he explained, "and my mither lives across the stair to your landlady, so Mrs. Leggatt spiered of me if I would meet ye since ye are new to Glesca."

Bartle's mind always went blank when he thought what would have happened if Sam Heggie had not turned up for him. As it was, Sam snatched his bag and slotted before him to lead the way.

They caught a vehicle that had neither engine nor horse but that nevertheless moved at an alarming speed along lines. But it was the buildings like cliffs that startled Bartle more than anything else. He could not understand how these crowds of people could go about their business apparently unconcerned with what was impending all round them. The height of the buildings distorted his gaze and to him they seemed either to slant forward menacingly, as though to smite, or to lean back like someone about to totter.

"Ye'll like Partick," his guide assured him once they had dismounted. "It's near enough to the university and there are country places round it. Mrs. Leggatt's reel handy for the tram. Here it is. She's on the top—-just like us."

He disappeared into a doorway without a door, like the mouth of a cave, in a tall grey building. Bartle followed him so slowly that Sam leant over the spiked bannisters to see what was happening.

"I canna come up yon," Bartle said thickly.

The two dents in Sam's cheeks popped, just as though the ball had been pressed in still further on either side by an invisible finger,t hen he clattered down the stone flight to be beside him.

"Ye'll have to walk up because Mrs. Leggatt's can no walk down to ye," he pointed out with devastating reason. A tenement child, he surveyed him curiously. "Ye're no used to stairs mebbe?" he suggested.

"I've never been up stairs in ma life," said Bartle, the words breaking from him with the force of vows.

"Ye'll have to get used to them in Glesca," Sam told him bouncingly, "Glesca's naething but stairs," and with this cheerful piece of news he bounded up them, two at a time, and rapped on a door between earth and sky with a vehemence that sounded to Bartle, so far below, like a fiend knocking up hell.

"Here's your lodger," he heard him say.

He was never to overcome his fear of going upstairs, for they were something to which he could never become accustomed. Because familiarity made small difference, he knew this fear had little to do with himself. It was something left behind for him by someone else, something that had been there all the time, which he had merely made up on.

When he moved through the streets at night, saw a drunk man lurch across his path, heard the jangle and crash of traffic, watched the light from a lamp-post streak the heads and greasy shoulders of those below, revealing avid faces, he thought to himself, "How Jamie would have hated all this." But even as he turned in at Number 107, Barrowflats, he knew Jamie would have done nothing of the kind. Jamie would not have stood at the bottom of the stone flight of stairs wondering which foot he should start off with. Jamie would have been up them in a trice, knowing the sooner he was up the sooner would he be able to come rattling down to mingle with the absorbed life crowding both pavement and street.

On the first day at the university he saw Alfred Wain. Alfred Wain saw him, but nothing further passed between them. He was a first year student, like Bartle; that was the only similarity they shared.

With his tall good looks and narrow head, he reminded Bartle of a fox. Prominent with his assertive red hair, his attractively captious temperament made him the leader of the dashers and gay sparks. Yet he was not merely the spoiled heir of a wealthy man, for the son of Sir Alfred Wain knew not to waste his time.

Lady Wain had arranged for Bartle to call at Victoria Quadrant on a certain Saturday afternoon. He knew she had settled the very hour to make it as simple for him as she could.

They lived near Charing Cross, on those upper heights where houses like palaces rose in tiers. He had given himself plenty of time and as he climbed towards Victoria Quadrant he neither hurried nor lingered. For he knew then that something fateful was going to happen to him that afternoon, that nothing could come between him and it, that haste would not bring it a moment sooner and no power on earth could delay it even for a second. He was being borne along by some invisible power towards a moment as certain as destiny.

He approached by the hill instead of by the sweeping terrace. The hill was so steep, broad stone steps had been inserted to help the climber. As he ascended, he knew he was facing Number Four.

It was always to give him the same impression that he received when he saw it first. Standing so high on top of the hill and facing due south, the afternoon light, and he was always to visit it in the afternoon, swept through its broad windows and seemed to lift it into some upper air, so that he never thought of the Wain's house having a ground floor or basement.

Although he was calling on Lady Wain, he did not dream of going to the porticoed front door. Instead he found the entrance to the basement steps. He used the area knocker and listened to its repetitive rat-tat as though it had been sounded for him. He noticed all the basement windows were stoutly barred. To the moment he knew when footsteps would answer the summons to let him in. He watched the door knob turn. The next minute he found himself looking into the face of Rachel MacInnes.

# Chapter Six

"WEEL, Bartle MacDonald," she said, glinting him a look, "ye havena wasted muckle time seeking me out. And how do ye ken I'll choose to walk out with the likes of ye?"

"I havena come to see ye, Rachel," he replied. "I have come to see the Lady. She gave me the day and hour on which to present maself."

The colour splashed her face and neck unevenly as she took a step back from him.

"So ye havena come to pay your respects to me, Mr. Lord All-Mighty," she said, her voice beginning to rise. He knew he had never been hated so much as he was by her at that moment. "Huh, ye, and wha do ye think ye are now ye're no longer at home? If ye think the Lady'll see a ragged loon aff the hill in her town house, ye're even more of a fool than ye look. So get ye aff and dinna ye dare to show your face at this door again——"

He let the words run on without making any effort to check them, for he knew Rachel could no more stand between him and his fate than a twig could divert a waterfall.

"Rachel!" he heard a man's testy voice sound from behind her, "what are you standing skirling there for? Haven't I told you to stop wasting your employer's time daffing at that door? Shut it at once. There's a draught that cuts like a knife when it's open."

"Ay, Mr. Blair. That's what I'm doing, Mr. Blair. I'm reel sorry to have fashed ye again, Mr. Blair. It's naebody at all."

But Mr. Blair had followed the draught to the door. He was a middle-aged man with a nose like a declivity that took up a great deal of his face. As it was long, thin and pendant, pinched in at the bridge, it gave him a supercilious look. A physical impossibility for him to turn up his nose, he expressed disdain by looking down it.

"Ma name's Bartle MacDonald," Bartle said to him over the head of Rachel. "The Lady said she'd see me this day and hour."

"Come in, Mr. MacDonald," Mr. Blair told him. "I'll take you this way since you're here. Lady Wain told me to show you in when you called. You're new to Glasgow," he amplified as beneficently as his temperament allowed, to indicate by this chattiness that he knew although he was taking Mr. MacDonald upstairs it was really downstairs to which he belonged. "Well, well, every day you're here will correct that, won't it?"

Bartle no longer felt he was being borne along by some invisible power, he was that power. That was why he was conscious of the blood charging through his veins as though he were a giant, why his head was filled with a roaring like mighty seas crashing round an island.

To his surprise Mr. Blair entered a room without knocking, announced him and stood aside to let him pass. Bartle found himself standing within. The crashing seas had now submerged the island so completely there was nothing to show that it had ever been.

He must have caught sight of her once or twice in the past at Barnfingal, a gliff as she passed in the carriage or a backward view as she sat beside the driver in the wagonette. But this was the first time that they had come face to face.

She was sitting at the piano, idly turning over some music on the rack before her. He knew she was the second daughter, the one called Miss Maysie, because the oldest had red hair. She was older than he but to him she appeared years younger, for he grew into a man as he looked at her. Everything about her was different to what he was accustomed, the very texture of her skin, the slightness of her bones, the fineness of her hair, the set of her head. Her fairness was quite different from Rachel MacInnes' fairness for instance, it had the sheen of gold about it and none of the yellow of butter.

"Come away, Bartle," he heard Lady Wain's voice as though it were calling from another world. "Bartle's mother opens The Shieling for us each summer," she said to her daughter. "Sit down, Bartle. You wanted to see Miss Gemmel before she left, didn't you, Maysie?"

"No," said Maysie, "not now."

"But you said you were sure she was going to do your velvet wrong unless you kept a watch on her."

"It doesn't matter," said Maysie.

She was called Maria after a great-aunt for whom no one cared over-much, and Maysie by her family because her younger brothers and sisters had found that easier to say than Maria. She would still be known as Maysie when she was her great-aunt's age, but even now, before she had reached her twenties, there was a certain decision about her speech that great-aunt Maria herself could not have bettered.

"Have you comfortable rooms, Bartle?" Lady Wain was enquiring. "Mr. Napier, the minister at Barnfingal, recommended them, didn't he? Ah then, you will be in good hands."

Bartle turned in her direction. Something had happened to her since last he had seen her, or rather something had happened to him. She was no longer the Lady, but her mother. Perfection had taken another guise, that was all, even as he made the discovery that perfection could both expand and contract.

"You know we have Rachel MacInnes with us," continued Lady Wain. "She is bound to feel lonely at first, just as you are bound to feel strange in a new place. It would be nice therefore, Bartle, if you could see something of each other to begin with."

He began to arrange his thoughts into sentences, to tell her that ay, he would see Rachel on her nights out. He was glad to do anything Lady Wain asked of him.

"Can't you see, mother," he heard her daughter say, "that Bartle doesn't think Rachel is the kind who will ever feel lonely anywhere?"

"Of course I would not dream of asking you to interfere with your studies in any way," Lady Wain hastened to explain. "I only thought it would be a pleasant arrangement for you both."

"Not for Bartle," interposed Maysie at the piano, letting the sheets of a piece of music flutter so that they made a little cutting sound. "He doesn't like Rachel."

"Dear, dear," said Lady Wain, looking vaguely from one to the other, "I didn't know that. Don't you, Bartle? Naturally then you won't want to see more of her than you can help. I'm sure there is no harm in her, a little heedless perhaps but service should steady her. Of course we'll say no more about it. And tell me, do you like the university, are you settling down?"

He longed to tell her that even if he hated Rachel, he would count seeing her a small thing because of the Lady's wish. But they talked so quickly in town that by the time he had grasped one topic they had flashed to another, so that now he had the breathless feeling, although he was sitting still, of chasing something he could never quite overtake.

"My son has started at the university too," she said delightedly, taking his lack of response for tongue-tied shyness.

"Master Alfred will be taking a different course from me," he managed to muster in reply.

"Yes, perhaps. What are you taking, Bartle'"

"Mathematics and Latin are the chief twa."

"An Arts Course?"

"Ay. "

In the stately room burnished with autumn sunshine, a boy's voice reached Bartle from a hillside in-the past, "The word is 'my' not 'ma.' And after this say 'live' not 'bide' when you're talking to me."

"We know Professor Barbour—I shall speak to him about you when next we meet. You are coming out to be——?"

"A dominie, if I win through."

"Of course you'll win through," Lady Wain assured him out of her ample store of confidence. "Bartle and Alfred have the same birthday," she explained to her daughter, and now Bartle knew why the mother had wanted to see him alone. "I always think of you on my son's birthday," she was saying to him; "because I didn't send a remembrance this year was not because I had forgotten. I waited until I saw you in Glasgow. I have arranged with Blair, Bartle, you know he showed you in just now, to accompany you to an outfitter's where you are to be fitted with a suit. I want you to wear it every day at the university, not on any account to keep it only for Sundays. You understand, don't you? Settle with Blair on your way out the day and time that would be most convenient for you." She pulled the bell-cord. "You know that if there is ever any way in which we can help you," she was smiling to him with the smile that seemed to bless, "all you need do is get in touch with me. Barnfingal means so much to me, the happy holidays we spend there, that I want you to feel about Glasgow what we feel about Barnfingal."

She saw it from the top of a hill, from the garden that had been formed from waste moorland, a bumpy road far below, a few cottages, sleepy under their thatch, scattered here and there, the picturesque huddle of roofs of Gow Farm, the schoolhouse round which children played. Even at that distance, on a still summer's day, she could hear them when they were "let out." It reminded her of a poem she used to know, "Still sits the schoolhouse by the road." It was all safe, secure, sure, uncomplicated as childhood. The blueness of the loch, the grandeur of Fingal on the other side— that reminded her of the psalm "I to the hills will lift mine eyes." It was all as simple as the lines of a poem or a psalm you have always known, so that they fall naturally into place because you have stopped thinking of them. "The earth is the Lord's and the fullness thereof," she would quote joyfully when she saw the haystacks standing in Gow Farm fields. Even when Fingal was obliterated by mist, and rain pelted, when the children chafed because they were not outside, she would sing, "We'll be happy in the house upon a rainy day," and tell them how glorious it was going to be when the sun broke through the clouds. Just as it always did and was.

"Yes, Blair, I rang for you: you will remember to arrange with Bartle before he leaves about a suitable afternoon."

"Why, mother," exclaimed her daughter, still at the piano, "what a shocking pun you have just made!"

"Have I, dear? I didn't notice. Good-bye, Bartle—for just now."

Bartle tramped quickly down the hill from Victoria Quadrant. He still walked in town as he walked in the country, putting the whole of his foot down at the same time. The hill was steep as a cliff and he strode with such force that his face shook.

If he thought about Lady Wain, his thoughts about her daughter might settle into some semblance of order in the interval, ravel themselves into a ball he could begin to unwind. For he knew then that even in a lifetime he could never reach the end of these thoughts, or could untie himself from them.

Lady Wain's picture of the place where he had been born had come as such a surprise to him that it was in the nature of a shock. He took everything about Barnfingal as much for granted as he took the milk that came out of a cow, or the kick from a horse with a red ribbon tied on its tail. And suddenly he had seen it as Lady Wain saw and thought of it: a picture so different to his own that he could scarcely reconcile hers as the place he had known all his life.

Bartle realized that Lady Wain's impression of Barnfingal was like a bloom. She did not see within to the stone, core or kernel that had formed the fruit. There it was always either high summer or harvest home to her, with the sun hot on the nape of her children's necks or the fields white with marguerites or lying wanly golden shorn of their grain.

And what was it like to her daughters He knew he was only feeding himself with thoughts of the mother to stave off his hunger. Barnfingal had none of the blessedness for her that it had for her mother. She was wearying of it, as she would weary of toys she had outgrown, that would be passed on to her smaller brothers and sisters while she became aware, instead of toys, of the power in the hands that had played with them——

Would she ask her mother where he lived in Barnfingal? Would she ever have noticed the cottage that stood between the schoolhouse and the roadman's? But she would not know which was the roadman's——

Would she say to her brother, "Are you not going to speak to mother's poor lonely boy from the Highlands when you see him at the university?"

Bartle stopped short in his march downhill so abruptly that he felt his body jerk forward as though he were about to lose his balance. He suddenly heard himself use to Maysie Wain an expression he scarcely knew he knew, an expression Jamie might use to describe Rachel MacInnes.

The release of that one word had the effect on him that loss of weight has on a caterpillar before it becomes a chrysalis. He felt lightened and at the same time bound. He wanted to hide his thoughts for Maysie Wain even from himself, and all he could do was use them to spin a cocoon that emeshed him more and more.

He met Mr. Blair at a large outfitter's in the centre of town. Bartle was at the prescribed meeting place, the principal door of the emporium, in plenty of time to avoid any chance of keeping Mr. Blair waiting even for a second. When the meeting did take place, he was whirled to gent's suitings before he had time to turn. Here a melancholy individual, with a tape measure round his neck, fitted him into different suits according to Mr. Blair's instructions while they kept up a telegraphic conversation with each other.

"To be charged to Lady Wain's account. Not only a suit, mark you, but two of everything from his skin upwards."

"You'll find vests on the ground floor—ask for Mr. Prentice."

"That's too tight for him."

"Well, well, with all her spending she never seems to make holes in what he makes. That's too big for him, we'll try this. Any truth about Mr. Scougall's son and You Know Who?"

"Always coming about the place. But I let in more than him, let me tell you."

"Bigger fish?"

"Bigger by far."

"Think she has any preferences herself?"

"As like to Sir Alfred as a grossett to a gooseberry—all preferences. The thing is: are her preferences likely to be like her father's? No, that won't do. Lady Wain'll have nothing cheap."

"You'd be likelier to answer that than anyone."

"If you ask me: ructions."

"No? You don't say? There now, what could be better? Just needs there and there—not easy to fit, is he? Broad for his height, but he's not small. And if it came to the bit, who'd Lady Wain favour—her or him?"

"Him behind his back and her to his face, so she'll get the redding-stroke. Yes, we'll take that one."

Bartle followed Mr. Blair about the shop in a maze while this and that was not only ordered for him but instructed to be sent to Mrs. Leggatt's address. They finished up in a tea-room where Bartle came out of his maze to prepare himself to ask Mr. Blair the question without whose answer he dare not part from him.

"Mr. Blair," he said, avoiding looking at him so pointedly that he squinted, "yon Mr. Scougall's son's after Miss Hetty, is he no? No the other one I mean." He could not mention her name lest he gave everything away.

"He's after Miss Hetty all right. Has been ever since they went to Mr. Richardson's dancing-class. But they're not all after Miss Hetty," he said with his air of the professional. "Wouldn't be surprised if Miss Maysie has a bigger court before she's done."

Bartle moistened his dry lips to force himself to ask, "But Miss Hetty's the one with preferences, is she no?"

"Yes. Miss Hetty might throw her bonnet over the mill for a man, but not Miss Maysie. She'd have the man risking not only their bonnets but their necks for her!"

Bartle felt such a relief at this statement that the very atmosphere round him seemed to lighten.

\* \* \* \*

Accustomed to the squatness of cottage rooms, everything in the Leggatts' flat appeared to him gaunt with height. Ceilings seemed to disappear altogether and the space played tricks with your voice. His room was the parlour, the best room in the house, where he had his meals by himself. The over-stuffed furniture that had been taken so much care of in the past it had scarcely been used, the coarse antimacassar on the back of the armchair that squealed when it was moved, the thickly patterned wallpaper that was so dark it could not fade, all struck him as sombrely magnificent.

He seldom needed to go into the kitchen which the Leggatts used as their living-room. When he did it always reminded him of a ship, perhaps because of the pulley ropes like rigging. He found that to think of himself as aloft a ship helped his fear of stairs, did not make him feel so dizzy when he looked below into courts where everything was dingy grey, from the cats to the grass that grew between the railings and the battered dustbins.

The Clyde was not far away, Mr. Leggatt worked in one of the shipyards, and the foghorns became a familiar sound to Bartle in that first winter in a town. But he never thought of the Clyde as a river. A river leapt between its banks when the snows melted, and frothed in spate below the bridge at Dormay, or veined Fingal's side so that you could see it across the loch. But the Clyde did none of these things. The colour of a knife-blade, it was as metallic as the hulks of the ships it bore, as the grey tenements that made the streets into traps, as the paving-stones on which footsteps and traffic clanged.

Once or twice after rain, when the streets and roofs glistened with wet, he smelt, borne up the Clyde, a new smell that always left him dissatisfied because it was not stronger. He knew it was the sea he was smelling, the sea that rocked round Wrack, that was silvered with fish or gleamed with holy seals, and harboured the wreckage of long lost ships.

80

His life at the university was so different to anything he had ever known that it was as though, once there, he entered another plane, the rhythm so changed from that to which he had been attuned that he might have reached another sphere where flights of figures and thoughts were concrete as things. He could tell when Lady Wain spoke of him to Professor Barbour, because from that rime the professor took some trouble with him, helping him over initial difficulties that were more formidable to him than to his fellow students. He formed no friendships with them however but, accustomed to solitariness, was unaware of any lack.

There was another life that only he knew of, that secret inbred life when he thought of Maysie Wain. The urge to think of her was as strong in him as the instinct that drives certain insects to forsake the protection of their natural cover and expose themselves to the open, that forces them once they are full-fed to travel long distances, across rough ground, in strange unlikely places.

"Since ye are no going home for the vacations, I'll redd out your room while you're in it," Mrs. Leggatt said to him, "if ye'll take your books over to Mrs. Reggie's that day to be out of the way. It's spring—that means cleaning time again."

He had not thought of spring coming to a city, where there were none of the myriad sounds that proclaimed it as in the country, the chirping, bleating, squeaking sounds. He suddenly had a yearning so acute that it was like a sickness for his home, with its greenness and strong fresh smells, but he knew he could not return until his first year at the university was over.

And when it did come, when he was swinging down the post office brae, fitting himself into it all again, as though it were a garment he had left behind, much of the exhilaration of returning home had gone. For he knew without being told that the Wains were not coming to The House that year.

He stood in the kitchen doorway of Croft Fionn, trying to familiarize his eyes to the half darkness within. His mother had been bending over a basket of cloths she had brought in from bleaching: she straightened herself to look at him.

"So ye've got back," she said in her toneless voice.

That was what he had expected her to say. What he had not expected was the feeling of hostility out of her that amounted to a barrier between them.

"Ay, mern," he agreed, reverting to the over-conciliatory tone of his childhood. He cleared his throat. "One of the professors tellt me I should do better next term—I've begun to take a hold."

"Ye've been a long time beginning," she remarked to that. She flapped a cloth in the air and ran her fingers along one edge until they held it at two corners. "How muckle did ye see of Rachel MacInnes when the pair of ye were in Glasgow?" she asked, looking at him over her shoulder with eyes that he knew were well accustomed to the twilight of the room.

"Naething at all," he replied. "Just once, at the back door, when I went to see the Lady yon time."

"Did ye ken she's lost her place?"

"Na, I didna ken." The news somehow winded him. "How did she do yon, mern?" he asked when she said no more.

"They say she's going to have a bairn. I ken they've been saying more than that ahint ma back, with you in the same town as she." She gave a quick hard laugh. "Dinna ye heed, Bartle. I ken it's no true and they'll ken that from me afore they're muckle older." She began to fold the cloths corner to corner. "I might have kent if there had been any truth in it, Donald MacInnes would be the first to be at ma door to force ye to father his daughter's bairn."

The roughly reared barrier between them had collapsed. Never had he felt so close to his mother as he did at that moment. Excitement took possession of him as he crossed the floor to stand beside his grannie that she could grow accustomed to him. How small her leanness made her look, with her flesh caved in on her bones. He felt her hand feeling him: it was dry and with as little substance as a withered leaf. He knew she liked to feel him standing there beside her, like an extra wall: he also knew that she was confusing her son's son with her son.

"Ye and your grannie can have a fine crack the night," said his mother, watching them, "when I'm out at the van."

"Ay, just like Raxdale," grannie commented once they were alone together and he began to tell her about Glasgow.

"I bide in one of the houses like the side of a mountain," he said. "I have to climb stairs to get into it. I dinna like stairs. Do ye, grannie?"

"I would not climb a stair if it was to cost me my life," she returned.

"Why no, grannie?"

82

"Because I would not," she said querulously.

She was too old now to share new experiences with him. He realized that the thread on which her days hung had broken; there was no longer any continuity for her, just breaks.

Soon after he had returned home he saw Jamie, who ran past from Brae Farm one evening and summoned him by chapping on the window. They went to the edge of Mar Woods, where Bartle sat on the dyke and Jamie swung on the low branch of a tree.

"Ye ken about Rachel MacInnes?" Jamie began at once.

"Ay," answered Bartle. "I kent when I came home— mother tellt me."

"Rachel tellt me," announced Jamie.

Bartle screwed up his eyes to look at him better.

"Ye've seen her, Jamie? I didna ken she'd been home."

"She didna gang home. She came to seek me out."

"And what did she want with you?" demanded Bartle.

"To get me to believe I was her bairn's father. But I tellt her I could count up to nine."

"She would have left her place by the time she saw ye?" pondered Bartle.

"Ay. She was in an awful way. She wantit me no only to father the bairn but marry her into the bargain. Can ye see me telling ma uncle Rob I wantit to get marrit." Jamie jerked himself higher on the branch of the tree. "Do ye ken Torquil Lament—the son and no the father?"

"Him of Naver Farm near to Dormay? What of him?"

"He's sweet on Bess," said Jamie, mentioning his elder sister, "but uncle Rob's put the fear of death on both of them not to see each other."

"Naver Farm's bigger than Brae," reflected Bartle, "what's to hinder them marrying?"

"Our uncle Rob, wha doesna want to lose his housekeeper. Annie's too wee. She's no good about the house, like Bess is." The branch he sat on creaked like an unoiled wheel. "Annie tellt me to tell ye she was asking for ye."

"Tell Annie I was asking for her," remembered Bartle.

When he was filling a dish of water for his mother at the well one morning, Bartle saw Rob Malcolm approaching in one of Brae Farm carts. Straddled across the ditch at the roadside, he waited for the cart to pass, for Rob Malcolm was not the type of man with whom you exchanged the time of day. He was surprised therefore to hear the horse stop when it drew alongside and the man's voice saying,

"That's yourself, Bartle."

"Ay, Mr. Malcolm," he agreed with too much willingness. His hands dripping, he turned to look up into his face. He gave Bartle a curious feeling sitting there on the plank stretched across the cart, as though everything and everyone had ebbed from him, leaving him so much surrounded by emptiness that he looked sucked.

"And how's your finger?" asked Rob Malcolm, swaying a little as he surveyed him as though he were still being jerked by a moving cart.

"Ma finger?" Bartle repeated uncomprehendingly.

"Ay, the one that got caught in the trap. It was ma trap, ye mind. Ye and Jamie were trying to let the fox awa'."

"Yon?" Bartle laughed and held up his right hand for him to see. "I never mind it's awa' now!"

He had been very small when it happened. He realized now he must have fainted but he had thought then he had gone for a little sleep as Rob Malcolm held him. Again he could feel the buttons on the man's jacket pressing against his head where the hair his mother had kept cropped grew like bristles——

"Ye must give Brae a visit before ye gang back to Glasgow," Rob Malcolm was saying. "Ye and Annie are friends. What about tomorrow night then? I'll tell Bess to expect ye."

"What was Rob Malcolm speaking to ye of?" his mother asked curiously when he entered the kitchen.

"He wants me to gang up to Brae tomorrow night," said Bartle, placing the newly filled basin carefully on the dresser.

"What for?" demanded his mother.

"To pay them a visit," returned her son.

She digested this in silence for a minute or two, then she said,

"He does, does he? And what's at the back of his mind, I'd like to ken. Aweel, Bartle, ye can gang. But if Rob Malcolm thinks ye'll ever take up with his wet-eyed Annie, he's mistaken. We want none of yon bad Malcolm blood here. Ay, ye can gang, Bartle, but mind what I tell ye. No promising, or looking as though ye'd like to promise. It'll be years before ye can even think of marrying."

"Ay, years," Bartle agreed thankfully.

# Chapter Seven

THE bad Malcolm blood revealed itself in neither of the daughters of Brae. Bess was a handsome, well made girl, the kind of girl a man would pick for his wife, and Bartle knew if it had not been Torquil Lament of Naver who had sought her out, hidden away as she was at Brae Farm, it would have been someone else.

That the girl was labouring under a feeling of resentment was obvious; she never opened her mouth when her uncle was present and banged as much as she dared as she went about her work. But for the short time before he came in, she was bright and responsive to their rare visitor. Her few freckles, which were as attractively spaced as beauty spots on the creaminess of her skin, did not sprinkle her face as the more youthful Annie's did hers.

Annie was so gentle a soul that she only smiled when addressed and scarcely spoke at all, just sat on her stool with her hands in her lap, her brown eyes looking from one to the other as each talked.

Dugie surprised Bartle by being much younger than he had expected: he had always taken it for granted that Jamie's big brother was immeasurably older than either of them. Now he had made up on him as it were, and was startled to find he was bigger than Dugie.

Bess, Dugie and Annie must have resembled their mother's side of the house, Jamie was the only dark Malcolm of the four. Small and quick in every movement, he always reminded Bartle of the black trout darting at the peaty bottom of the mountain tarn.

Perhaps it was because he was an only child himself that he was aware of the four Malcolms as a family, corporate, each as necessary to the whole as a side to a square. But when their uncle entered, he realized this feeling of unity they gave out was the unconscious strengthening of the herd against the herdsman. He might drive them where he willed but if they kept in a pack they had a certain personality where he was concerned which they could not possess as individuals.

Their uncle's presence drew like a damper on the children. As Rob Malcolm was a silent man, Bartle, never loquacious himself, found conversation something of a burden and was glad when the time on the loud-ticking clock allowed him to push back his chair and say he had better be getting along now. Jamie was on his feet almost before Bartle had risen in his alacrity to accompany him part of the way.

"If you don't stay where you are," his uncle said threateningly to him, "the world will happen to you." He spoke in Gaelic, obviously under the mistaken impression that their visitor would not know what he was saying. "Annie will see ye a bit of the road," he said peaceably in English to Bartle, "will ye no, Annie?"

She put her stool dutifully below the table and followed Bartle out of the farmhouse. He walked slowly that she could be at his side, to correct the impression he had of her always tagging after Jamie and him. He felt big beside her, and removed from her as a grown up is always removed from a child. At the march gate he stopped to look down at her.

"It's I wha must take ye home, Annie," he said kindly, "and no ye me. So will I see ye round the bend?"

They retraced their steps and he said goodbye to her in full view of the stark farmhouse that no one would expect his farewell to be warmer than it was. He watched her walking to her home, the new-found dignity of a woman every now and then interrupted by a little skip, as though she were excited or talking to herself.

Before he returned to Croft Fionn that night, he went to The House. His mother had told him the Family were not coming to Barnfingal that summer because the younger children had had measles and it was thought the seaside would be more bracing for them, but she had opened it once or twice to give it an airing.

Even if the gate had not been padlocked, he would have climbed over the wall. He found himself in a waste piece of the grounds, hidden from the avenue by rhododendron bushes, where the moor still pushed below the dyke. He elbowed his way between the bushes on to the drive. He wanted it all to burst upon his gaze as it would burst upon theirs when they drove up the avenue. He also wanted to know if it were possible to see Croft Fionn from the grounds.

The drive was shaded where it began by bushes and trees, silver birches that had not been cut down and that formed a pretty thicket on either side. But once past a certain corner, it swept into the open with the house standing well back behind level brilliant green sward.

The hunter's-moon was up and it was bright as day. But although it was as bright, the light was quite different from that of the sun and threw different shadows. So that Bartle, walking for the first time with certainty here, saw it all drenched with a sheen as though from another world and never thought that he was not seeing it as it always was.

There was a small round glass-house on the edge of the lawn. He went up to it, his footsteps suddenly silenced as they walked on the grass. This was where the Lady would sit in summer, with the rustic door opened, and have an uninterrupted view of the loch and Fingal, while nearer home she could catch glimpses of the road as it wound up and down and round corners to Dormay.

He turned to see what she would see when she sat there, and felt as though a mountain blocked his line of vision although the prospect stretched for miles. It was no mountain but a hillock and the lie of the land that completely shut from sight Croft Fionn from this, height.

He walked up to The House as though drawn in spite of himself, for he did not know that he wanted to look inside, or to see it at closer quarters. The moonlight banked against the windows, and he had to press his face against them to see the slatted blinds were all down.

An indescribable sadness took hold of him as he wandered uneasily round the house, like a ghost that is tethered to the spot it haunts. He felt as out of place here as a changeling might feel in a world of mortals, or as a human would find himself in some angelic sphere.

Bartle could see that his grannie's mind wandered constantly. Although she never looked up as Kirsty or any other woman entered, when she heard his step, as heavy now as a man's, it seemed to startle her. Often as he entered the kitchen he would see her waiting suspiciously and covertly, but when she understood who it was she would be at her ease again. Sometimes children ran past the cottage, and then she would become at once eager. It was almost as though she expected the footsteps to stop and a solitary little boy to stand in the doorway.

Even at night now she slept happed in her chair at the fire. She was no longer able to be moved to bed and to be helped up every morning, so his mother thought it brighter for her to sit at the fire than lie on her back in bed day after day.

As his holiday drew to an end, it dawned on the grandmother that something untoward was taking place around her. Thoughts like fuddled bats flew round and round the toppling structure of her brain. Her heart misgave her when she saw the old black bag had been brought out from under the bed. The uneasy thought that this was not the first time it had made its appearance afflicted her memory.

"I'm aff to ma bed now," she heard her grandson say.

She eased herself in her chair. He was only away to his bed, there was nothing to fear.

"Ay, ye have a long journey before ye the morn's morn," replied his mother.

It was true, he was going away tomorrow. Kirsty always spoilt things. The old woman was afraid to fall asleep in case her grandson slipped away without her seeing him. She thought she sat awake all night but she dozed repeatedly.

Suddenly she saw her husband standing in the kitchen where he used to stand, before the fire, with his legs apart and his projecting underlip, his roughened face and strong, short-fingered hands, Her mind went blank for a moment hollow as eternity. Then quite unaccountably she thought of her grandfather, of their nailing a lock of his hair to the door when he died to keep out evil spirits.

Morning stirred and Bartle came in from washing at the spring as usual, his hair wet and the neck of his shirt damp. He hung his towel to dry over the string stretched across the fireplace. You would not think he would have done that unless he expected to use it again; on the other hand Kirsty had early taught him to be orderly. The grandmother remembered she used to think many a time there was such a thing as being too tidy. No, there was no doubt he was going away, for Kirsty gave him two platefuls of porridge to fortify him for his journey.

It had been different when he had left her the first time. Then her pride at her grandson going to college had taken away the edge of parting with him, but now the thought of his leaving her filled her with dread. She clung to him with her old, knotted, brown hands, her tongue clucking desperately in her mouth. He was conscious as he kissed her goodbye that she was 'a' cruppen thegither'. At the door he turned and looked back.

He had once seen a tree struck by lightning, had seen its leaves wither instantaneously. He remembered that now as he looked round at his grannie, huddled in her chair as though she had withered into nothing and only her clothes remained.

The letter was lying waiting for him exactly as he imagined it, on the magenta-coloured tablecloth in his bed-sitting-room at Mrs. Leggatt's. Still standing, he opened the envelope carefully and drew out the double sheet of good ivory notepaper to read what was written in Lady Wain's generous hand.

She was sorry she had missed Bartle since they were not at Barnfingal this summer, so would Bartle come to see her at Victoria Quadrant on Saturday first at three o'clock.

He had none of the tumultuous feelings today that he had had the last time he climbed this hill, for he knew he was not going to see Maysie Wain that afternoon. Yet as he neared the top, something tightened in him, like the coiled spring of a machine that, once released, would have tremendous force and resilience.

He knew that Maysie Wain was watching him, standing a little back from the window, with that secret smile flipping across her face. He could tell the very window although he did not look up, he would rather have died than been seen looking—the one on the top story at the corner. It was barred inside: that would mean it was the nursery, and they had made it safe for children.

A maid he had not seen before answered his summons at the area knocker. Her cap, apron and blue print made him remember Rachel MacInnes. She took him up the basement stairs and handed him over to Mr. Blair.

Bartle felt that his fairly intimate contacts with Mr. Blair last year called for some geniality when they met this, but Mr. Blair obviously felt otherwise. As his air of well-bred disapproval was now characteristic of him, when he chose to dispense with the well-bred he expressed something like contempt. Again Bartle was reminded of Rachel MacInnes, this time unhappily.

He heard someone racing up and down the keys of a piano as he was led upstairs. Lady Wain was alone in the same room in which she had received him last year. That meant there must be two pianos in this house. He could hardly bear to look at the one in this room because Maysie was no longer sitting at it.

"Come away, Bartle," Lady Wain greeted him. "Sit down there, where I can see you. How disappointing we could not manage to come to The Shieling this summer, but your mother was so good and aired it just as though we had been coming. You went home, didn't you? I'm so glad: how delighted your mother must have been to see you, and your grandmother. Did they see a change in you? I declare you have grown, Bartle."

He knew at once there was a difference in her, not towards him but in herself. So much of the joyfulness had gone from her, so that although she was the same to him as always, he realized she had to think now about what she had felt in the past. She was embroidering with coloured silks but looked at him repeatedly as though to make him feel he had all her concentration.

"You will have heard that Rachel has left us," she remarked, and took several stitches without looking up.

It was on the tip of his tongue to say, ay, that he had, more fool her to lose so good a place, but the words never came. Stunned he gazed at the Lady. Now he knew why so much of her joyfulness had fled. He picked it up from her as his mother might pick up stitches from someone else's knitting. The father of Rachel MacInnes's child was no servant like its mother, but Lady Wain's own son.

"I remember you did not care for Rachel, did you, Bartle?" she enquired, running her thread over a small piece of wax.

"Lady Wain," he said, moving forward his body which felt big in the slightness of the chair, "Master Alfred is the bairn's father, is he not?"

Startled she looked up at him, the blob of wax hanging to her thread like a golden knot. And now when she spoke, she spoke so lightly her words merely fluttered, as though not to impress themselves on the air.

"Who told you that, Bartle?"

"Nobody, I just kent."

"Have you seen Rachel since?"

"No."

"And — do they know at Barnfingal?"

90

"They ken she is going to have a bairn, but not wha the father is. Nobody's ever thought of such a thing. And if Rachel MacInnes tried to get them to think it, the likes of her is too well kent to be believed." Compassion filled him as he looked at her, and his heart cried out that there should ever be occasion to feel compassion for her: now he knew why she had been glad of any excuse not to return to The House this summer.

"If she hasn't told her own people, she'll have told no one. It would not be worth her while."

"You mean," he sat back a little in his chair, "you mean you've made it worth her while to keep quiet?"

"Not that, Bartle. It was only right adequate provision should be made—for the child. That provision will not be stopped should she marry. Master Alfred's father must never know, Bartle."

"No. Never, Lady Wain, There's no reason why he should—ever."

He was speaking very much as she was speaking, using as little breath as he could to fan the words into audibility. It was as though they were not so much talking to each other as signalling.

"Deed, Lady Wain, at Barnfingal they thought it would be me, with me being in the same town as her. Just as Mr. Blair thinks."

He saw her clear grey eyes looking at him in a troubled way.

"I know, Bartle. When I realized the trend of his thoughts, I said at once you could not be mentioned in the same breath as Rachel. But he still thinks it." Helplessly she continued to look at him. "There is only one way of stopping him thinking it, and that is to tell the truth."

"No, no, Lady Wain. What purpose would that serve? Let them fasten what they will on to me, it's handy and it does no harm. It's you kenning it's not true that matters." She saw his face was shining with the adoration upon it. "No one need ever ken it was not me." His lips pursed, as though to fold in their secret.

"No one does know who it is except my son, myself and my two daughters," she replied.

His heart stouned within him at even so slight a reference to her second daughter. Maysie would know then, her mother would tell her, that Bartle knew who was the father of Rachel MacInnes's bairn, that Bartle said he did not mind Mr. Blair and others thinking it was he since that prevented them ever discovering who it really was. Lady Wain saw his shining face look as though it were illumined.

In Mrs. Leggatt's bed-sitting-room he turned over and over in his mind the thought of Maysie Wain in the light of this new happening, as he would toss the scythed grass at home into a swathe of hay. He even carried on imaginary conversations with her. "Mebbe I would have done if for your sake, I'm no telling, but certain I am I did it for your mother, even if there had not been a you." But he knew that was merely bravado, and his mind would stall at the very thought of there not being a 'you'. He found he could as soon think of himself as non-existent than think that of her. That frightened him a little, the realization that he was dependent on her not she on him, as though he were the begotten and she the begetter.

During that winter he heard from his mother that his grandmother had died. "There is no need for you to come home," she wrote as though in afterthought at the end of her letter, "she will be put by the morrow."

The news of his grandmother's death chilled Bartle. He knew she was very old, that her mind had gone, but hearing of her death ruined a childhood confidence in something unknown. It was as though he had heard the almighty norms themselves had made a slip or been found asleep.

His heart was in his mouth when he thought of her dying. He saw the thatched cottage standing by itself on the highroad, saw the wooden door left slightly a-jar, saw as if he had been there the ghostly winter mist stealing in noiselessly like a vapour, saw it clamming the old woman's empty mouth, twisting down her throat.

He was not conscious of the wind in Glasgow as he was in his Highland home. Here when it did blow he was aware more of its effect on things, the window of his room rattling in its frame, as though a strong hand were shaking it, of the whirl and rattle of a chimney-can above the slates. Sometimes of an evening he would raise his head from his books and, listening, think how extraordinary and inexplicable it was that he should be here in this tall lean room, himself the one point of silence in a city that clanged with sound. And as his fingers ran up the edges of a book to lift the cover and let it fall again, he would think that he was like that city that clanged, round the silent thought of Maysie Wain.

One blustery night in March, when the strong hand was banging and pummelling the window rather than shaking it, he had one of these incredible moments that always left him feeling slightly stranded, as though on some remote shore. He was staring at the door at the time and when he saw it open and someone suddenly stand with his back against it, it seemed all of a piece with the incredibility of his thoughts, as though the door had only opened and shut in his mind.

"Well, Bartle, and how's yourself;"

"Jamie! "

But it was only when he felt his friend's rain-chilled hand against his warm one that he knew Jamie was neither apparition nor fetch. Mrs. Leggatt came clattering into the room with dishes chinking and jumping on the indented tin tray. She accepted his visitor's presence as more toward than he did, glad to do something extra for their lodger who was as quiet and seemly and made as few demands as any landlady could wish.

"Ye'll put me up the night, will ye no, Bartle?" asked Jamie before she left the room.

"Mr. MacDonald will be reel happy to oblige," she answered hospitably. "Now make your tea, the pair of ye. Ye will be hungered after your journey."

As she shut the door behind her, the window shook as though cannon balls were being rolled against it. "Whatever's yon?" enquired Jamie. He was wee and wiry and so alert that even when he was standing still as now he seemed to be dancing to get away. He was so exactly as Bartle remembered him that it was almost like seeing a piece of yourself standing there, making familiar the unfamiliar room.

"Just the wind plying at the window," returned Bartle. "It's high up here."

His speech had altered since he had been in Glasgow, he spoke more consciously, saying 'you' for ye and 'yes' for ay when he answered professors. Now he was careful to revert to the pronunciation Jamie would expect from him.

"Ay, ye're gey high. As near to heaven as ever I'll be! I said to maself as I climbed your stairs." He went to the window and held back the curtain to look out, his small dark face sparkling with excitement. "Grand and high. Ye're up in the world, Bartle, as I'll tell Annie when I gang home!" He came and seated himself at the table, toppling over as he did so the pile of books Bartle had hurriedly thrust there to be out of the way. "Hungert did she say. I could fair tear the food with ma teeth! She's a long drink of water, is she no, but I like her all the same—let me come in by maself to give ye a surprise! Yon's yon window again! Ay, ye're up in the world all right." He was bolting his food and choking down great mouthfuls of tea. "Did I tell ye our uncle Rob's dead?"

"No!" gasped Bartle. "Ay, but of course, ye would no be here if he was alive. Dead did ye say;"

"Ay, dead as the grave-stone that will never be put over him."

"What did he die of, Jamie?"

"No in his bed like other men. Our uncle Rob was no like to other men." His gaze was on Bartle the whole time. "Ye ken the tarn at the back of Brae?"

"The one the curlers use when it's frozen?"

"Ay, it. It was frozen this year but yon day the curlers were no using it. Na, but our uncle Rob was." He wagged his head at the door. "Do they ken the Gaelic through yonder?"

"Na," said Bartle, "never a word."

Jamie at once switched into Gaelic although the window chapping in its socket made such a row that no one could have heard a word he said outside the door. He was used to speaking English to Bartle since their earliest days at school. That was the language used in Croft Fionn because his grannie's Gaelic was not the same as the one spoken in Barnfingal. "A queer kind of language," his grandmother had once confided to him, "that a pody can no make head or tail of." Bartle now understood Gaelic better than he could speak it.

"We were up on the hills, the three of us," Jamie was recounting, "our uncle Rob, Dugie and me, seeking out the sheep. It had been one of these black frosts that grips the ground at this time of year, and there was a wind like a whip at your face. I was glad when we came upon a sheep if only to put my hands under her wool. Uncle Rob put the anger on me when he saw what I was doing, and cried out that the pair of us were as much good to him as a couple of new-born lambs. He sent us home and said he would finish himself, calling after us we were not to take the short cut across the tarn but to go the whole long way round, although that added two miles to our journey. Not that he cared if it had been two hundred. It must have been too hard even for him, for he was not long by himself before he thought of turning home. He took the short cut over the tarn and would have been back at the same time as we, had the ice not given way below his feet. The old drove road goes not near the tarn and never a sight would we have seen of what we saw had Dirk, his dog, not come nosing us to go where he led. There he was, near enough to the shore, on the home side, his head and shoulders out of the water, holding on to the ice. But he could not for long keep that way for the ice was forever breaking in his hands with the weight of him. He shouted to us to bring him a spar of wood that lay beside the curler's hut. The ice would have held us, for we are lighter far, the pair of us together, than he ever was. But he had told us already that day not to cross the tarn, and we knew that our uncle Rob was the great man for seeing we did what we were told when he was the teller. So we had to watch him there, one saying no word to the other or to him, until he could hold on no longer. He went down quietly enough, all the shouting out of him, as though someone had a hold of his feet. The water was black as a pit and his head scarce made a ripple. The last thing we saw of him was one of his hands gripping at nothing. It is not the truth when they say they rise three times, for our uncle Rob never touched the top again. Mebbe he was not the rising sort. We waited to see if he would come up and when never a sight of him we had, I went back to Brae to tell Bess and Annie they were without their uncle Rob. I told them what Dugie told MacIntyre of Balloch when he made his way to his croft to tell him to come quick, for we feared our uncle was in the tarn. Dirk, his dog, had led us there and when we reached it we saw never a sight of him. Only a wee black hole broken in the ice. That was the queer thing, Bartle, it was such a wee hole.

"Dugie and I had no Sabbath clothes but that night we made ourselves respectable for the road and off we went as far as the manse. The minister came into us and said, 'Lads, you'll have come to see about your uncle's burial once they are able to reach him from the tarn.' But we told him that was not why we had come at all. We had come to see about the lifting of our mother from the gable-end of the house where our uncle had had her buried. We wanted her put in the graveyard beside our father as close as the one grave. He would not be feeling the chill on his right side when they lowered her in beside him. As for our uncle Rob, we did not know where he could be laid as the Brae lair was full—or would be when we were placed there with our families. But the minister said a decent spot must be found for him, although he was no kirk-going man, so they settled to place him on the north side amongst the MacIntyres and Shields and other newcomers to Barnfingal. And Mr. Gow of Gow Farm stepped over our march dyke as he would never have done in our uncle's day and said to Dugie, 'You and Jamie are young to manage a farm. The oak knows the acorn but the acorn can have small knowledge of the oak. Let Brae remember that willing hearts will make short of the road between them and Gow.' Torquil Lamont had wanted Bess so badly that his father was prepared to come to Brae and ask our uncle Rob for her and, when he would not let her go, take her away with him. She is of age and could have gone her way, but Bess would never bring herself to leave Annie and the rest of us. When there was no uncle Rob to ask, Mr. Lament said he would spare Torquil for a year or two to Brae when he married Bess, for Torquil's older than Dugie, and he has other sons to help him with Naver. Annie kept starting up at night, thinking she heard uncle Rob at the door, but we told her she would know he was dead for sure when they got him out of the tarn. There was Dirk—he did not return to Brae the night it happened and never entered the house again. We would see him going as far as the gate where the carts come through but back he would always come, as though he had not found what he set out for. He was always uncle Rob's dog, and old now, blind in one eye, although the other one soon told him when either Dugie or I was near. So one morning early Dugie shot him without Dirk knowing it, for it does not do for a dog to be without its master. There has not been a gathering like the gathering at uncle Rob's burial since the coming of age of the laird's son. Every father and his eldest son from Auchendee and Mhoreneck and as far as Naver was there. We knew why they had come, not to bury the dead but to hold out their hand to the living." Jamie's face was working. "And after it was all over, Dugie stood out in the graveyard and thanked them for coming and asked them back to Brae. He and I led the way, and when we reached the door he went forward to open it, and turned himself round in it to face them. 'Welcome ben, neighbours,' he said."

# Chapter Eight

THE wind had dropped when Battle awoke, and the window stopped its chattering. It was not fully light outside but what did manage to penetrate, striking in shafts between the curtains carelessly drawn, lightened considerably the muffled room.

Bartle lay and let it all form round him again. The room, austere in the half light, gave him the stripped feeling of a landscape after storm. It was spent but still vibrant with what it had been through.

Something had happened since last he had wakened here. Jamie of course. It was the room's effect on him that confirmed his presence before he raised himself on his elbow to look round at the boy lying beside him.

He need not have been so cautious. His visitor was in so deep a sleep that Bartle realized neither thunder nor lightning would have wakened him. He lay with his face half buried in the bolster, as he did at home. There was nothing particularly youthful about his face, it was only its smallness that made it appear like a child's, as it would when he was an old man—if Jamie lived to be an old man. Bartle suddenly sickened.

Mrs. Leggatt promised to let their visitor he until he wakened by himself. Jamie, now he was in Glasgow, was going to stay a day or two, and Bartle determined to take him over to see Sam Heggie that evening. It seemed hard that it should be he, Bartle, who lived across the stair from Sam when he and Jamie were such obvious kindred spirits.

As lie tramped to the university that morning, what Jamie told him charged through his mind with all its tumult packed behind it. When Bartle asked him if he would study now to join him at the university, he had replied, "I'm too far away from it all now. You begin to learn when you should leave school, like you did, Bartle. But I could never go back to the dominie now. Besides I'm too old for a scholarship—I feel like my own father!" He picked up one of Bartle's books, looked inside it and then pushed it from him. "There, you see, it's Greek to me. But it doesn't matter the same, when Brae belongs to Dugie and me." His words began to pelt again. "I'm somebody now—I'm Jamie Malcolm of Brae."

Bartle realized that Jamie was unlikely ever to be haunted by the picture of his drowning uncle. He had told him that at one point uncle Rob had made such a stupendous effort to save himself he had nearly succeeded. "I feared I would have to take the spar of wood to his hands," he had said, and his last words before he fell asleep were, "I would no have liked to have done yon. Yon would have been murder."

When Jamie returned to Barnfingal, Bartle was aware of an emptiness he left behind, as though he had not only taken away himself but something that belonged to Bartle. For the first time now while he sat by himself having his meals, he was conscious of the solitariness of the room. The Leggatts missed Jamie too, for like all those brought up on a farm he had constantly veered towards the kitchen.

Bartle's second year in Glasgow passed more swiftly than his first. He was into his stride now at the university. Indeed in all his mathematical subjects he was so far ahead of his class that he had the same feeling of loneliness he had when Jamie left him, like a home sickness. He felt he either topped or tailed those who should be his brothers, he missed the heat and comfort of being with them. He never found himself in the body of the kirk, he either came too early before the service had begun or so late the doors were shut in his face.

He went to the graveyard when he was home for his summer vacations to see his grannie's grave. The church, a modern building, shared by Barnfingal and Auchendee, lay half-way between them at the lochside, but each clachan had its own graveyard. Barnfingal's was on the side of a hill, with the stump of ruins of what had once been a church protruding from it. The graveyard itself, standing on the bald hillside, was overgrown, but it was not because it was a wild place, seeding of itself, that made Bartle wish his grannie did not lie there.

He knew the graveyard in Wrack would be wilder with a stonier wildness: he also knew that was where she would have liked to have been put by. Because such a thing was out of the question would not prevent her wanting it.

His grandmother must surely have told him about the graveyard in Wrack, for he saw it in his mind's eye with a vividness as though he had seen it in reality. The island was rocky and every advantage had been taken of the church yard, where there was some soil, until the mounded graves seemed to overtop the crumbling dyke that enclosed them. Only the hardy sea-pink grew there and the rough gravestones were splashed with gull's droppings. Few bore the names of men, for the restless sea claimed the fishermen as its toll.

Not in Barnfingal soil, that had once stirred with the roots of trees and was now green with turf, would his grannie have chosen to be laid, but in that earth whitened with bones and shells that had powdered into dust and sand.

He was passing the schoolhouse on his way home when he heard his name called, and looking back saw the dominie standing in the doorway of his house. He retraced his steps and the dominie came towards him, so that they met at the gate. He was smaller than Bartle had expected, a burly square man with his head set on his shoulders like the block of stone surmounting a gate-post.

"Well, Bartle," he said pleasantly, feeling in his back pocket for his capacious handkerchief, "surely it is not like you to cast a stone at this house, passing without chapping at the door. Take a last look at your old school for by the time you return next year a new one will stand in its stead. The Board are building us a fine big schoolhouse for the bairns to rattle about in like the last sweeties in a bottle. This glen has been emptying ever since I've come to it twenty-odd years ago. Twenty-odd years more at this rate there should be nothing but roofless crofts and the Board's fine big schoolhouse. I had Professor Barbour stopping at my door on his way to the salmon fishing at Mhoreneck in spring—he seemed to think you should make something of yourself. Are you doing any vacation work? Well, bring your books along one even and let me see what you are doing."

Bartle wished he could feel more at home with the dominie but it was as though he could not surmount a certain something between them. Unconsciously he must have felt this to a lesser degree with his mother, for once she said to him, "Ye're missing your grannie, are ye no?" and he realized he had not spoken for long enough. She was even less talkative than he, but their lack of conversation was different to the silences that might have fallen with his grannie. There was no communion between him and his mother, they could not share even the same silence.

The Family came back to the Big House. That made Barnfingal as full for him as a heart that beat and pulsed with life. He was not to know, when he went to the miller's cottage to visit old Mistress Stewart, that he might not see the love of the heart, the light of the eye in the form of Maysie Wain on his way home.

But he did not fall in with her. Instead the summons came for him. He answered a knock at the door one evening to find the coachman from The House standing without. He said a few words to him, probably that Lady Wain wished to speak to him, but Bartle did not hear them. He went forward to the wagonette, as though he had received a call, keeping his gaze trained on the Lady's face because he was not strong enough to look at the daughter at her side. A small agile Wain son was holding the reins in the seat beside the driver's, looking round when he dared to show how practised he was and how easy he found it.

"Bartle," Lady Wain was smiling down at him, "we are taking the carriage to Dormay tomorrow. We thought your mother might have some shopping she would like you to do there for her—anyway, we should have plenty of room for you. We shall stop then for you tomorrow morning, round about eleven—why, it does not even take us out of our way."

He stood at the roadside until the wagonette had driven out of sight. It was so wonderful a moment that it seemed to protract itself into eternity. Forever and forever would a vehicle drive into as far as he could see, diminishing but never disappearing, with a nodding parasol beside a flowering gown.

Maysie had suggested they should stop on their way at the cottage by the roadside, it had been Maysie's idea he should accompany them tomorrow when they took the carriage into Dormay. She had made some haphazard excuse, that he must find it dull and little to do at home after Glasgow, but he knew that was not why she had made the suggestion. She knew he loved her, she was content to be loved by him, she wanted him near her although they might never speak a word.

"Real thoughtful of the Lady," his mother said when he told her. "I want naething at Dormay, but ye'll enjoy the hurl. Now, Bartle, ye'll say good-morn to her through the window when ye gang out, and then ye'll gang and sit beside the driver."

"Ay, mern," he agreed. He was at the low, deepset window-sill where the big Bible was kept. He raised the heavy black cover like a lid and noticed the black lining leaves were mottled and marbled with damp.

"What's that ye're doing there?" she asked.

"Naething," he said hurriedly, and dropped the cover as though guilty.

"The Bible's no naething," she returned. "That book belonged to your father, Bartle, and his father before him. It shouldna be shut as muckle as it is. I would like to see it open across your knees. It should be easy for ye to read with all your book learning, no like it was to them."

"Ay, mern," he agreed, but even to please her he had the greatest reluctance to open the book again. He wanted to keep the cover shut down on it like a lid for all time. To raise it he felt would be like raising the stone over a grave—you were not sure what would come out.

His mother came with him to the door when the carriage drew up next morning and went forward to speak to the Lady while he took his seat beside the driver. He heard the murmur of Lady Wain's voice, the sudden crack of his mother's words in answer, but he made no effort to hear what either said. The stillness that lapped him round he knew lapped Maysie. They were that stillness, as safe in it as in the inside of a shell which seas could swamp and tides tug but it remained the same.

He had seen her as he looked into the carriage before he took his seat outside. Their eyes had met. She was dressed in some pink material, with a lace yoke at her neck. He knew she thought it the prettiest dress she had at The House——

The coachman beside him pointed with his whip across the loch. "Do ye see yon burn running up the hill?" he asked. "Well, yon's the Drum march dyke." He was a Mhoreneck man, who worked at the Drum Arms in the pretty village that clustered like a bunch of flowers at the castle's gates. The Drum Arms apparently provided the wagonette and the carriage which the Wains used when they were at The House for their holidays. Bartle found himself looking at the rubicund coachman with uncharacteristic distaste. What had he to go prattling on about so much for? It upset Bartle to think the Wains did not own the carriage and the wagonette, as he had always thought they did. As for the coachman, the Family did not spell for him the Wains he served during the summer months, but the Marquis of Drum, whom he had hardly even seen, and his furthest out, most insignificant connection.

In Dormay the carriage drew up at the hotel, an imposing building facing a piece of open ground, with the river on one side and its garden on the other. Everyone as far as Mhoreneck, at the head of the loch, knew that Mr. Drysdale, the proprietor, had once ordered gypsies to move the encampment they had struck under the trees at the river, because he considered their presence offensive so near to his new hotel. The gypsies had moved their low tents, rickety cart and shanky pony from under the trees and settled, for as long as gypsies do settle, outside the hotel entrance. Everyone as far as Mhoreneck knew that Mr. Drysdale could do nothing about it as the piece of open ground was common. Bartle, as he gazed at the long hotel with its expanse of windows and doorway like a conservatory, wondered how they had dared.

Lady Wain told him to have his meal, she called it luncheon, at the hotel. He felt rather than saw Maysie's impatient dissent. He knew she was going to say to her mother, "You shouldn't have done that. He's not a servant." He did not want to take up the time having a meal with others when he could be by himself thinking of her, but he had to accompany the coachman when he drove the carriage round to the back.

He escaped from the kitchen as soon as he could, walking past the tweed mill to the bridge over the falls. The thunder of the cataract in his ears, he leant over the parapet to see the rocks lined with the swirl of the waters, and pitted and pocked with stones. But even the thunder of the river could not drown the sound of his own heart in his ears. Fascinated, he gazed below at the tumble and spume of the floods. Would his secret thoughts of Maysie Wain do to him what the water had done to rock and stone? But his thoughts were no longer secret, she knew he loved her. His thoughts were like the torrents in spate, when neither river bed nor bridge could curb them….

And now because he knew he was going to see her very shortly, he felt a sensation he had never felt before, as though he were growing where he stood to fill every mote and pore of his body. Abruptly he left the bridge.

He went into a little shop to buy a present for his mother with his herd's wages of two years ago, which he had not touched since he had been in Glasgow. He thought of a teapot, and the old woman gave him a variety of two to choose from, stretching behind her to take them out of the window, one with a sprig of heather painted on it and the other the falls of the river. He thought the white heather one the prettier but the spout was chipped so he took the other instead. He stood outside the shop with the newspaper parcel under his arm, looking into the window to use up the time before he could return to the hotel. The white heather teapot had been put back on its shelf but there was a circle in the dust where its neighbour had been.

He judged the time so effectively that when he returned the carriage was outside the entrance and Maysie was showing the hotel porter where to put their various packages and parcels. One of the horses was restive and Bartle went over to it. It was all falling out as though it had been planned down to the smallest detail.

The horse shook its head over his shoulder and he put back his hand to fondle it. Maysie came and stood beside him in her pink dress, stroking the white streak down the horse's face. They looked into each other's eyes. Each knew that it did not matter what either said, words were but a screen put up between them and the rest of the world when their two minds moved as one. He had grown so big for his body that he felt outside of it; and she was where he felt he was, about her, round about her.

"Horses are always impatient to be on the journey. Have you noticed that?" Her hand was stationary now, covering the white star on its forehead. Her hand itself might have been a star.

"The more mettlesome they are, the more eager to be off"

"Her name's Lady. We like her better than Diamond, although she is more chancy."

"She is not used to the traces—even yet. Her sort never becomes used to them. She wants her own head."

Their hands met on Lady's face, earth touching the starry heavens on a horse's warm brow.

"That is untrue," Bartle said.

"I did not speak," she gasped.

"You were going to say it was kind what I did—being blamed for Rachel. You were going to thank me."

"And so I should—so we all should."

"You are not all. You should know that whatever I did for you I would always be in your debt. You know everything there is to know about my love for you."

She heard the words fall from his lips as though each was forged with one stroke, white hot, on the anvil of his mind. They had been molten in the furnace all the time and it had taken this moment to bring them forth. Her mother's voice, the hotel proprietor's gruffer tones, struck her as inconsequential as puffs of wind in comparison. It was as though she had been living, until this moment enclosed her, outside of things instead of at their heart.

* * * *

Bartle placed the china teapot on the dresser for his mother to find. He was glad he had thought of buying it for her, because for some obscure reason he felt guilty about his mother. It looked a little dusty but he was afraid to put it in water in case the painted river and red evening sky washed off.

She said nothing when he entered after bringing home the cow. Through the darkness he saw something gleam whitely on the dresser. She had not found it yet. Nervously he watched her form moving nearer the dresser, then moving away. She had not noticed—yes, she had. She had taken it up in her two hands and was asking, "What's this?" as she carried it to the window to peer at it more closely.

"'The Falls of the River, Dormay'," she said, taking her two thumbs across the china. "Ye shouldna have done that, Bartle," her monotonous tones came through the gloom. "Ye should have kepit your money by ye for Glasgow."

He felt he had to say something.

"There was one with white heather on it," he hazarded, "but its spout was a bittie chipped so I took yon one instead."

"Ay," she answered, "white heather would have been more ordinary like."

Kirsty had a bottom drawer in which she kept a bedspread her mother had knitted in nine different stitches and a flounced petticoat she herself had made long ago. But no occasion had ever arisen fit enough to shake the bedspread from its folds or to don the petticoat. She kept the teapot on the dresser but Bartle knew she would never use it. It was too good. Besides, no pot made better tea than the old brown one she had had all her married life.

"It's true what everyone has been saying," she remarked. "The Lady tellt me."

"What's true, merm" he replied.

"That there's going to be a wedding in the family. Her eldest daughter. That'll be the one wha's called Miss Hetty. To a Mr. Scougall's son. He's been with them up at The House. The Lady said they have kent each other syne they have been bairns."

"I heard tell of that when first I went to Glasgow," he said, feeling it due to his mother to tell her what he knew. "They said then her father didna want her to take him but to make a better match for herself."

"The Lady seems pleased enow. He's a ship owner's son. Yon wasna Miss Hetty with her this morn. Yon must have been the second one, Miss Maysie."

"Ay, mern," he agreed, feeling he could hardly breathe.

"She's reel bonny," said his mother.

He could not answer.

He had the feeling, which strengthened the more he thought of it, that not only Sir Alfred but Maysie thought little of the first engagement in the family. She considered it a dull thing to do, to become engaged to a man you knew when he was a boy, just like one of your own brothers.

The wedding took place that winter and even Bartle, cut off as he was from what happened without his own very circumscribed existence, heard news of it. Mrs. Leggatt told him about "yon big wedding in the town" when she brought in his tea one night; and, learning that the family had a house at Barnfingal for their holidays, kept a photograph from one of the newspapers for him to see.

He could hardly bring himself to look at it in case it included Maysie and was inordinately relieved when he saw it was only of the bride and her groom. He felt he could not have borne to have seen her face and form printed in a newspaper for thousands to see who did not know her as he knew her. He wanted no picture of her to fold away in his pocket when he wore her memory imprinted on his heart as she appeared only to him.

He found he was able to commune with her, and he knew when that happened she must be thinking of him as he was thinking of her, as he was always thinking of her. These contacts with each other were like lightning flashes revealing the same landscape from an entirely different airt each time. Thus sustained, he lived from one such experience to the next until the cycle of the year brought round again his summer vacation, home—and her.

"The Lady has sent down a message for ye," his mother said when he returned one day after helping in Gow Farm fields. "She wants ye to gang up the morrow's afternoon and she'll give ye down produce from their garden. Her goodness is great, but what can she give us from their garden that we can no do without'"

He knew that was Maysie's idea, to take him to The House. He took so long to set out next day that his mother had to ask him if he minded about the Lady?

As he entered the grounds by the gates, he suddenly remembered when he had last been here how he had jumped from the dyke into a piece of waste land that had encroached from the moor beyond the boundary wall. Perhaps it was only because he was viewing everything in broad daylight, or because he knew his entry now would not be questioned, that it all struck him for the first time as appearing almost ordinary.

He saw Lady Wain sitting in the little glass-house by herself and went over to speak to her. She was wearing a straw garden hat pretty with flowers. Something about the vague sweetness with which she turned to greet whoever approached stabbed him to the quick. He was suddenly appalled to realize that Lady Wain must be as old, if not older than his mother. What had age to do with such a one, timeless as the flowers that blow each spring, self renewing as a river at its source, bright as the beams of the parent sun? She spoke to him in her smooth way, telling him to call at the back door where Mrs. Urquhart would have the basket ready for him, thinking out everything that he should find it easy.

But after he had left her, he did not go to the back door. There was time enough for the basket Mrs. Urquhart had ready for him, time enough for everything else under the sun, when the present was so full of the present it trembled like water about to brim over.

He struck off from the avenue, scarcely aware, so sure was he of his way, that he was using a lightly worn path. He crashed through the sparse undergrowth, as though to herald his approach, a man entering a child's domain. The little house was so cleverly contrived it merged into its surroundings and could easily have been overlooked. This was where the younger Wain children "kept house," where they would have tea-parties and secret picnics and hide notes to themselves this year which they would forget to look for next.

The door was open. It had a door, and windows, for it had not been insecurely erected by children but built properly by workmen out of logs of wood. As he approached he saw inside. It struck him as oddly elaborate for children, with curtains at the windows and a hearth where they could light a fire, built-in presses, even a sofa that was too shabby for anywhere else but that scarcely looked worn to him, a table and chairs.

Maysie was sitting at the low table, reading a book. From the doorway he looked down at her and she, as though sensing she were not alone, raised her head.

"It's you," she exclaimed, lightly conversational. "You gave me quite a start!"

"You've been waiting for me," he replied.

She was taken aback by this assertion, and looked it.

"And what makes you think that?" she countered a little breathlessly.

"If I had gone away without coming, you would have seen my back from here and reached the gates before I did."

She laughed as she looked at him, looked away hurriedly and then announced:

"What are you standing there for, neither in nor out? You must make up your mind to come in or go away."

He entered by the two steps. The floor was wooden and high to raise it from the damp of the ground. He shut the door behind him, and a large triangular splash of light rushed outside as he did so. He crossed the floor to sit down beside her at the table, thinking that the ground under the planks of wood would be like the ground

Rachel had lain on when she visited him on the hillside.

"I didn't tell you you could sit down," she said defensively.

"You didna need to," he replied.

"Well, and now you're here, what do you want?" she demanded, her voice beginning to flounce again.

"You."

All pretences dropped from her as she gazed at him, his knee brushing against the stiffened material of her thin frock. Her voice when it next spoke had shed its would-be bright tones and sounded deepened in the wooden interior.

"You are very sure of yourself," it stated.

"I'm surer of you," he said.

It struck him as odd that at such a moment, filled as it was with such excitement that the very air seemed to throb with it and have a force of its own, he should find himself correcting an impression he had just formed. It was as though he had found himself doing a trivial sum in his head while he was drowning.

The ground under the wooden floor he now stood upon would not be like the turf where Rachel had lain. If the hut were removed, there would be revealed a plot so withered and parched it would take years to restore it to its virgin state—if ever it could revert to what it once had been.

# Chapter Nine

"THE carriage passed on its way to Dormay," his mother remarked two nights later. "It was taking the second lass back to Glasgow—or wherever her eldest sister bides. The one wha's marrit. She is having a bairn, and they fear for her, so her sister has gone to be by."

Astounded, Bartle listened to her words. In the dark kitchen, beginning to blacken with night, only objects nearest the red glow of the fire had substance: the hump of his grannie's chair where no one sat, his mother's boots she had unlaced and removed her feet from, one of his own stockings hanging from the string stretched across the mantelpiece. In the encroaching darkness they each assumed a bulk, as though they were filled, of which daylight would empty them.

"Ye mean the Miss Maysie one," he heard his own voice sound as though disputing. "She can no have left Barnfingal. Her sister's no near her time."

"Weel, that's what one of the servant lasses told Kenny at the post office when she was down fetching their letters."

The very deliberativeness of her tones had the effect of infuriating Bartle. It was as though he were being thrown a lifeline the thrower should know was too short or too frail to be of any service.

"She has just gone to Dormay," he said, aggressively for him. "She'll be back the night."

"And what would she be doing at Dormay after mirk?" demanded his mother. "Na, the carriage came back without her at the back of four."

"She and Miss Hetty are no close like some sisters," he asserted, as though making a final grab.

"Aweel, she's awa' to her, so the servant lass thought they must have had word that Miss Hetty had taken a turn."

"Then the Lady would gang," he insisted, as if that would corner his mother.

"It is Miss Maysie wha has gang, no the Lady," she returned flatly. "Like as not she is glad to fling awa' when she can. They say she is no like to the others but finds it dull up here, and that it is a happier house without her."

"She has everything her heart could desire," he said, his voice harsh.

"Mebbe," she replied, "but ye are often less content when ye have everything than when ye have naething."

So overwhelmed was he by what he had just heard that he had to go outside, for he felt no interior could contain the tumult of his emotions. That she should leave him without word filled him with apprehension. The dread thought would obtrude that she had gone away on purpose not to see him again, but why should she do such a wicked thing? They had lain together as man and wife, nothing could unbind into twain what now was one. For her to leave him was to attempt to leave herself, and as futile. She must know that such an action was as self-destroying as unsheathing a two-edged sword; the more space it was given, the more harm it could do.

He went to the edge of the jetty. He felt at the brink, at the very mouth of cataclysm, and the sight of the loch spread peacefully before his gaze, with moonlight rippling the water, roused in him a revulsion akin to hate. He raised his eyes to the mountains on the other side, to denunciatory Fingal which wore storm clouds as its crown and snow wreaths as its cap and from whose rocky ramparts whistled the blast and shock of weather. But tonight it leant against the pale sky with a blue bloom upon it softening its crags, filling in its gullies, and smoothing out concaves.

His footsteps accompanied him along the hard road when he left the pier path at the edge of fields. They cracked like pistol shots in the silence of the night, his own footsteps—was he to be dogged only by himself throughout his life, was he never to feel someone walking by his side?

"Bartle," came his mother's disapprobating voice from the box-bed when he entered the kitchen, "what has got hold of you? What were ye doing out at this hour of the night?"

"Having a walk to myself," he muttered, lifting the sneck of his own door.

"Ye'll take your walks in the daylight," she retorted, "if ye have nought better to do with your time. But ye'll no gang stravaiging at this hour of night, and giving the house a bad name."

The afternoon before he was to return to Glasgow he made his way to the Big House, branching off from the avenue before he reached the bend to find the little hut in the clearing. The curtains were down but the door was open. He crossed the mossy path to look inside. He scarcely noticed that the table had interlocked chairs on top of it, and that everything left out had been packed away into as small a space as possible, just as he paid no attention to the child busily employed inside. Instead he looked round at everything, taking his time to survey the scene, as a warrior might gaze at the armour in which he had met the bright glory of battle, and think how sorry it looked.

The girl, on her knees at a small opened tin trunk, glanced round and saw him.

"Oh," she exclaimed, pausing in the act of folding a piece of cloth, "who are you? What do you want?"

"Where's your sister?"

She was about twelve years old, compact as a pebble or a berry, not a flower found on some mountain-top near the snows, its white petals trailed with blue veins.

"I've several sisters," she announced in a business-like way. "Which one do you mean?"

"Maysie."

"Maysie's with Hetty," she replied, returning to her packing now her child's transitory interest had subsided. "Maysie's been away for ages. We're returning home the day after tomorrow."

"Will you give her a message when ye win home and see her?"

Curiously she looked round at him.

"Yes, of course I shall," she agreed. "What message do you want me to give her."

"Tell her I was back."

"Is that all? Yes, I'll remember." Something reached her from this man as she stared at him over her shoulder, something black with unhappiness. "What—what name shall I say?" she enquired.

"You don't need to say any name. She'll ken."

Even when he was gone, it was as though he still stood there, or as though the door were shut and bolted from the outside. Lorna suddenly dropped the lid on to the trunk and ran out into the open. She was surprised to find the sun was shining brightly outside, just as it must have been all the time.

112

She hated returning home after the holidays, back to school and clothes that muffled her up. The station-master was there to welcome them, in his glassy black hat, to his big dirty station that reverberated with trains all shunting in the wrong directions. Pandemonium crowded round her as Lorna stood on the platform, clutching all the things that were too precious to pack, ferns and a piece of quartz that Marcus and she were sure was a diamond, when she became aware of a terrifying stillness in the pandemonium.

He was back, the man who had come to the hut the day before yesterday, standing beside a grimy pillar watching her. She disassociated herself from those she was with and reluctantly went towards him.

"She didna come to meet you?" His voice was imperative.

"Who? Maysie? Of course not. She's with Hetty I told you, and Hetty's at Helensburgh."

A sigh subsided from him.

"She wouldna come then. I thought——" He did not say what he had thought but his face lightened as he looked at her and for the first time she noticed he was quite fair. He took a step back from her, as though afraid of appearing intimidating. "You'll mind to give her my message?" he pleaded.

"I've already said I would," she returned. She spoke loftily because she knew how much power lay in her hands and wanted him to know she knew.

As the weather turned colder, the door at the close mouth was swung to in order to keep the building warm. Each time this door banged, the repercussion volleyed up the stairs and broke against the top flat. Bartle would sit in his room each night, waiting for it to shake, to herald the postman climbing to Mrs. Leggatt's with the last mail. When at last he rose to go to bed, he would count the hours that stretched between him and the following morning's post. Sunday gaped like an abyss until he discovered that letters could be sent by special messenger on a Sunday from the general post office, so that at any moment of any hour on a Sunday it might come——

He waited until the new year when he knew he could wait no longer. He wrote himself then, addressing the envelope to her before he began the letter as though to confirm to himself what he was doing. He asked that he might see her and as soon as possible.

She answered him by return but even when he saw the envelope on the table he did not hurry to pick it up to find out what it held. Either he sensed what its tone would be or it had come too late. He walked round the table before he touched it and sat with it opened in his hand, staring at the words in the pretty writing, before he formed them into sense.

It was written in the third person and intimated that Miss Maysie Wain would see Bartle MacDonald on the evening of the 17th for a short space at eight o'clock and he must come to the front door.

Mr. Blair let him in, looking levelly above his head when he addressed him and speaking in so distant a voice that Bartle did not feel present. "As Lady Wain has not been well this winter, Miss Wain will see you about the matter," he announced, before leading him to a room on the ground floor.

It was a much smaller room than that in which he had been previously, and she was already there, waiting for him. When he thought back to that evening, it was always of the room he thought first, as an old campaigner might re-trace in his mind the he of the field before the battle had been fought—and lost.

The walls were lined with books, all behind glass against which the gaslight flattened itself. Bartle had once seen Sir Alfred Wain quite close in Barnfingal, he wore spectacles and had looked at the boy through them without noticing him. This room had the same effect on him that Sir Alfred had had, he felt himself glance off it without making any impression. Even the large coal fire burning in the elaborate grate did not warm it for him.

"Thank you, Blair," said Maysie. These were the only words of any cordiality Bartle was to hear her say. The heavily curtained door had no sooner closed behind the servant than she leapt from her seat at the fireside to face her visitor, "How dare you do this," she said, her words so clenched with anger that she seemed to have some difficulty forcing them apart.

He looked at her in a bemused kind of way, as though not sure of his bearings.

"One of us had to do something," he said.

114

"What do you mean by that? What are you here for? If you think you can blackmail me, it won't take very long to make you understand you cannot, so I advise you not to begin."

"I've no come to blackmail you," he said, his voice empty at such a thought. He looked down at her, so still that he seemed massive beside her, who had all the brittleness of one strung to breaking point. "How could I blackmail you without blackmailing myself?"

Her face contorted with her emotions.

"You!" She was frightened to raise her voice, and spoke in husky whispers that grated with feeling. "You! You surely don't place yourself on the same plane as me. What have you to lose; Nothing,because you are nothing."

"It was you who placed me on the same plane as you. You have yourself to thank for that, not me."

"I have, have I? I don't take advice from you. How dare you ask to see me, how dare you send messages to me through my sister."

"If you had answered my message through your sister, mebbe I would not have needed to have written."

"What have I to answer, to you or anyone?"

"I have come here only to speak for myself. You have something to answer to me."

"Have I? Indeed. And what may I ask?"

"You gave yourself to me."

He felt her hand stop his mouth, the hand he had once thought like a star. He knew at that moment that she hated him so much she could have murdered him had she had the strength.

"You can prove nothing," she said between her teeth.

Again his voice went empty with astonishment.

"It's a waste of time proving what we both ken."

She turned from him, as though she could not bear such proximity, and went towards the fire where she stood with her back to it. It outlined her as though she were painted on red paper.

"What do you want? Why have you come here? Why did you ask to see me? Remember, not one penny do you get from me."

"What would I want your money for?"

"What are you here for then?" Her voice and attitude were defensive, as though she were waiting for something and was prepared, the moment she received warning, to tilt at it before it could take a stand.

"Professor Barbour says if I do as he expects me to do in my examinations, he will speak for me to another professor he kens wha is working on certain experiments the now."

He saw her deflate as she gazed at him, as though unable to believe her ears.

"And what has that to do with me?" she demanded.

"I would be his assistant. Ye and me could get marrit."

The fire behind her roared up the chimney with the sound of a forge. This was certainly not what she had expected. She seemed to fall to pieces as he stared at her and when she came together again, it was into someone different from the person first conceived.

"You think, you dare to think that I would ever marry you———" she said at last.

"You've lain with me. Where's the difference between that and marriage?"

"Don't you see, can't you understand," she cried, "that I'm not like you and never will be, just as you would never be like me. I would as soon think of marrying you as I would think of marrying a servant."

"I was either like to you or you were like to me, or mebbe we just both met, when we were one."

"I tell you I'm finished with you, and I'll deny with my very last breath that anything was ever begun. You don't talk about such things in my circle."

"You shouldna do them then."

Her lips were tightened into a straight line.

"I fail to understand you. You must go, and go for good. If I am troubled with letters or messages from you in the future, you not I will be the loser."

He turned towards the door, feeling for the handle in the folds of the curtain. Suddenly her nails dug into his hand.

"You haven't promised me," she said roughly.

He looked down at her.

"Promised you what?"

"That you will never, by word or deed or gesture, attempt to get in touch with me again."

He continued to look down at her. As she was immediately beneath him, his eyes appeared to be closed.

116

"I dinna need to promise ye anything," he repudiated behind his lids. "Ye ken."

Her feelings broke through any control she had left.

"I know nothing about you, nothing," she cried out, as though her words were blows and she was assailing him with them. "There has never been anything between us, never—either before or after. There couldn't be. We're not the same."

"Ay, there was. Mebbe no now, because ye've broken it. But there was. And no all the words ye say can smash what was."

Her fingers tore at his hand.

"You'll promise me, before you go, you'll promise me never to get in touch with me again."

"I'll do nothing of the sort. If ye think I'll fash ye again, gang on thinking it for all I care."

* * * *

Now he had to do without that world where he thought of and dreamed over and lived for Maysie Wain. Somewhere in hideous space it was gyrating on its own axis, fluctuating and tottering but forever spinning, a world that would never again embody him, although no other atmosphere could fill his lungs with such life and strength.

It was not that he no longer walked in that bright air, the virtue had gone from the air he was able to breathe. She had not only robbed him of herself but rifled him of something he had looked upon as indivisible as his own personality, something he had taken so much for granted that it was only now he had lost it he realized he had once possessed what others did not possess.

It was as though he were a water-diviner who found himself deprived of the force that twisted the hazel rod in his hands. He was a harp that no longer sounded as it had been strung to sound, a traveller who could neither return the way he had come nor take a new road, who waited for conveyance in a town where the temporary had the nightmare quality of doom.

He had seen a landscape obliterated by snow so deep that landmarks were no longer landmarks. That was what he felt when he viewed the landscape of the present, saw what had once loomed large on his horizon now flattened into unmeaningness. These were snows that would never melt until something happened to him, for he realized he was the airt from which this freezing wind blew, that it was he who was colder than the atmosphere, his earth that lay buried under icy wastes.

Such was the sameness that surrounded him, endless existences might have passed instead of several months when he heard from Lady Wain. She asked him to come to see her on Saturday afternoon, because she knew a Saturday was more convenient for him than a week-day.

It was April and the sky blue as summer above the arc of houses like white palaces in this dazzling light, for the wind was from the north. On such a day as this at Barnfingal, he knew, there would be a sudden scurry of snow through which the startled cuckoo would sound. But neither the thought of Barnfingal nor his present whereabouts made the slightest impression upon him.

As he reached the pavement carriage-step of Number Four Victoria Quadrant, the tall front door opened and two girls came out. He saw the elder of the two was Maysie and the small one the sister to whom he had twice spoken. He watched them in a dull dumb way, the flower and the berry growing on the same twig.

"Oh," Maysie exclaimed at sight of him, and he could no longer have told whether or not she had purposely chosen that moment to make her exit. Not that it mattered, not that anything mattered now. "Good afternoon, Mr. MacDonald. My mother is expecting you." Her hands were hidden in a tiny muff and he fixed his gaze on it that he need not see her face: the muff was not made out of fur but some smooth kind of skin. He wondered why he felt sick as he looked at it. "You'll find the house in a great flutter I'm afraid," her bright voice claimed him, "because my engagement is to be announced on Monday."

He took a step nearer her, his gaze still downcast.

"What's your muff made of?" he asked urgently. He could feel her start with surprise.

"My muff?" She took one hand out of it and raised it with the other. "Sealskin of course. Why do you ask?"

That was why he sickened when he looked at it. He did not her seals were considered sacred where his grannie came from. Still he did not look at her.

118

"Have you nothing to say to me?" she asked, her voice low, bending towards him. "Lorna," she said to her sister but he knew her gaze was still on him, "go down the crescent and I'll make up on you."

"Nothing," he said so emphatically he spoke too loudly, "so the bairn needna taigle herself."

He mounted the steps and as he stood waiting for admittance knew that she still stood bending towards someone who was no longer there. He thought he had heard her cry out his name, but in this world wherein he was trapped, as though in the workings of a clock, and where nothing was of any significance, it did not seem to matter whether he had or not. He remembered thinking clearly that in Barnfingal on such a day as this, when the wind drove the snow against dyke and stone, the sheep would hump themselves on the other side for shelter.

It was only when the door was opened that he realized he had come to the front and not to the area. He was unmoved by Mr. Blair's taciturnity. Ushered into the room where she had always received him, he saw Lady Wain sitting at the fireside.

"Come away, Bartle." she welcomed him, "and take a warm seat. How cold it is—you are glad to have been out only that you can come in! I had to see you, Bartle. What wonderful news this is."

He no longer saw her thoughts or was swept forward on her glad surges of feeling. The face he turned towards her was blank.

"Professor Barbour has told me," she said. "About the Gartness Gold Medal. Did you telegraph your mother?"

"No."

"Why not, Bartle?" She saw such an idea had never entered his mind. "You'll have written and told her of course."

"I'll tell her when I reach home."

"But that won't be for months yet," she protested. "I do feel it deserves a telegram—but perhaps she might think you were ill when she saw the wire."

He changed the position of his feet on the floor.

"Na, she wouldna think that. I'm never ill. But there would be na one to send with the telegram syne the bairns are all at the school."

She did not think she had ever heard him quite so broad. Kindly, she looked at him with her mother's eyes, this boy out of a mere but and a ben who, Professor Barbour had told her, was the most brilliant student ever to pass through his hands, with the rare gift of visualizing figures.

"Professor Barbour thinks so highly of you, Bartle," she continued. "I believe he has told you that he will find you a post where you will have every opportunity to use your talents."

"Ay, with Professor Stalker," He cleared his throat. "He is in the early stages of certain experiments."

"So Professor Barbour was saying, important experiments that may have world-wide significance before they are completed. To think that you will be working on them from practically the beginning. I am as proud of you as though you were my own son, Bartle." He smiled to her in response, but even although he knew she spoke the truth, her ardour failed either to reach or warm him. "I remember you, you see, when you were small—oh, it wasn't so very long ago but it will seem far away to you although so near to me. There was something about you that—wound yourself round me," although you were always so sturdy, she thought. "Perhaps it was having the same birthday as my Alfred—I never think of his birthday but I remember you, Bartle. And then you were so very generous about that matter of Rachel." She was looking at him in a vague perplexed way. "I have always felt I wanted, I always hoped to do so much for you, and as things have turned out you have always done so much for yourself and others, on your own as it were." She was aware there was something different about the boy today, she felt as though she had not met the person she had started down the road to meet. Or perhaps she was still thinking of him as a boy and forgetting he was a man now. "And dear Barnfingal," she exclaimed, brightening herself with a change of topic, for now she was speaking merely for speaking's sake. "Dear Barnfingal. Our ties with Barnfingal are stronger than ever now because my daughter, that is our second daughter, is engaged to one of the Marquis of Mhoreneck s sons."

She had a feeling of such stagnation out of him that it was as though all his faculties had suddenly stopped short. She glanced at his face and saw he was looking quite stupid. He was over-impressed, that must be it—she must remember he was Highland and the Highlander venerated his laird as though he were royalty. "The second son," she said smoothly, "the one called Ninian."

"Ay, the second one's called Ninian."

"You'll know the Drum family of course, Bartle, living on their land."

"Na," he uttered, and he was so impressed his breath seemed to go, "I've never set eyes on one of them, but I've heard tell of them from those wha have." He stood up and she saw that he had grown into a big man. "They dinna use our road," he explained. "When they gang to the castle at Mhoreneck, they gang by Tomben. They never use our road—like ye do."

"No, of course they won't." She felt such insistence called for confirmation. "Dormay would be quite out of their way."

"Our road's rough and bad and stony for carriage wheels."

"Sir Alfred always says it is more like the bed of a river than a road!" she smiled. "Still, Bartle, as I always say its very roughness keeps it private. All the traffic goes by the other side of the loch and leaves your side and ours to ourselves, doesn't it?"

"Ay, to those wha have to use it."

He felt that road again beneath his feet when he returned home after leaving the university for good. He passed the post office croft, where the bramble bushes tore at unwary passers-by over the dyke. The bush-like trees grew like moss there, in the shadow of the bank, and the garden was choked with nettles and dockens, so that if you stung yourself with a nettle, there were plenty of dockens to rub on the sting.

His mother was coming out of his room when he entered the Croft Fionn kitchen.

"So ye've got home," she said, as she always said. "Ye did well for yourself, Bartle. The Lady wrote and tellt me, and the dominie came ben when he was passing."

He put down the black bag on his grannie's chair.

"I've got a school," he said. "It's at Faal—yon's further north, a wee place but bigger than Barnfingal, in the Loch Garbh district. A house gangs with the school, mern—will ye come and mind it for me?"

She passed behind him to fetch their cups from the dresser.

"Barnfingal's big enow for me," she replied. "I'm too old to start, Bartle, and I've been here too long to move."

He closed his eyes with thankfulness that she was not going to accompany him.

She infused their tea, picking up and setting down each object with the absorption of a workman with his tools.

"Ye have a house to yourself now," she remarked thoughtfully, swilling the tea round the pot before she poured it out, "and a good wage in your pocket. Ye'll be thinking of marrying, Bartle."

He felt as though someone had dropped a black sack over his head.

"No, no," he said wildly, "not that."

"Ye're young enow," she conceded, "but ye were aye sober for your years, and no too young to think of the future now ye're in a settled post where ye'll be for the rest of your life." She pushed a plate of her large triangular scones towards him. "When ye do come to think of taking a wife, Bartle, I dinna think ye could do better than gang down the road for her."

"Gang down the road?" he repeated uncomprehending.

"Ay. I'm thinking of Daisy Thomson."

He had a picture of a little girl in a light-coloured frock sitting on the floor stringing beads.

"She's but a bairn," he said protestingly, as though Daisy Thomson had stuck like that ever since.

"She'll be a ripe age for ye in a year or two," said his mother, "when ye'll be the right age to get marrit." She lifted a scone in both her big hands but before she bit into it she remarked, "Daisy's over young yet for us to ken how she'll turn out, but she canna gang far wrong with a good father behind her."

Bartle went to the schoolhouse that night to see the dominie. He thought that wiser than waiting for the dominie to come to him. But he put it off so late that he arrived when Mr. Shaw was about to close up the house for the night.

"Come away," he greeted him genially, "like bonnie Prince Charlie, you're rather late of appearing but none the less welcome." He took him into a room where the lamp had not yet been lit, nor would it have been, Bartle knew, if his arrival had not made that necessary. "I saw your passes in *The Glasgow Herald*, man—like the one hundred-and-nineteenth psalm they went on forever." He burnt his fingers with a match and made an unpsalmlike ejaculation. "And I had Professor Barbour coming in to see me on his way back from the salmon fishing this time, as pleased with you as though you were a thirty-pounder on his rod. That was before your finals, mind. When are you taking up your work with Professor Stalker?" The lamp was lit at last.

"I'm no taking up yon work. I've no accepted it."

The dominie jerked his head to look at him. Above the smoking glass funnel Bartle saw his broad face abnormally widened and lit by the light so close to it.

"You haven't accepted it," he demanded. "Why not? Did something better turn up?"

"I have accepted the post of dominie at Faal—that's in the Loch Garbh district."

The lamp began to smell the stuffy room of oil.

"I know where Faal is, so you can save your breath explaining where. A cross-roads on a moor, with a smiddy, a schoolhouse and a kirk, and a sign-post pointing the different roads out of it." He turned out the smoking lamp instead of adjusting the wick. Through the dark his voice reached Bartle. "I was right from the beginning," he was saying, "although I would have given my soul to have believed I was wrong. You'll never come to anything."

# Chapter Ten

INSTEAD of being scattered like pebbles, as Barnfingal was, up the brae and along the road, Faal was gathered into a bunch in a clearing of Roy Forest. A large triangular patch of green filled the opening where four roads met before branching into four separate directions across moor, through forest, towards the dark pass, and to the loch. The children used this green as their playground and round it the village clustered, as though for company when so much that was unexplored lay at the back, where the silence smote or whispered, rustled or raved.

Because it was gathered into a community, it was stirrier than Barnfingal. There were no shops, not even a post office or Jeannie a' Things, but the smithy forge lit both summer and winter day with its dusky glow, a cobbler's hammer sounded on and off, and a saw-mill could be heard grinding and turning from the river.

The whitewashed cottage under its deep thatch, like Croft Fionn, was not so prevalent here, where many of the buildings were small houses rather than cottages, some with attics looking out from under peaked roofs. This was laird's land. Faal House, where the laird's family had lived for centuries, stood not far distant, and like the shepherd with his sheep the laird knew everyone by name in the dwellings on his land.

Shut off by itself, it was neither lonely nor inaccessible, for it was near the village of Achbuie, on the great north road, which had a big hotel built, as big hotels were built at the period when the railway was a novelty, facing the station. The district had therefore what Barnfingal had not, a tourist season during the short summer months, although all Faal saw of the tourists were small parties passing to climb one of the mountains, or straggling to Achbuie after having walked through the savage pass, or bumping past in horse-drawn vehicles, for the roads were too rough for the newer motor-cars, to picnic at Loch Garbh.

Barnfingal had its one road that wound round the loch and its old drove track over the hills, which years of moss and turf had done their best to reclaim as their own, but the Faal district was dissected with thoroughfares of every description, from the

124

old Thieves' Road to bridle and pony paths, from the tree-shaded Lady's Walk to the Captain's Mile.

Not that Bartle ever took any of them, for he never went far from the schoolhouse, to explore heathery moor or discover picturesque waterfall. He never saw the huge clumps of mountains any closer than between the trees that stood like an army round Faal. They were pines and when the sun set it stripped them into avenues of pillars, dyeing with its light their long pink boles into ruddy hues which was why the forest was known as Roy, or red.

It was but the relic of the forests that once clothed the vast plain and crept up the mountainsides: in the lochs and lochans that lavishly sprinkled the district could be seen tree stumps that had been rooted in that past age.

It was the trees that made the landscape here so different to what he was accustomed. This countryside had none of the denuded feeling that Barnfingal had, with its bald green hilltops, as though turf was all the centuries had managed to crop to cover rock stripped bare to the bone. The bearded trees there grew mostly near the loch and were planted in woods, not stripped outposts still surviving when the main body of their army had long since been vanquished by time and man.

And because of the trees the light fell differently to what it fell at home, where it drained from the loch and drenched the hilltops, or on a dull day struck some barren mountainside, making it stand out with the splendour of a revealed place. Here it striped, not swept, the ground, slanted, filtered and crept.

The snow did not cover up everything so completely as it did at more exposed Barnfingal. The slightest wind wafted the white powder from the light foliage, and under it the snow could only speckle the ground, thickly carpeted with pine needles. So that when Bartle heard the snow ploughs were out on the great north road and the children from Mulloch Moor could not come through the drifts to school, he saw in his mind's eye, instead of the freckled landscape outside his windows, the snow making everything the same at Barnfingal, the small smoothed away by immensity.

His scholars liked him and he liked them. They brought sugar to him and he made jam for them out of the berries in the school garden; then they brought their pieces for him to spread. They liked the dominie because he spread the jam into all the corners.

Few bursary scholars ever left the little woodland school for college or university. The object of their dominie was not to fire them with ambition or stir them with a love of learning, but rather to make that learning as easy and smooth for them as he could. Although he used neither tawse nor rhetoric, he was seldom taken advantage of, and the shyest newcomer was never timid of him. Mr. Turner, the gamekeeper, was wont to say that passing the schoolhouse now Mr. MacDonald had taken over was like passing the kirk on a week-day. When they grew up, some of his scholars were to wonder what was the secret of such unenforced control: they never came to a satisfactory conclusion whether it was that Mr. MacDonald had treated them all as adults or permitted them to treat him as a fellow child.

It was always an effort for him to return home to see his mother during the summer vacations, such an effort that he felt it like an uprooting. He formed the habit of returning immediately the term ended that he need only spend the first part of the holidays at Barnfingal and could return to Faal as soon as possible.

While he was home he no longer went near Brae, to give them a day's work in the fields. Dugie was married now, to one of Torquil Lamont's brown-eyed sisters, so that it was said the sheep of Naver and Brae could not have told whether they belonged to a Malcolm or a Lamont. When Jamie saw Bartle he would say to him, "Annie said to mind ye to her," to which Bartle always replied, "Ye must mind me to Annie."

"I'll mind to tell her I minded ye of her," Jamie once turned on him savagely to retort.

Unlike the great majority of dominies, school-masters and marms, Bartle looked forward to the annual visits of the inspector. He was a spruce, white-haired man with a white moustache trimmed into ferocious lines as though to counteract the blueness of his eyes. The first year of his inspection while Bartle was dominie, he had difficulty in finding accommodation in the district and Bartle put him up in the practically empty house that went with the school. After that, it was taken for granted between them that he should spend the night there, although neither stressed the matter lest it got about that the inspector was a friend of dominie MacDonald's and so would send in indulgent reports of Faal school.

126

"It always surprises you that I don't drink," Bartle remarked to him good-naturedly one night when they were together and he had given him his customary tot of whisky.

Mr. Miller looked into his glass in an embarrassed way.

"Well, you don't, do you?" he said lamely.

"No," replied Bartle, "and I never have. That surprises you too, doesn't it?"

Mr. Miller cocked his blue eye at him.

"That was the only reason I could think of why you, with your unversity honours, were to be found buried up here. I used to come across it again and again in the islands in the past—a teacher of outstanding attainments hiding away in some remote spot because spirituous liquor had led to his downfall."

"You used to visit the islands?" enquired Bartle, to steer the conversation as far from himself as he could.

"In my young days. That was when Her Majesty's Inspector was given instructions by My Lords of the Education Department in London. 'Where is Skye?' some official once wrote in the margin of a minute. They would have been put to it to find on the map some of the islands I used to inspect!"

"Did you—ever—reach—a little island called Wrack?" asked Bartle. He spoke reluctantly, as though not sure whether or not he wanted Mr. Miller to know anything about it.

"Wrack? I remember it well. Very primitive, or was in my day, but it will be the same now. What is a decade or two to rock? It's in the Roman Catholic belt of course." Bartle's face was bland to impassivity as he stared into the unlit hearth. "So remote, Protestantism never reached it. The only soul on it when I was there who wasn't Roman Catholic was the male teacher from the mainland. Yes, I always remember Wrack because of the ruins of a chapel there—it must have been a substantial building in its day, for such a place, with a chancel or choir at the east separated from the body of the kirk by an arch. I discovered the mortar had been made of burnt shells and was of thin consistency but harder than cement. Legend has it that it was built by foreigners from a wrecked ship in gratitude for having been spared and received well by the natives. The fishermen still set their lines at a particular spot where the ship is said to have foundered and which is known to this day by the name of the Infanta deeps. That takes us back to 1588 and the Spanish Armada. Several of the children I inspected were as black of eye and hair as any foreigner. I always remember there was a family in Wrack who believed they were descended from seals!"

The dominie was smiling politely in his direction without actually looking at him.

"One wonders how such ridiculous fancies could ever have taken root," he remarked remotely.

"We would probably find sense in the very essence of nonsense if we only dig back deep enough," the inspector replied leniently. "Time passes so swiftly, and brings so many changes, that we outgrow customs and beliefs as a child outgrows his elder brother's clothes, but something always sticks, particularly in these seldom visited, outlying regions where the years pass but to return. There they are still wearing their elder brother's clothes. It's quite a different life they live away yonder to what we do down here. There are some islands where they take the second sight as much as a matter of fact as we take ordinary sight."

He saw them, as the inspector talked on, his voice bearing to and from him as though on waves, islands bright green, like a fort or ruins that have been turfed over, and islands bare as the hulks of abandoned ships. He kept his inward eye on them, as though he thought if he fixed his gaze on the horizon it would prevent him taking the stony path from the shore to the churchyard a little way inland. He could feel the rocky ground below his feet, the strength of the sea air against his face. With the desperate effort it takes to force oneself awake from a dream, he made himself think again only of islands in the distance.

* * * *

That summer was hot and even in autumn the garden still hummed like a hive, for changes came tardily to this small clearing sheltered by its screen of trees. School had only shortly started after the holidays but it seemed a long time since he had been home to Barnfingal. On this afternoon he had locked up the schoolroom for the day and was back in his house when he heard a knock on the door. It was Jamie Malcolm.

128

"Why, Jamie," exclaimed Bartle, holding the door wide, "come away ben." Once his friend was inside he shut the door slowly behind him and more slowly turned to face him.

"Ye ken why I've come," cried Jamie, his words jumbling together with excitement.

"Yes," Bartle said heavily, "I think I know why you've come."

The lobby where they stood was awkward with its too large hall-stand, and Bartle pressed forward into the small sitting-room. Jamie backed before him.

"I'm on ma way to join up." His fists kneaded the cap between them. "Ye'll come too, Bartle. We can gang thegither. I dinna care what it is, the Cameronians or the H.L.I. or the Black Watch. We'll gang to Glasgow, the pair of us. We can bide with Mistress Leggatt and enlist thegither. Mebbe Sandy'll come too, if he's no awa' already."

Bartle sat down on the slippery sofa. He suddenly felt old, and as though his bones weighted his body.

"I can't come, Jamie. I've been to Perth already. I went—as soon as war was declared. They won't take me.

"They won't take ye?" repeated Jamie, his voice thinning with wonder. "But they must, Bartle. Ye've nought wrong with ye. Ye're bigger and brawer than me, or yon wee skelf Roddy Fisher and they've taken him."

Bartle said nothing but held up his right hand. Jamie's dark brows ran together as he stared at it.

"Why, of course," he said at last, "I never thought of that. It's your trigger finger that's gone."

"That's what they told me. I would have done anything to have gone." His voice suddenly disappeared, and he looked round wildly as though wondering what he had said. He knew what he had felt and he felt so strongly that sometimes he was not sure whether or not his feelings, without his behoof, had taken the form of words. He had felt that if he did not take this opportunity to enlist in the army, he would be submerged for life—or was it death—in this unvarying static state, as though embalmed in a glacier that took years to move an inch.

"I'm reel sorry about that," said Jamie, "reel sorry. They'll no find anything wrong with me, will they, Bartle? I'll murder them if they do. But they winna, for ye mind how ye aye said I'd get awa'? And here I am on ma way! It's no so bad for ye no coming, Bartle, ye've your school to leave, but I've naething to hold me back, naething I mind leaving. I'm no a farmer like Dugie. A farmer has to bide and I want to gang. There'll be plenty of time for biding when ye're put under the earth! I might as well be a soldier as be anything. Mebbe I'll make such a good soldier they'll keep me in the army after the war. Ye never ken! They say it will all be over by Christmas but I canna thole to believe that. As long as it lasts long enow for me to get into it. It's aye the way, is it no? Naething happens for long enow, and then everything happens at once!"

Bartle was looking at him in a fascinated way, Jamie his usual cocky self, crowing away, swelling himself out into double his size with the importance of the moment. For at that moment Bartle knew that Jamie would never come back.

He remembered when he had looked at him asleep at Mrs. Leggatt's, he had suddenly sickened when he found his thought finished for him—if Jamie lived to be an old man. Now he knew why he had sickened. Jamie was going to be killed.

He felt he could not bear the burden he was carrying. The present was so loaded with the future that it was cumbered by it. He moved into the kitchen to put the kettle on, and Jamie followed him. He found himself addressing him with care, applying himself to speak naturally, as though he had to make a stupendous effort to separate Jamie from his wraith.

"And how's Annie?" he was mindful to ask as he poured the boiling water into the teapot.

"Annie's fine," replied Jamie. "At least she's just herself." His face puckered as he considered his younger sister. "It's getting serious about Annie," he confided, "she's no trysted yet."

"Give the lass time to grow up before ye fash yourself about her being trysted," advised Bartle.

"Ye're twenty-five," Jamie said sternly, "and Annie's three years younger than ye. She's as grown up now as she'll ever be. But she has aye thought on one lad, and doesna seem to take to lads, and they dinna seem to take to her. They never come to the bend in the road to see if she'll walk out with them, and if they did she wouldna ken what they were after. Annie's no like Bess. She kent what a lad

130

was up to almost before he kent himself. But will I tell ye why I never feel too low about Annie?" he enquired, brightening.

"Ay, ye'd better tell me," said Bartle, smiling good-naturedly to hide that he felt he was balancing precariously between two worlds.

"Ye said she'd get awa'," Jamie told him. "Ye mind, yon day on the hillside before ye went to Glasgow for the first time? Well, that means Annie's going to get marrit, and be all right."

"Of course it does," agreed Bartle.

He had a picture of a little girl walking to Brae Farm after she had left him. The compassion that he felt for her made him unhappy because he knew it could bring no happiness to her. Nor could he wish that she had always remained the little girl he had watched skipping to her home. Youth did not strike him as a radiant time, as childhood did not strike him as a state of unthinking happiness. He thought of those who passed through both transitions as enclosed and frail as egg-shells in a world that had not one of the features of a nest. Who was it who had once mentioned to him something about burnt shells proving harder than cement?

"Annie will be all right," he said.

He was glad when Jamie left next day, to enlist as soon as possible before the war had a chance of stopping. A generation seemed to have slipped between them, separating them as finally as though one were already dead.

The laird was already in France, the Grant brothers had enlisted and the cobbler's son went, as well as the smith across the way. The first aeroplane any of them had ever seen flew over Roy forest, scaring the animals in the fields below. One man in an aeroplane such as that had destroyed a German Zeppelin. And Mr. Miller came on his annual inspection, as though everything were the same as it had ever been.

He set the older children an exercise while he examined those in their first year orally. There were only three of them, two little boys and a smaller girl. Effie was in such a scare that she reminded Bartle of nothing so much as a rabbit which, petrified with fright, presses back its ears. Her face was the size of a sixpenny bit and when she was frightened it seemed to dwindle to the size of a threepenny while her eyes grew bigger. She was a shepherd's daughter who came from a lonely cottage on Mulloch Moor, which accounted for her bursting into a storm of tears on her first day at school when she found herself amongst so many strangers. Bartle now smiled to her reassuringly, while he thought to himself, You silly wee doo, the Inspector's not going to eat you!

"Begin the multiplication table of three times three," Miller ordered her.

Effie was not looking at him. She dare not look at him. Her gaze was glued to her dominie's face which did not bristle with moustaches nor was overhung with the white thatch of bushy eyebrows, but was mild and smooth and known.

Trust Mr. Miller to know the sore parts! Bartle was thinking serenely. Poor little Effie could not manage her two times yet and even four times was easier than three. Tommy MacNab next her was nudging her to begin, but Effie would have been insensible to prompting even if his elbow had been a scythe.

"The Inspector means you, Effie," Bartle said kindly. "Three times one are——?"

"Three," Erne answered him, her gaze still on his face.

Now what about three times two? thought Bartle.

"Three times two is——" panted Effie.

Six of course, thought Bartle, very surprised she had got that length.

"Six," Effie said obediently.

Startled, Bartle gazed at her. Three times three are nine, he thought deliberately. He heard the child say it as though repeating it after him. Three times four are twelve, he conned to himself. "Three times four is twelve," she recited breathlessly. Three times five is fourteen, he tested. "Three times five is fourteen," he heard her say. No, fifteen, he corrected in the silence of his thoughts. "No, fifteen," she said aloud.

By the time she had reached three times thirteen being thirty-nine, Bartle knew Effie was doing what Mr. Shaw had once accused him of doing, finding his results without working them out. She was reading his mind.

"That child has a remarkable flair for figures," Mr. Miller commented to him after the examination.

"Most remarkable," Bartle agreed with perfect truth.

"She appears fascinated by them," continued Mr. Miller. "I believe she would have gone up to three times ninety-nine if I hadn't stopped her!"

After that incident Bartle began to take particular note of Effie. There was one thing about their dominie the children felt rather than noticed, and that was that they were all the same to him. He knew what work to set each child, but beyond that, each child had no further individuality for him. Now as he separated Effie from the sums he wrote on her slate and the capitals he formed for her to copy, he became aware of someone who was hanging on his every word and look and gesture.

He would see her waiting for him when he took his place at his desk each morning. He was conscious of her child's eyes when he turned round suddenly from the blackboard.

She was not robust like most of the other children, but a sick looking thing, like the white petal of a flower, who always looked cold even in summer. Then she wore a checked dress that hung limply as though its small wearer had had all the starch taken out of her, and in winter thick black stockings and coarse boots, like weights to keep her to the ground in the face of the winds that ransacked Mulloch Moor.

Because of her shyness, it was difficult to know whether or not she was taking in what she was being taught, and Bartle had fallen into the habit, if he had to show her anything new, of showing it to her by herself when the rest of the school had run shouting outside for their mid-morning break. As he sat beside her on this certain day, he found himself wondering if her backwardness were not caused by expending too little thought about what she was being taught because she was expending too much on the teacher. He was about to speak more briskly to her, to try to waken her from her day-dreaming, when she suddenly burst into tears.

"Now, Effie," he said, "it is not nearly so bad as all that. If you would but listen to what I am saying, you would find it quite simple."

Her tears were such that she could not speak, but he felt her put both her hands over his one where it lay on the desk, as though to cover something she could not bear to look upon.

"Why, Effie," he exclaimed, comprehension beginning to dawn upon him, "you're upset because I have one of my fingers off. I lost it long ago when I was John MacLintock's age. I've forgotten all about it. It isn't in the least sore, and I never feel the lack of it. Think of all the pains and aches I have missed not having that finger!" he joked, as her small body continued to shake with her sobs. "All the times I might have snecked it or cut it or jabbed it!"

She bent her head over his hand and began to kiss it, in an agony of love to make it whole again. He could feel her nose, wet and cold, against his knuckles.

"You know, Effie," he said, "if I had had that finger, I would no longer be sitting beside you as I am doing this morn. I would have been in the trenches. But because I have no first finger, I couldn't fire a gun and so I was no use to them as a soldier. That's what trying to let a fox out of a trap has spared me!"

She lifted her head to look at him, her tears streaking her woebegone face.

"Oh," she said then, "you would have gone away. I could not have carried that," and her small face quaked as though she would begin all over again at the very thought of such a happening.

He had no wish to be the recipient of such adoration, and tried to rob the situation of her intensity by treating her in as matter of fact manner as possible, but when he saw her strung up in case she earned his disapproval, sitting on her hands, or twisting her thin legs round one another, he could not be other than gentle to her. He realized now she had cried on her first day not because of the strangeness of her surroundings, but because she had seen his hand when he put it over hers to show her how to draw the figure one "straight as a soldier".

He saw the game of Snakes and Ladders when he was at home. It was lying on the shelf which he no longer needed to stretch to reach. Was that what being grown up meant—seeing within your reach what once you would have given your soul to have, when it no longer meant anything to you?

A smile on his face, he picked down the brightly coloured box, and thought of Effie. He felt a little guilty thinking of Effie for the first time on the last day he was at home, when he knew each day apart would stretch long as a lifetime to a child. He determined to take the game back to Faal and give it to her. Perhaps, he thought hopefully, looking inside, she would become absorbed in the gift, like any other child, and forget about the giver.

But Effie did not answer Here when he called the register on the first day of the term. He heard she was recovering from the whoops. A cloud seemed to reach him from her, a cloud so black that after school that day he walked to the shepherd's cottage, the flat box under his arm, to hand it in for her.

There were no dogs about the place, so that meant Erne's father was from home. Instead of the customary warning bark, he heard instead the crying of a very small baby as he waited at the door. The shepherd's cottage was a stout stone building, to stand up to the blast of moorland winds. Bartle's house in Faal, like most of its neighbours, was built chiefly of wood. This perhaps accounted for the temporary feeling about it he had had from the beginning, although he felt his tenancy of rather than the house itself was transient.

He listened as someone, a woman from her tread, crossed the floor to answer his summons at the door. The next moment he saw looking up at him the startled face of Rachel MacInnes.

# Chapter Eleven

"RACHEL!" he exclaimed.

"Bartle MacDonald," she said at the same moment. She was the first to recover. "What are ye doing here?" she asked uneasily. "Awa' aff with ye, Bartle. Ma husband Will is a reel jealous man and it would no be good for ye if he found ye here."

"Not good for you, you mean," he corrected automatically. Rachel's thoughts were like the china doll in a Halloween cake, formed but featureless. "I have the school at Faal, and when I heard Effie had the whooping cough I came to hand in this game for her."

"That's reel kind of ye," she returned, taking it from him. She looked at him in a troubled way, as though wondering what to make of him now he was here. "I sometimes wondered when I heard your name was Mr. MacDonald if ye were the Bartle MacDonald I used to ken."

"Why should your husband be jealous of me?" Bartle demanded.

"Ach, he's the sort of man wha's jealous of any other man," replied the pliant Rachel.

"Did you tell him I was the father of your bairn?" pressed Bartle.

"I tellt him it was a Barnfingal lad wha was in Glasgow at the same time as I was. I tellt him ye had gone to Canada. I never said your name, Bartle. Thank God I didna, with ye no further aff than Faal school. But I wouldna like him to find ye here, lest he finds out where ye're from and begins putting twa and twa thegither. He's a great man at putting what isna there thegither and making a muckle heap of it, so I'm feart what he would do if he ever got his hands on to something."

"Dinna fash yourself," said Bartle, reverting to how he used to speak as though to give her confidence, "he can no find out what isna there." So much taller than she, he leant against the doorjamb, his hand well above her head.

"Everyone here thinks Effie is his bairn," she said, still disquietened.

"Ay, that's the thing to let them think," he acquiesced.

"Syne Jamie Malcolm wouldna father his own bairn, I was lucky to get a man wha would," she continued righteously.

"Reel lucky," he agreed, "but Effie's no Jamie Malcolm's bairn, as ye ken well enow, Rachel. I ken wha Effie's father is. Alfred Wain," he inserted, before she could think out someone else. He felt a little bemused as he realized that the game of Snakes and Ladders, which had originally belonged to Alfred Wain, had now found itself into the possession of his child.

Her cheeks flamed scarlet as she backed a step from him.

"Bartle MacDonald," she said huskily, "ye never kent yon from me. I never tellt anyone, no even ma own mother, lest she clyped it to ma father, and he went to Glasgow and made trouble with the Wains." He knew she had not told even her parents in case her father had taken from her the money she received from the Lady. "Syne ye didna get it from me, wha tellt ye?"

"I found out," he replied evasively, "but it's as safe with me as though I didna ken it. The Wains have been reel good to ye, Rachel."

"No better than they should be," she retorted, giving her head a fling. "My, when I see their name in the papers and mind wha was the father of ma Effie, it gives me quite a turn. Yon Miss Maysie—I never could bide her— she marrit on the Marquis of Mhoreneck's son. Weel, her bairns and ma Effie are related, whether she likes it or no. And her so high and mighty."

He whitened at the sound of Maysie Wain's name.

"She has no children," he replied coldly, as though to put distance between him and Rachel.

"Has she no?" she asked with interest. "Aweel, when she has, the son of the Marquis of Mhoreneck's son will be first cousin to ma Effie."

"I wouldn't go building on that if I were you," Bartle said roughly. "You were due nothing from the Wains and Lady Wain aye saw you had something."

"Ye'll be telling me next where I have a mole, Bartle MacDonald, ye seem to ken so muckle about me," she retorted. "Wha's saying anything against the Lady? She got me into hospital to have Effie and I never needed to gang home. Ay, she aye saw to it I had something and the something didna stop when I marrit, but na one kens about it but me and her—and ye seeming-like. Even Will doesna ken. Master Alfred's at the front now. I ken, because I saw he was mentioned in despatches in the papers, with a photo in looking so like himself I wantit to laugh. Ay, ay, there was never anything muckle wrong with Master Alfred."

"You've other bairns now," remarked Bartle, feeling the sooner Rachel was brought back to the realities of the present the better.

"Ay, twa and another on the way—there's aye one on the way," she said contentedly.

The apologetic little figure of Effie, making herself even smaller than she was as though not to be in anyone's way, strayed into Bartle's mind.

"Your husband," he said, "will naturally care for his own bairns better than he does for Erne."

"I've never askit him," Rachel replied defensively.

"He's bound to," insisted Bartle. "You said yourself he was a jealous man. He would never take it out of Effie that she wasn't his, would he, Rachel?"

"Effie doesna ken she's no his," Rachel said indignantly. "What would he gain taking anything out of a bairn wha doesna reach his knees" she demanded. "Na, na, ma Will's a man," she gloried, "and if he wants to take anything out of anyone, he'll take it out of me, as he's free to do syne he is ma husband."

Bartle walked slowly back to the schoolhouse. He was glad to return to Faal, where the wind harped through the trees like fingers at an instrument, sounding airs and touching chords that awoke no response in him. Not like a stone cottage on a desolate moor. His grannie had once told him that when a certain woman, who was believed to have been a witch, died in Wrack, she had been buried within the seamark. After his brief visit to the stone cottage, it was as though something long buried was left exposed, something the tide of his thoughts could no longer cover.

Mrs. MacNab was at her garden gate when he passed, speaking to Mr. Turner, the gamekeeper, and the cobbler who was standing in his next door garden. Bartle paused to pass the time of day with them. He always took trouble to speak to people because he felt such effort was called for on his part. It was not shyness that enclosed him but absorption. He knew perfectly well that if he himself did not break through this absorption, he would find himself sooner or later marooned with the world unable to break through to him.

138

"We were talking of Roderick MacBeath," Mrs. MacNab said hospitably to make him feel at home in their conversation.

"Ah yes, Roderick MacBeath," said Bartle, lowering his voice and shaking his head in sympathy, for Roderick MacBeath had died last week. He lived with his pale-eyed wife and their brood in a barnlike cottage up at Tomanbeg. Their home had a scraped look outside, as though the many MacBeath children were hens who long ago had scratched all sustenance from the soil it stood on. There was a MacBeath for every form in the Faal school, but not one sat where he or she should have sat according to age, for all had the same kind of light-headedness. Although so numerous, Bartle was sorry for them as he always was for the minority, because they were the one family in the district who were Roman Catholic.

"The priest did not win to him in time," Mrs. MacNab nodded over her crossed hands comfortably holding her elbows.

"And no wonder that was," said the cobbler, "seeing the length of the road he has to travel from Alltdu."

"It's a fearsome thing for a Roman Catholic to the without a priest at his side to nudge him into heaven, by their way of it," remarked Mr. Turner.

"So it is," agreed Mrs. MacNab, "and their mother was in great distress of mind, Lally was telling me, with their father chilling on the bed and no priest at the door."

"Lally is the brightest of them all," ruminated the cobbler. "Would you not say so, Mr. MacDonald?"

"So he is," affirmed Mrs. MacNab, as though there could be no two answers to that. "No back to his mind at all. He is just like a milk-jug when you ask him a question—it pours until it is empty. 'Your father would be quite dead by the time the priest arrived?' I said to him. 'Dead as a herring,' he agreed. 'The priest could do nothing then when he did come?' I said to him, to see what answer he would give, though well I ken a priest will aye find something wrong to do. 'Deed yes,' cried Lally, 'Father Owen has made it all right with Saint Peter.' 'However could he do that now?' I asked of him. 'Father Owen wrote a wee note to Saint Peter,' Lally said to me, 'and he folded it up wee and put it atween my father's lips. And Father Owen told our mother she was to have no fears that St. Peter would not find it and understand why our father had no priest at his side when he died.' "

"Did you ever hear such superstitious tomfoolery in all your life?" demanded Mr. Turner, outraged.

"A priest never walks on the sole of his foot but only on the edge," said the cobbler.

"They are deceivers and liars, the whole black pack of them," said Mr. Turner. "I'll warrant Father Owen does not believe that shibboleth nonsense. He has had some sort of education."

"An education in Roman Catholic lies and Popish snares," pronounced Mrs. MacNab.

"But he will not stop short at pulling the wool over an ignorant woman's eyes."

"A priest never stops short," said the cobbler, "he goes the whole length every time, until he comes to the end of the rope and finds it a noose."

"Let him put in his own head then," retorted Mr. Turner, "but it should be forbidden by law that he meddles with other folk. What do you say, Mr. MacDonald. Do you not agree it is a scandal?"

"What is scandalous about making a woman happy?" asked Battle.

He was aware of three pairs of eyes fixed upon him as though he were the offending priest.

"She is living in a fool's paradise," protested Mr. Turner.

"A fool's paradise is surely, better than no paradise at all," said Bartle. He spoke as he always spoke without heat, and was startled to see the excitement such temperate words enflamed.

"Mr. MacDonald," Mr. Turner asked him bluntly, "do you, an educated man, mean to tell me you see nothing scandalous about all that mumbo-jumbo?"

"Mebbe it is not mumbo-jumbo to Mr. MacDonald," said the cobbler, staring at him hard, "syne he thinks a fool's or a Roman Catholic's paradise is better than none at all."

"I was not talking about myself," Bartle hastened to say, but he suddenly found himself wondering, would he not prefer a fool's paradise to none at all? "I was thinking of Mrs. MacBeath. Surely it is better for her to be comforted than to think of her husband bubbling in hell."

"It can never be better for anyone to believe lies," Mr. Turner told him strenuously.

140

"No, for it is just putting off the evil day every Roman Catholic will have to face when he sees the truth staring back at him," propounded the cobbler.

"All I meant," Bartle said carefully, smiling to him, "was that a pinching shoe is better than no shoe at all!"

"Your foot would tell a different story once it is out of the shoe," returned the cobbler. "By that time it is fitted for nothing but what pinches it and could not walk straight if it tried."

Despite their displeasure, Bartle still considered Father Owen had done right, but he did not press the point since obviously it meant so much more to them than it did to him. When he saw the priest passing on his way from Tomonbeg, however, he invited him in to have a cup of tea, for he knew Father Owen would get nothing at the MacBeaths. The faithful were so scattered in his far-flung parish, visiting must prove an arduous business for one pair of legs. If it were, Father Owen did not complain. His rough red cheeks gave an impression of good health that seemed to festoon his priest-black clothes so that it was never noticed he was shabby. Bartle liked him for his good nature, and looked forward to his visits, for Father Owen now made it a practice to call on his way back from Tomanbeg. He never once spoke of religion on these occasions, and Bartle was careful not to raise the subject with him.

Alfred Wain was killed at the storming of the Messines Ridge. Bartle was at Barnfingal when he heard the news. It made him remember Alfred Wain, with his white ears, and sent his thoughts flocking to the Lady.

When he went to fetch the Croft Fionn cow from the herd, the waiting men and boys would tell him the last time Master Alfred was up that way. Things were not the same as they used to be, with the Wains coming back each year as faithfully as the summer itself. But last autumn Master Alfred had returned to Barnfingal with Sir Ninian, his brother-in-law, with whom he was biding at Mhoreneck, and had a day's shooting on the moors. Davie Thomson would have thought that Master Alfred had had his fill of shooting in the trenches. Young Kenny Anderson and the two MacInnes lads had been up with them as beaters. All agreed this would be a grievous blow for the Lady and Sir Alfred. An eldest son was an eldest son, and no younger brother could ever quite take his place as he could not his father's first name. That was their eldest lad and their youngest awa' now. Ay, do ye mind Master Charlie? It was at Barnfingal he died. That was all any of them minded about wee Charlie, and the braw hearse for but a bairn. How time flies. If Master Charlie had been alive the day, he would have been old enow for the war——

As Bartle heard their voices come and go, he thought of Lady Wain and what this news must mean to her. Her sorrow beat through to him so that he could hardly bear it. When school started and he saw Effie, he would gaze at her, trying to trace some Wain, but nowhere could he catch a gleam or flash in that form as wispy as a handful of hay. Unless her hair, but even it was pallid, not white-fair like her mother's, nor definite enough in colour to be called red like her father's. She did not enter and leave like the other children, making her presence felt, but always seemed to hover, like the feather so light it follows the swish of the broom but is never swept away.

Annie Malcom was married now. His mother kept him advised of the various stages of Annie's courtship each year he went to Barnfingal. A soldier friend of Jamie's had entered into correspondence with her and sent his photograph. Annie had sent hers. They were married on his first leave and Annie was now in England. The last time Bartle was home he learnt Annie's husband had been invalided out of the war, and was back at his work making bricks.

When he knew Jamie was dead, Bartle felt he must go to Annie. He took that as much for granted as though it had been arranged between the three of them. The journey south was complicated by many changes. Vast catacombs of blacked-out stations knelled with departures as final as any destination. Here war was not a shock that took you unawares when you opened a newspaper or saw the laird home on leave. Here you were at war, and it was at your throat.

He arrived at Annie's in the morning. He counted out carefully the houses, a row of one-storied buildings all stuck together, whose fronts looked like their backs, for there was nothing but the number to tell him which was Annie's. He wondered how she could breathe here, in this built-up flatness, after the windy uplands of Brae, in a house that struck him because of its very similarity with its neighbours as inimical as a trap.

142

She answered the door herself and even before he realized it was Annie he saw she was with child. She was not expecting him and he heard her say his name with a flood of recollection in its two syllables. She took him into the kitchen where his bigness felt awkward because it was all unfamiliar, the black built-in fire so different from the open hearths at home. He noticed a photograph of Jamie framed on the high mantelshelf, and even Jamie looked unfamiliar because he had been photographed in private's uniform.

"Why, Bartle," cried Annie, her eyes spouting, "and is it no like ye to come to see me? I might have kent ye would be. Jamie, Bartle, Jamie——" She put her hand up to her heart, as if to separate it from the child she was carrying.

"Ay, Annie, Jamie. We both ken what the other feels, so we'll lift it between us."

"Ay, Bartle, ye ken. Ben was reel fond of him, but he had just met Ben. Ye kent him when he was wee. We were all wee then. I can gang further back with ye than I can with Ben." Her voice throbbed with her feelings as she busied herself making tea for him, and the child he remembered as Annie was swallowed by the woman. "Ben says if our bairn's a lad he's to be called after Jamie. Can ye no wait, Bartle, until Ben comes home for his tea? I have to give him his dinner awa' with him each day because he can no manage home for it. Aweel then, ye'll have to gang long before that. They say the war's going to stop. Dugie has three bairns now—ye would be up at Brae when ye were last home?"

"I gave them a day at the shearing," he replied.

"Do ye mind how the newly sheared sheep used to pour through the gateway like milk?" she said, her face wreathed in smiles as she remembered.

"Ay, and Jamie giving the last one a skelp to hurry it on!"

"I'll see ye have something awa' with ye for the train journey," she promised. "All this way—just to see me. Dugie says there will aye be room at Brae for any bairn of mine. Ay, but it does my heart good to hear ye talk as they talk at home."

The kitchen smelt strongly of waxcloth. He thought of this place becoming familiar as home to Annie's children, who would find the way they spoke at Brae and the way they did things there unlikely and strange. He turned to wave back to their mother as she stood, bulky and unwieldy, in the narrow doorway.

* * * *

He only remembered it was his birthday when he felt Lady Wain thinking of him. She still thought of him on his birthday although the son he had once shared it with was dead.

That was the only milestone that marked the passing of the years. His annual visits home had become such a part of his life that they now merged into its even tenor without causing any change of key. But on his birthday he came to the end of something as he added another year to his age, like a stone on a cairn.

He would look at the boys and girls ranged in rows below him, thinking how each one had moved back a form since his last birthday, how those who sat in the front row had not been there last year, and those who had sat on the furthest back bench of all had run out of the schoolroom door for the last time.

And always his wandering gaze on these expeditions would light and fix on Effie. She was the one person in that room who had any individuality for him, who stood alone in his thoughts without the accompaniment of those with whom she did sums or conned history.

She had outgrown her childish adoration of him. At least he supposed she had outgrown it. Certainly she had disciplined it until it no longer embarrassed him or upset herself. A quiet girl, she seemed to live a contained life of her own that made her older than her contemporaries, and although liked by her fellows she never seemed quite one of them. Bartle felt he could have picked her out as different even if he had not known her story. She achieved a picture of great neatness, neatness with such a shine to it that as she grew steadily older the shine was noticed rather than the neatness. Her hair was brushed until it looked burnished, and even when the fashion of the bob reached Faal hers was not cut, but tied behind her head with twin bows. She worked hard at her lessons and was undoubtedly his most promising pupil. He realized this promise was due to wanting to shine in his eyes rather than to a natural bent towards scholarship. On the first day of school after the summer holidays, she would bring up to him a smaller brother or sister, tell him his or her name, and gently unloosen the child's hand clinging to hers. These were the only occasions she approached him; on all others she waited for him to speak to her.

As he looked at her on this particular birthday, he realised with a sensation so strong it had the impact of a shock that she was sitting on the furthest back form. This time next year she would not be there.

He was appalled to find how appalled he was by such a realization. It was as though his future were being emptied of the one living thing in it.

"Tell your mother," he said the next day, standing behind her, "that I think you should return to school for an extra year after next summer. In your case it decidedly would not be wasted."

She answered him, "Yes." She always did answer him either yes or no, if she was not reciting something from a book. A stillness came out of her, but he could not tell whether or not it was the stillness that trembles on excitement, for no longer could he read her like a book. Perhaps that was because she was no longer in her primer. He found himself wondering if she could read him, or if his page too had become obscure and recondite.

"My mother says I am to tell you," she said the following day, "that she and my father will bide by what you think best for me."

Not since he had been in love with Maysie Wain had he felt such a rush of feeling break over him. He knew that properly he should have waited until at least next year before he had made such a proposal, but he knew also that he could not have waited another day. The present was only bearable when he had cleared this thing from the future that lay but a few months ahead.

During the extra year she had at school she sat with the boy MacLintock and did lessons with him. He was older than she, the son of the manager of the saw-mill, whom Bartle was preparing for the Technical College in Glasgow. As John was not so bright as Effie, the preparation was proving arduous for him, even with a teacher as patient and painstaking as dominie MacDonald.

Bartle wondered what was going to happen when the school year drew to a close, when his star pupil withdrew from his sky and left him without light or guide. He could not imagine such

145

darkness: when he thought of it, he came to a full stop, face to face with emptiness. If he could only think of some way, some ruse to keep her within his 'orbit for but another year—these years of three-hundred-and-sixty-five fleet days that streaked like a comet as a child grew into a girl.

He was thinking of her as he walked back across the green and was so deep in thought he did not notice Mr. Gilchrist waiting outside the cobbler's for him to draw near.

"Good evening, Mr. MacDonald," the minister greeted him as he passed.

"Good evening, Mr. Gilchrist," replied Bartle, starting at being addressed. "I did not notice you," he explained, retracing his steps. "I have been across at Miss Telfer's, helping to skep a swarm of bees. She is lucky—'a swarm of bees in May is worth a load of hay'."

"Ah-ha, most fortunate," agreed Mr. Gilchrist. For one who spent an appreciable part of his time in public speaking, his speech was spluttered with unfortunate ahems and audible hesitancies, like barriers he had to take before he could get into his stride. "Mr. MacDonald ahem—will you—I mean I would like a word with you."

"Why, of course," Bartle said willingly. "Will you come in—excuse me if I go first."

He wondered what Mr. Gilchrist had to say to him. The thought did pass through his mind that the minister might be approaching him to become an elder. As he led the way into his sitting-room he wondered what he should say: he did not think he wanted particularly to be an elder.

"Mr. MacDonald," began Mr. Gilchrist, without sitting down, "do you not think—ah-ha—I'm afraid you are seeing far too much of a priest to be good for you."

Astounded Bartle stared at him.

"The only priest I see," he said, when he had recovered from his surprise, "is Father Owen, and the only times I see him are when he has been visiting at Tomanbeg."

"Father Owen," said the minister, with a disagreeable smile, "must have been visiting Tomanbeg an unhealthy amount lately, from all accounts, if—ahem—each time he is seen going into your house he has been up the hill."

"Every time Father Owen is seen coming into my house," replied Bartle, nettled, "he receives a cup of tea, to refresh him on

146

his journey. He will continue to receive it if he chooses to call every day on the calendar."

"Mr. MacDonald," said the minister, "for your own good I think it only right to tell you that your continued hospitality to a priest is causing unfavourable comment in the neighbourhood."

"Mr. Gilchrist," replied Bartle, "I think it only right to tell you, for the good of the neighbourhood who have seen Father Owen enter my house no more than four times a year, that I am becoming a Roman Catholic."

Mr. Gilchrist did not look more shaken than did Bartle as he heard how his sentence ended.

# Chapter Twelve

Owen gave Bartle booklets and treatises to read to strengthen his convictions. Bartle had not known he had convictions. He had thought that was what he lacked, but the priest appeared to think not only that they were in a robust condition but that he had had them, without knowing it, all along. In his opinion they needed stabilizing rather than shoring. Bartle for his part was glad to read anything of a strengthening nature.

He knew he must go home as soon as possible to tell his mother that he had been admitted to the Catholic church. She was the only person to whom he owed that, and his life-long experience of her had taught him that where she was concerned unwelcome news did not improve with the keeping. He made up his mind therefore to return to Barnfingal that Saturday, sleep the night at home and travel back to Faal on the Sunday that he could start school at the usual time the following day.

Since he could not state the reason of his visit until he saw her, he did.not advise her he was coming. He walked from Dormay in the late afternoon. It was a bright day with that brightness he always associated with Saturday afternoons since he had been a boy, when the sun used to shine more dazzlingly and the loch more shimmeringly just because it was Saturday afternoon. He saw from the twigs on the ground that a gale had been blowing, and knew it would be the teuchit-storm on which the teuchit, or green plover, is blown home. He always thought of the teuchit-storm when he saw a green plover, thought of their being driven before the wind and unfurling themselves from the storm when they reached once more familiar lochan or peaty pool.

He saw the stout gable-end of Croft Fionn after he had swung down the post office hill and turned the corner. He suddenly thought how small was the cottage where he had been born, its only garden the flowers netted on to its rough whitewashed walls. That had never struck him before, although he had returned each year since he had grown to be a man. It was as though he had always taken it for granted in the past, while today on this unexpected visit he came upon it as a stranger would.

His mother was not inside when he entered. He knew she could not have gone far or she would have locked the door and taken the key with her. He went to the dresser and unhooked their cups, placing them on the table and setting it for tea. Somehow he felt he did not want to sit down until his mother returned; this was her home, no longer his. The low fire talked to itself as it subsided and the kettle on the swee began to hum.

He heard her footsteps on the gravel outside and went towards the door. He had left it open so that she expected him when she entered. Her cheeks were the redness of raw meat and her high-chested figure, buttoned into its dark clothes, was vigorous and strong. His mother, he realized, looked younger now despite her grey hair than she probably was, just as in her youth she would have looked much older.

"Why, Bartle," she exclaimed, "and what has brought ye home? Ye've no lost your school, have ye?" she demanded suspiciously.

"No, no," he returned, and smiled at the thought to reassure her, "nothing like that, mern. I'll make tea for us now you're back, shall I?"

"Ay, ay," she agreed, "ye make tea for us. If ye have no lost your school, what has brought ye home?"

"Because I wanted to see you."

"Weel, ye're seeing me." He was pouring the boiling water into the old brown teapot and the steam rose between them like a veil.

"To tell you that I've become a Catholic."

If he had any doubts how she would take his news, he had none now. The silence in the kitchen stunned his ears.

"Say yon again."

He would not have recognized her voice unless he had seen her standing before him.

"I've come home to tell you, mern," he said gently, apologetically, "that I've become a Catholic."

"Ye'll do nothing of the sort, Bartle MacDonald," she said, excitedly for her. "Are ye hearkening to me? I'm your mother, and no son of mine will ever do such a thing."

"I have already done it," he replied. "I am a Catholic now."

"Then ye're no longer any son of mine."

"I did not think you would take it like this," he said slowly, speaking out his thoughts. "I knew of course you would not, naturally could not care for it, but I did not think it would make all this difference to you."

"Did ye no? Then think again. I never could bide her, yon old cailleach, and the years I had her on ma hands." Her voice droned as she remembered. "I canna mind ma life without her. Skirling in her corner, aye honey-sweet to Kirsty, and all the time she was poisoning ye against me. Ye dinna need to deny it—I aye kent ye cared for her more than ye cared for me what brought ye forth. There was aye something unnatural about ye. So that was what she was up to, was it? When I used to come back after being out, I'd see the guilty look on both your faces but I never kent it was because she was teaching ye heathen practices and Popish prayers."

"Mem, you're not to speak like that, Grannie had nought to do with this. I swear before God she hadn't."

"Your god's no ma God. Dinna take mine on lips that pray to images. And as your God is no worth the breath that says his name, dinna speak of him to me."

"We're both looking at the same thing, only through different windows."

"No, we're no, Bartle MacDonald, and I'll thank ye to remember that. Ye take after your grannie. Ye dinna take after me. All right then, gang your grannie's gait and see where it will bear ye. I thought I had got rid of all her crucifixes and beads and nonsense, but na, I might have kent the old cailleach would beat me in the end. When I was dressing her in her dead clothes, I came across a charm she had hidden from me all these years. 'Aweel,' thought I to maself, 'ye've cheated me for years while ye were living, so I'll cheat ye of what I ken ye would like reel weel to be buried with,' and I threw the wee hair bag with its bean and a puckle of fern seeds into the loch."

His ejaculation of protest was involuntary.

"I didna ken then that I should have kept it for her precious grandson," she cried out at him. "I didna ken then that he would like it to say his prayers to."

"I didna want it," he refuted, "I don't believe in things like that, but she did. You have to mind that she was old and even when she was young ignorant, brought up on an island away from the rest of the world."

150

"Where they were all Catholics."

"You can't blame her for that," he took her up as sharply as she was taking him.

"I'll tell ye what I do blame her for, Bartle MacDonald, and then I'll never say another word to ye and I never want to see your face again. I blame her for going to the kirk and thinking of the chapel. I blame her for making a show she was taking the wine at communion when she was doing nothing of the sort. I blame her for crossing herself when our backs were turned, and being softer than butter to our faces. I blame her last of all for teaching ma son to forsake the true faith and turning him into a heretic."

"I deny emphatically it has anything to do with grannie."

"I dinna believe what a Catholic tells me — he could no speak the truth is he tried."

"Listen, mern, if it had—do you not see I would have done it long ago?"

"Ye're like your grannie. She was a grand one at biding her time. I've said ma say now. Ye can gang."

"Mern, you cannot mean that you'll never speak to me or see me again."

"I'm no Catholic, Bartle, so ye should ken by this time that I mean every word I say."

"Kenny from the post office and Davie Thomson saw me on the road hom," he told her, changing his tactics. "You don't want them to ken that we've fallen out. Let be bide until to-morrow, mern. Mebbe ye'll not feel it so hardly the morrow."

"Ye'll no bide another moment in this house. And dinna ye gang cheating yourself that I'll no feel it so hardly the morrow. Ye've forgotten what I've no forgot—the morrow is the Sabbath. I'll feel it worse every Sabbath than I feel it on a weekday. Do ye think I care what Kenny of the post office thinks? Everyone in the place will have to ken—no that we've fallen out but that ye've fallen by the way. Ye'll no be able to show your face in Barnfingal again."

He reached as far as the door.

"Mern, will ye no say goodbye to me," he pled.

"Ye're no longer ma son," she said, her voice void of feeling. "There's no call for me to say goodbye to someone I dinna ken."

He went out and snecked the door between them.

* * * *

He should have felt guilty when he went to Mass in the chapel at Alltdu, but he did nothing of the kind. His one feeling of guilt was that he enjoyed it so well, for he wondered if it were right for religion to be enjoyed, but Father Owen assured him that it was, that gospel meant glad tidings, and the more joyful such glad tidings made him, the more fit was he to receive them.

Now he went to Father Owen's house oftener than the priest came to his. Their friendship more than compensated for the loss of Mr. Miller, the inspector, who no longer stayed with him when he arrived on his rounds to inspect Faal school. That this coldness was due to his change of religion, Bartle knew, but it seemed a small price to pay, anything seemed a small price to pay for the happiness such change of religion shed over each day, which he found waiting for him every morning the moment he awoke and which made his lips smile as he slept.

Happiness was no longer to him like music in another room but something so personal that he knew it would still clothe him in the busiest city or the loneliest outpost. His one dread had been he might be forced to leave Faal, because that would mean he would have to leave Effie, but even that fear was behind him now.

He fought to remain on as teacher of Faal school as he had never fought for anything in his life before, banking on his popularity with both parents and pupils to outweigh prejudice. Opinions were divided fairly evenly on the question, but in the end the Ays for him had it. He had declared himself at once which counted in his favour; and there was something so straight and open about his uncomplicated face, his very fairness made him look neither secretive nor sinister, that he was trusted in spite of having "gone over to Rome". Even those who had voted against him most strenuously held little or no malice against him, and he was discreet enough not to do anything to flaunt the fact that he had won the day. Mr. Gilchrist, the minister, now supplied religious instruction in the school. It struck Bartle as curious that, now they were no longer of the same religion, he should find Mr. Gilchrist pleasanter and had more respect for him both as a minister and as a man.

152

One afternoon, before the summer term drew to a close, Erne stayed behind to speak to him. She had a message for him from her mother. Effie would not be coming back to school next term, but her mother wondered if Mr. MacDonald would go on giving her lessons out of school hours and she would see that he was paid for them.

"Tell your mother that of course I shall," he agreed, sitting beside her in the silent schoolroom, "and that I wouldn't dream of taking payment. But no one else need know that," he added hurriedly. He realized Rachel was prepared to pay for Effie's extra schooling out of the money she had saved from Lady Wain.

He looked at the curve of the girl's cheek as she sat in profile beside him, at the pretty hair that feathered the smoothness of her brow with little curls where it had grown in short. And as he looked at her as a child, he loved her for the woman she would so soon become, as he knew when she was a woman he would always love the child he could remember in her.

"Effie," he stirred himself to say, and it was the schoolmaster that forced him to speak, "next term you should be going to the secondary school at Alltdu."

Her hands were touching the books before her on the desk, hands small as a child's and fine as a lady's. They now moved spasmodically.

"No, no," she said in alarm, "father would never hear of any such thing." Her relief that her father would never hear of any such thing reached him like a gush of water from a spring.

"Why not?" he enquired, strong enough to dally with the subject now he knew it was not likely to be entertained.

"Because I would need to be boarded out at Alltdu whilst I was attending school."

"The Grant boys attend it without being boarded out, travelling there and back by bus."

"Yes," she agreed, and the hands on the books clasped themselves as though in an unspoken prayer of thankfulness, "but they do not bide so far away as Mulloch."

There was a certain limpidity about her, like the shine on the waters of a clear burn, like the shine over everything on a Saturday afternoon.

"What does your father want you to do?" he asked, as an excuse to keep her beside him. He knew enough about the household of the shepherd's cottage to know that what the father said determined the day.

"My father expects me to go into service," she replied.

He realised that the prospect did not appal her except that she would be sent away, and as she had been reprieved for another year she was going to dwell on that year, holding each day to her as loving fingers would hold each bead of a rosary.

He knew Rachel did not want her to go into service, that it made her suffer to think of the daughter of "Master Alfred" in so lowly a position. He could feel her mother's perturbation as though Rachel were present and he silently counselled her not to distress herself, but to leave the future to solve its own problems.

"Mr. MacDonald," the child was saying beside him. "I would like you to be for knowing that I know Catholics are not bad folk, or all daft like the MacBeaths. They cannot be since you are one. I am thinking myself of going over when I grow up."

"Now, Effie MacIntyre," he said emphatically, and saved himself in the nick of time caning her Effie Wain, "don't you ever let me hear you speak like that again. If anyone knew you were even thinking of such things, I would be turned out of Faal without being given time to shut my door."

"That I know," she assured him with the immeasurable dignity of a child, "and I would never say a word to injure you." Her voice implied that he should know that by this time. The certainty of her words frightened him: he knew at that moment she would go to the stake to save him pain. "But there is no harm to anyone saying what I think to you."

"Of course there are good Catholics just as there are good Protestants," he pursued, struggling to keep the situation on the schoolmaster-scholar plane, "and there can be bad Catholics just as there can be bad Protestants. But you must not even contemplate, Effie, changing your faith just because I have changed mine. That is no reason at all," he said with severity that was so uncharacteristic it carried no weight. "Our positions are totally different. You have been brought up as a Protestant, all your people are Protestant, it is right and seemly you remain one. I may have been brought up as a

154

Protestant, but all my grandmother's folk were Catholic. I have but returned, not broken away, and what I do has nothing to do with you, or anyone else for that matter."

She shovelled her books into her neat little hands and rose to her feet.

"There's no harm thinking thoughts and saying them if I say them only to you," she replied finally. He had the feeling he, the schoolmaster, was being dismissed by the scholar who knew more about the matter than he.

In the new term she came to him to have lessons after school hours. He was careful always to have her in the schoolroom: never, even in winter, to take her into his house. She would meet her brothers and sisters on their way home as she made her way to him. Some of the witchery of the twilight would cling to her as she entered the quietened schoolroom where he was awaiting her.

He would think of the road she had come as though she had brought it in with her, thinking of it as she would take it on her way home—down Lady's Walk where the road was so densely lined with trees it was like going into a green tunnel, out into the open, past Tomanbeg and so glad she did not live there. Now all alone with her thoughts, nothing but space, immensity and solitude all round her as she made her way to Mulloch Moor, where the winds tusselled and everything was on an epic scale, so that there alone she felt satisfied, giant's food for a giant's hunger, as long as she could be by herself to think her incontestable thoughts.

She came even in winter when the snow was on the ground, and then he would accompany her home although he never went as far as the shepherd's cottage but would stand a little way off to see that no harm came to her between him and it. She would turn at the door to look in his direction across the wastes of snow, but she never waved to him. It was as though she had left such childish gestures behind her in the schoolroom where the slate she had outgrown, the books she had conned to the end, were used by other hands.

In spring the trees stood out blue as flames against the green skies of dusk. The earth quickened with shoot and blade and bud. As he looked at Effie he saw she was quite tall now, a sheath that encased the winged petals of a flower.

"Our church always strives to keep our teachers within our fold," Father Owen said to him when they sat together in his house at Alltdu. "It was not so important the first year, but we consider it imperative that after the summer you teach only children of your own profession."

"That means?" Bartle questioned faintly, staring at him.

"That means you will be given the school at Tornichon and a Protestant teacher will take over that of Faal," the priest replied.

Bartle did not dream of disputing or fighting against the decree. But what surprised him was that such a pronouncement, when he thought of Effie, did not loosen despair in his heart. Instead he was filled with a curious peaceableness, as though he were rocking on a tide that could bear him only towards good.

"Tornichon!" he exclaimed. "Isn't that on the road to somewhere?"

"The only place it is on the road to is Fort Halliam where the monastery is," said Father Owen. He was always good-natured so that there was a cheerful humour even about his grumbling. "A pity, if you ask me, there is a monastery for the road to lead to! What can a monk do that a priest could not do better? They run a school of course, mostly boarders, but the standard of education is so high that many Protestants send their bairns to it as day scholars. I warrant Father Abbot would like to have you to teach his seniors mathematics!"

The benignant tide still rocked Bartle as he walked back to Faal from Alltdu. By the time he reached his house the sky behind the trees was beginning to glow with sunset. He went into the yard at the back to chop some wood for his fire. The hatchet half buried in the log, the geranium in a pot he had put outside to let the rain fall on it, the interior of his tidy shed, all seemed deepened into a particular significance that afternoon, as though despite each one's ephemeral quality it was there for all time. He remembered how from the beginning he had always thought there was something transitory about his home at Faal. Now he confirmed what was transitory was the tenant, not the tenanted.

Before he could draw the hatchet from the wood, Effie had entered the yard. She sat on the log, her hands in her lap, and amongst all these things that seemed rooted to their own shadows, he was aware that she had the same transience that lightened him, as though both shared the same upper air.

156

"Oh, Mr. MacDonald," she said, "mother said I was to tell you," but he knew she would have come even if her mother had not told her, "the family she used to be in service with have sent for me to come to Glasgow. They say they will have me taught typing and shorthand and book-keeping, and then I can find a fine post for myself."

He heard what she was going to say a split second before she said it. Sir Alfred Wain—he had died lately, Bartle knew. This was Lady Wain's way of doing something for the child her son had brought into the world.

"Mother said you would be sure to be interested," Effie was continuing, her hands clasped between her knees. "She says you knew of the family she used to be in service with."

"I am most interested," he replied, but he knew they were standing on a common ground where polite words no longer served to keep them distant. "And who will you stay with whilst you are in Glasgow?"

"Their old nurse, a Mistress Blair," she returned.

She would be the wife of Mr. Blair, the man-servant— Bartle had not known he was married to the children's nurse.

"That is splendid, Effie," he answered. "What a chance it is going to give you."

"Yes, for when I come back I will be grown." Her words outside had the same clarity and separateness of a robin's notes when all other birds are silenced. "You'll be away yourself after summer, Mr. MacDonald, will you not?"

It was as though he felt the soil of the common ground they shared stir beneath his feet as he looked down at her across the yard.

"How do you know that?" he asked.

"I felt it. That's why I was not troubled in myself when the letter came from Lady Wain. I could not have borne to have been at home with you in some other place. Now, when I return, I shall have grown."

He went towards her across the yard and as he neared she rose. Her fine hair clung like silk to his hands while he held her head to kiss her mouth. He was big and in his arms she had but a child's slight bulk, but he did not feel as though he were kissing only a scent. He could feel her living as spring, yielding yet ardent. He kissed her as though he could never have done.

"When you return," he said hoarsely, "come to me. Say nothing about it to anyone until then. I'll live for that day."

"I promise never to let anyone kiss me but you," she plighted. "I promise never to marry anyone but you. I promise not to say a word to anyone until I return home to you."

# Chapter Thirteen

THE schoolhouse at Tornichon was as exposed as Faal was sheltered. The whole district was uplands, not the uplands that surrounded Brae, fierce with heather and hag, a wilderness of bracken, but rolling, green wave upon green wave, as far as the eye could see. Barnfingal was a glen carved out by a glacier, the green of growing things there was intense and vehement as weeds. This was an open strath with a certain mildness, where the greens were soft, sometimes mellowing to the yellow of fields of buttercups, or threading into white cotton blowing on marshes. Light swept over these unshadowed reaches as though this were the first place it smote when it reached the world, and Bartle had the joyous feeling throughout the year as though here it were perpetually Easter morning. He loved his new home as he had never loved the house he had tenanted in Faal, because he could think of sharing it with Effie, because he could prepare for the time when she would be his wife, making a seat where they would sit to watch the sun sink.

He had written to his mother to tell her of his change of address, but she did not reply to his letter. When he did hear from Barnfingal, it was of her not from her. He received a telegram telling him she was dead.

He knocked at the door of the roadman's cottage on his way to Croft Fionn.

"Come ben, Bartle," Davie Thomson's wife greeted him, "I was thinking it would be ye. Take a seat to yourself—ye must be tired after long yon walk. Ay, your mother, Bartle. She died on Monday. It was cancer—the quick kind. The doctor kent about it, but no one else. She would no have ye or anyone else tellt. Teenie Robertson saw her on the Saturday and said she was looking reel bad, but ye ken Teenie's cawing ways. When she was no at the kirk on the Sabbath, Davie went ben on his way home in the even. He found her reel bad, and came for me. I would have done anything for her, ye ken that, lad, but I had never been inside Croft Fionn and I thought mebbe she wouldna like to see me there. So I sent Davie for Morag Stewart. She bided with her until the end, and it wasna long in coming. It was a pity about your mother, Bartle, her and me being near neighbours and never seeing each other I mean, for I aye felt we would have got on well thegither—if things had been different." He did not ask what things. "She's all ready, Bartle, but they kept the lid aff the coffin for ye to see her. Davie has seen to the funeral for ye—he kent ye would like him to."

"Ay," Bartle said thickly, "that was good of him, Mistress Thomson." He knew his mother had made it clear that anyone but he must see to her funeral.

"The morn at eleven," Mrs. Thomson was saying. "I'll give ye the key, Bartle. Ye'll want to go along now, but come back and spend the night with us, and tomorrow night as well—for as long as ye choose."

"It's reel good of ye, Mistress Thomson," he replied, turning the big cold key over in his hand, "but I'll spend the night at home."

He pushed the door open after he had unlocked it and went inside. The kitchen was even dimmer than usual because someone had pulled to the curtains at the tiny window, and for the first time in his life he saw the hearth without a fire. Instead of caves in the corners and a pit below the box-bed, the darkness was more evenly distributed, so that as his eyes grew accustomed to the twilight things in it bulked blackly without their shadows.

The coffin rested on the four wooden chairs in the house. He touched back the sheet covering her and looked down at his mother's face. Her cheeks were sucked in like his grannie's used to be when she was alive, and she looked as old.

He went suddenly to the open door for air and leant against the jamb, wishing he could have seen on his mother's face some of the shine of her heavenly home as she turned towards it.

Davie Thomson came that night on his way back from work. He stood, with his thick beard that always made Bartle think of him as a fisherman, while they discussed in low voices the final arrangements for the funeral tomorrow and settled that Bartle should return with him now to have a meal "down the road".

"Your mother tellt me to tell ye, Bartle," he said before they turned to leave, "that she couldna mind all she said to ye yon last day she saw ye, but she wantit ye to ken mebbe she didna mean all she said."

"She used to have such bonny hair—Kirsty," he said to no one in particular when Bartle locked the door behind them.

160

* * * *

The day after the funeral Bartle spent by himself in Croft Fionn going over his mother's belongings and possessions. It did not take him long for there was little to go over. She had promised Morag Stewart the teapot he had bought her with his herd's wages. He grouped everything into small tidy clumps to go to different households in Barnfingal, The only thing he was taking himself was the seaman's chest which stood under the window.

He drew it out to see it better, smiling down at it as he remembered what it had meant to him as a child. Just a rough old box with a hinged lid that had once been painted green, its wood whitened with exposure underneath, where he had never seen it before. He held it up to the light—it had seemed so big and cavernous when he had been a child that he had confused it with Davy Jones's locker. Someone had scratched his name on it: Jno. Jackson Jnr.

As he knelt at the window holding the square chest in his hands, he thought of Erne so strongly it was as though she had actually drifted into his arms, of Effie and the children they would have. Suddenly the rotting old box, the kitchen dark even at mid-day, the corruption of his mother's illness unto death, all flowered and blossomed and bourgeoned with spring.

He heard a motor car drive up outside, and waited for someone to tap on the door to ask the way, but no one came. He put down the chest and stood up, irritably over-conscious of that person outside who drove to his door but neither tapped nor went away. He looked out of the window and saw it was a small shining car. Maysie Kuld sat alone in it, at the driver's wheel.

He recognised her at once although she had her back to him. She had driven the car into the slight curve of the roadside opposite, beside the well, that any other traffic could pass her on the narrow country road. Now she was sitting, waiting for him to go out to her.

His face darkened as he turned from the window. Let her wait until Kingdom Come. As though he would go a step out of his way to speak to her. He began to busy himself again in the kitchen, his face lightening as he realized any power she had ever had over him was now broken for good. His heart had not turned over when he saw who it was, nor had he to fight with himself not to go out to her.

It must have been an appreciable time later, for he had forgotten all about her, when he heard movement at the door, and looking round, saw Maysie Kuld standing in the doorway.

"How dark it is in here," she exclaimed involuntarily.

As though feeling she was at a disadvantage, she moved from the doorway to the settle where she sat down. The cottage had something of the effect on her that it had had on her mother when she first entered it many years ago. Maysie felt it was like something underground, and so strong was this impression that she imagined she could smell the mould of roots and dampness of earth. Like something underground, or submerged by stagnant waters.

"You don't seem very pleased to see me," she enjoined in her light laughing voice.

"Why should I be?" he asked, eyeing her unblinkingly. Drawn back into himself, he was unaware that he looked proud.

She was exactly as he remembered her. The blundering years had not turned against her nor changed her in any way that he could see: the same fair hair the colour of honeysuckle, the same small features moulded by delicate bones, even the same slightness of figure. It was as though nothing had happened to her since he had known her, and this absence of change in her after that she had once wrought in his life almost shocked him.

"It is always nice to see old friends," she replied provocatively. When he made no answer, she seemed to tire suddenly as though there were no point challenging what remained unprovoked. "Why didn't you come out to speak to me?" she enquired, her voice no longer either light or laughing. "You knew I was there. I know you knew I was there."

"I knew you were there because I looked out of the window and saw you," he replied impersonally. "I didn't go out to speak to you because I have nothing I wish to say to you."

The peremptoriness he had taken so much for granted in the past had completely died from her voice when she next spoke. It gave a little as she whispered,

"You hate me very much, don't you?"

162

"You don't hate what means nothing to you at all," he said evenly, "you don't even dislike it. It doesn't affect you one way or another."

Colour ebbed over her face, leaving it paler than usual.

"I have never forgotten you," she said.

He was holding the wooden back of a chair and looked down at his hand as if to see what it was holding.

"Haven't you?" he replied, brief with disinterest. "I have forgotten all about you for long enough."

Her face with its perfection of feature chilled with her thoughts as she realized he was not saying such things simply to hurt her, but because he did not care whether he hurt her or not.

"My mother has never forgotten you," she said brightly, conversationally. "She always speaks and thinks of you on my brother's birthday."

"I know she does," he answered, his voice warming. "I have never forgotten, I never could forget Lady Wain."

"We lost our father—I suppose you know that, you always seemed to know everything about us." She returned to the only subject that really interested her— himself. "I remember, during the war, my mother could not understand why you were not at the front. It was I who told her you had a finger off. She had never noticed that. But I knew everything about you, Bartle."

"Do you?" He had turned from her, and began once more to "sort out" the articles in the dresser drawer, studying each for the fraction of a second before placing it on one of the four clumps he had built up on each chair. "Then you will know that I never think of you."

"I said knew, not know."

He had no comment to make, so made none. She sat watching him until she stirred herself to say,

"You lost your mother. I'm sorry."

As the one thing that affected him about her was that she sat in his mother's kitchen now she was dead as she would never have done while she was alive, he still had no comment to make.

"You know that Rachel got in touch with us about Alfred's child."

He stopped what he was doing to stare at her.

"No, I didn't know that," he said, startled. "Did she?"

"Yes. She told us that you were the child's teacher and had got her on well. It was good of you to take trouble with her."

"She has never been any trouble to me, only a joy." He looked into the open drawer again. "What did Rachel want of Lady Wain?"

"She told her she didn't want her to go into service, so mother wrote back and said to send her to Glasgow and we would have her put through some course or other. Of course what's-her-name——"

"Effie," he supplied.

"Yes, Effie—she doesn't know who her father really was."

"Naturally not. She thinks it is the shepherd Rachel married."

"Mother has seen her. I haven't. She is a pretty child apparently. Do you see any family likeness?"

Again he considered her, thinking how curious it was to remember that Maysie was old enough to have been Effie's mother.

"She is very like Lady Wain's grandchild," he replied.

"That's what mother said," she remarked. "At least I gathered from her that Alfred's illegitimate child is more of a Wain than any of her legitimate grandchildren!"

He did not trouble to smile at her levity; she saw he was not amused by it. Now she came to think of it, she had never heard him laugh.

"You have never married," she said wonderingly, watching him.

"Because I have not in the past is not to say I shall not in the future," he replied calmly.

She absorbed this piece of information in silence for a little while, as though turning it over in her mind to see what she could make of it. When she spoke again her voice was stilted and formal.

"Professor Barbour used to tell us he had seen you."

"Professor Barbour only saw me once," he corrected. "He was passing through Faal at the time."

"He told us he had gone out of his way to see you. He told us he wanted your help with a mathematical problem."

"Yes," he agreed, remembering, "there was a wee thing he couldn't quite see his way through."

"And you were able to help him."

164

"I chalkit it up on the side of a cart."

"You must often regret that you never did what he wanted you to do—work under Professor Stalker."

"I have nothing to regret. If I had, my life would have been quite different. It would have fallen in different places, I would have been thrown in with different folk."

"And you are quite content with the folk you have been thrown in with?" The smile seemed to slip as she watched his face, giving her own a false look.

"More than content."

"You are very lucky. My mother always says of course that we make our own luck. Not that I believe that." Her gaze measured him intently from head to foot, her own uncertainty gathering strength from his certainty. "I still think it's a pity you were not thrown in with Professor Stalker. You know what he has been experimenting on all these years? The study of atomic energy—that means splitting the atom, doesn't it? Funny, isn't it, that the smaller the thing the more trouble it gives—and takes. Lifetimes spent on an atom! You don't ask anything about me," she said suddenly.

"Why should I?—you are no concern of mine," he returned.

"It's human nature to be more concerned with what doesn't concern one than with what does."

"You mean it's your nature."

She looked pleased to be taken aback.

"Is it?" she said challengingly. "And what do you consider is my concern?"

"Your own life, which includes your marriage."

"What have you heard about my marriage?" she asked hotly.

"Nothing. There's nothing to hear."

Dubiously she looked at him, moistening her lips as though they had suddenly gone dry.

"Nothing," she emphasized, "but you know what nothing can grow into in the Highlands. You have been brought up here and will have heard all about the Mhoreneck curse."

"What has that to do with you and your marriage?"

"I've no children, and I know what they say in these parts—that why I have no children is because of the curse." He recollected that because a Kuld had played a small part in the massacre of Glencoe, his family were laid under a curse that there would never be more than two direct heirs. "Ninian is only the second son, but Rufus is the eldest and he has three sons and Ian two. I wonder their father's tenants don't think the curse is going to die a natural death in the face of such competition! Unless they expect the holocaust of another war to arise simply that it may wipe out a complete Kuld generation! I hate the Highlanders, banking up old curses that but for them would have been forgotten long ago. Their house is not good to my house." He suddenly realized that her husband, Ninian Kuld, was of course Highland. "The only one I ever liked, far less loved, was you, Bartle. I got to the back of you as I can never get to the back of them. And even if I do happen to manage it in an isolated case, I'm not at home there as I was with you."

He looked at her, his lips pursed.

"Your love for me did not take you very far," he said dispassionately.

"It took me as far as any woman can go." Her voice grated with her feelings. "I gave myself to you."

"That was a sum that was reckoned up long ago. You drew the line underneath it yourself."

"Nothing cost me so much as that—to break with you. It was like breaking with a part of myself, the feeling, living part."

"I wouldn't deceive yourself if I were you. You were an adept at breaking things with as little hurt to yourself as possible."

He saw her face draw as she looked across at him.

"It was afterwards I realized what it had done to me."

"You would have realized nothing of the sort if you were not dissatisfied with your marriage."

"I told you that you had been listening to gossip," she said sharply. She did not flush, but looked hot underneath her eyes.

"I've heard no gossip about you. But you are sitting there telling me in everything but words that you find your marriage unsatisfactory."

She looked into the empty, brushed-up hearth, her head turned from him.

"I might as well not be married," she said.

The silence in the cottage was like the silence that falls after a stone has dropped.

166

"You still have what you married for," he pointed out, "a titled husband."

"I'm not saying a word against my husband," she took him up shortly.

"There is nothing to say."

"I didn't come here to discuss him with you."

"What did you come for then?"

"To see you. I heard about your mother, and was sorry. I wanted, I had to see you again, Bartle. There is so much for me to put right where you are concerned. I was responsible for your becoming a poor country schoolmaster instead of carving out a career for yourself."

He shook himself, as though he would shake her sympathy from him.

"I have told you I have no regrets," he announced coldly, addressing the empty space above her head.

"But I have regrets for you." Her voice pulsed as though trying to quicken and fill the emptiness she felt spreading all round her. "I've cut you off from the kind of life you should have led, from the people you should have met. Bartle, you'll have heard about the library at the castle?"

Astounded by the question, he replied, "Where every volume is bound in scarlet morocco and has the Mhoreneck crest on it in gold? Yes, I have heard of it."

"But you haven't seen it, or used it. Why should we part the moment we come together again? When you leave here, come to the castle. My husband isn't there with me at present."

In the silence of the kitchen, he heard the stone cottage creak as though it were a hut built of logs. His hands, hanging at his sides, suddenly looked disproportionately big.

"No," he said, as though returning over a gulf of years. "You wouldn't have asked me if he had been, would you?"

"Of course I wouldn't," she agreed lightly. "What woman believes in mixing up her past with her present, particularly when one's past is so much more important to one than one's present."

She was aware that he was studying her in a way she did not altogether like. She suddenly felt pinned down, hedged about by that look.

"You mean for the present," he said unpleasantly.

"What are you looking at me like that for?" she demanded, as though trying to change her position.' 'There's nothing wrong in what I am suggesting. Everyone does it nowadays, as you would know if you hadn't been living in a backwater all these years. It's Ninian who is cursed, not I—what a thrust out of nowhere at fate and all these Highlanders, with their long dark memories, if my child, should I have one, heired everything but the curse !"

"I'm looking at you like that because I don't like what I am looking at."

She rose to her feet, as though drawn up in spite of herself by the harshness of his voice.

"Don't you?" she retaliated, hearing her words ineffectual as hailstones on a window-pane. "And what in your opinion is wrong with me?"

"I think you are unclean."

He was as impervious to her as though he were glassed over. No warmth glanced from him, no glint of love found a chink through the armour of the years. He was not even fortified against her, he did not need to be on the defence or guard with her. As far as he was concerned she had no ammunition with which to mount any attack.

"I told you once before that you were very sure of yourself," she said, hating herself for the unsteadiness of her voice.

"And I told you that I was surer of you," he answered.

His words had a curious effect upon her. He had apparently reminded her of what was the last thing she wanted to remember. Colour flayed her cheeks, and every pulse she had suddenly sprang into activity so that her face seemed to move before his unimpassioned gaze like quicksands after they have been disturbed.

"It is an unwise enemy who underestimates the strength of his opponent," she said, trying to keep her voice gay as she made her way to the doorway. But even for that short distance she had the greatest difficulty to hold her ground. Such was the strength of her emotions she felt stifled and bound by them, as though she were a tree whose nightmare roots had spread themselves from the ground to coil about what they had borne.

Later that day, when Bartle locked the door on the emptied cottage before handing the key over to the factor, he did not feel he was locking up his childhood or writing finis to a bygone Chapter of his life, but rather that he had left nothing behind to shut up. He knew when he thought back he would think of the cottage as it was now, gutted of them and their things, with light splintering through the deepset windows, falling in tiny patches, cracking the darkness, the mottling, like damp stains, moving slowly over the walls as the sun travelled from one gable end of the building to the other.

Mr. Marshall, the factor, told him when he handed over the key they were not re-letting Croft Fionn but removing its roof and letting it fall derelict. There was nothing to attract tenants to Barnfingal. Bartle knew what was happening to it now was what would have happened in ordinary circumstances when his father died, but his father had not died in ordinary circumstances and the laird had continued to rent the dwelling to the widow and elderly mother.

Now Bartle knew when he remembered the cottage where he had been born, he would remember it as he had seen it last only with its thatch removed, like a hairless head. Day would beat upon what had lain hidden and obscured for so long, roofless walls expose where a hearth had once been, and weeds thrust themselves between stones and what had one time been a floor. The unheeding footsteps that passed on the road would not hollow as they had done when a door stood open, motor car tyres raise no echo amongst what had leapt to the roll of carriage wheels, the rattle of a wagonette and the stippety-stap of a pony's hooves. Little by little the ruins would subside, unhaunted by those who had once lived there. These fallen stones would be no mile or tombstone, marking neither a place at the roadside nor recording the unknown lives of people long dead; but shrunken with time and unbuilt by weather, any who did notice that a building had once stood there would think it had been some fank or byre.

He was glad to return to Tornichon, to see the light roll over the unshadowed landscape. He felt light had the same effect on this countryside that the sea he had never seen would have. It furrowed and ploughed these rolling green plains, filled every shallow concave hummock high and made an island of each mound top. The very verdure was ridged and tracked as though by waves, and the long, moulded slopes into which the ground naturally fell were like the back of some, green flounder, or the hump of a half-sunk whale, as the sun swung like a ship across the horizon.

The changes of season here were not definite as in other places. It grew paler rather than darker in winter. If there was a wanness about autumn, instead of the customary golden ripe vigour of harvest, it was a wanness of trans-lucence rather than of thinning soil. A wet district, summer had all the softness of spring, did not bare the land to the assault of the ever-mounting sun but sheathed it in misty rains.

And thus the days passed not unhappily while Bartle waited for Effie to return to him. He would hear the clatter of the children's footsteps as they came to school in the morning and the stampede as they left in the afternoon. He missed that sound during the summer holidays, and their companionship in the wide bare schoolroom, like the busy ticking of a clock. Now it was as though the clock had stopped; in the silence he realized he was alone and that the days took long to pass.

Perhaps that was why he began to shed the serenity that had clothed him in the past when he thought of Effie. It was almost two years since she had gone to Glasgow, but they had known it would be at least that time. Nevertheless his disquiet increased until it became unbearable and, in a cloud of alarm, he made the journey to Faal to hear of her.

Movement towards his goal served to rid him of some of the urgency that had prompted him to overtake it. When he saw the shepherd's cottage in the distance, he even slackened his gait, as though to assure himself that there was no reason for his hurry. Standing where it did, at the beginning of the moor, it looked as though it hung on the brim of the horizon. The one habitation in so much desolation, its very position had a propulsion about it, as though it were the airt from which winds blew.

He saw someone at the side of the cottage, on a bright green patch of grass, hanging clothes on an invisible line. The moor was beginning to redden with heather and above it the sky fluttered blue as a flag. As he drew nearer the someone grew from the

170

pygmy stature of a child into the bulk of Rachel, while the squares no bigger than pocket handkerclikefs she was pegging to the line billowed and flapped into sheets. By the time he reached the gate she had left the bleaching-green, and was returning to the house, the empty basket on her hip.

"Why, Mr. MacDonald, and it's yourself," she greeted him.

He noticed that unconsciously she had called him Mr. MacDonald, not Bartle. She was stout now, or rather had broadened considerably more than stoutened, and walked with a roll.

"Yes, Mrs. MacIntyre," he replied. "I am back at Faal and wondered if you had any news of Effie to tell me."

"A good friend you were to me about Effie, and no mistake," she exclaimed warmly, "giving her all yon extra schooling, and no taking a penny. I just hope ye dinna think all your work's been thrown awa'. I aye used to think she must fancy one of the lads at the school from the amount of time she spent on the ribbons in her hair of a morn, but I never kent it was John MacLintock."

"John MacLintock," he repeated after her, smiling faintly to reveal polite interest while his thoughts centred on the saw-manager's son whom he had once taught. He strove to keep him as he remembered him, his thickening boy's body, his slow look of incomprehension, leaning too low over his books.

"Ay, ye ken—ye taught him too," recalled Rachel. "The saw-manager's son. He was in Glasgow at the Technical College whilst Effie was at her classes. They saw something of each other. No one would have objected to that. That was natural-like. But the news we heard yester morn fair scunnered her father. Just when the Wains were finished paying for her to be turned into something real handy, when she could have lifted a salary instead of wages."

As though cutting off his own retreat, Bartle made himself ask, "What was the news that scunnered Mr. MacIntyre?"

She hoisted the empty basket higher on her hip.

"That with never a word to one of us, she has gone and marrit on John MacLintock," she said.

# Chapter Fourteen

"CAN I sit down?" he heard himself ask Rachel. He supposed it was his voice that spoke. The whole world, and his voice with it, had reeled from him, white clouds bellied like sheets, the very earth he was standing on shelved under him, while he found his gaze clinging to the clothes-pole which moved as though it were the mast of a ship. He tried to drown the words of the Psalmist, "All Thy waves and storms are gone over me," with his own cry, "O Lord, open Thy clouds and swallow me up," but even as he thought his thoughts, he knew he was neither going to drown nor be swallowed up.

"Why, come ben with ye and have a seat," Rachel was saying. "We're that out of the world at Mulloch, and I never stir from the door maself with the bairns to send ma messages, that I forget it is a traik to reach it. Sit down, Mr. MacDonald, and make yourself at home," hospitably she cleared a chair for him, "and I'll make ye a cup of tea."

Surely the cottage must be unbearably close, stuffy. It could not be he who felt so crushed for air he could not breathe. It must be this kitchen with a fire burning on a hot day, consuming what air there was, its flames white, as though blind, in the bright light.

He saw a wooden cradle piled with logs of wood pushed into a corner, and stared at it as he would have stared at a sinking ship. It was not going to be used again as a cradle and so had been requisitioned for another purpose. A cradle in a cottage and a boat rocking on the open sea—both were made of wood. That was what must have made him think of a boat when he looked at it. And a coffin—that was made of wood too.

"Effie is young to marry," he said slowly, as though picking his words with care, as though he had dictionaries open to choose from, while in reality he felt he had to scrape and grope for each one of the five he used.

"Ay, more fool her," returned Rachel, banging about the kitchen. "It just shows ye never ken even your own weans. I would have thought it of any of the others, but no Effie, even although their father's never given them any rope. But no her. She aye kept to herself, that's what I thought, different from the others. But she has no been at all—just like any other lass when any other lad crossed her path."

"You mean," he said, staring at Erne's mother instead of the cradle, "you mean you think they had to marry."

Rachel shot him a pitying look.

"Ay, of course yon's what I mean,"she said roundly."What would they be getting marrit for at their ages if it was no that they had to, and him even startit work? Her father says the MacLintocks can look after the pair of them and what's on the way, for he'll no raise his pinkie to aid them, and that she's no to think she can have it here. They're coming to Faal next week, brazen as bulls, but her father says he'll no let them across his door."

"The MacLintocks will surely not close the door on them," said Bartle in the same slow voice.

"Effie said in her letter they would gang to them. They have a bigger house than this, although her father says if it was the size of the laird's he would no have them."

"He feels it very keenly, her father, doesn't he?" remarked Bartle, concentrating on the shepherd as a helpless cripple might on a slightly lame man.

"He's black affrontit," Rachel informed him. "I kent what he was thinking before he tellt me when we were in bed at night, awa' from the weans. That bad blood will come out. He's thinking of the man I tellt him had gone to Canada. And he's glad she's no his, although he has fathered her in his home as though she was. But she was aye separate was Effie, mebbe because there was longer atween her and Andra than atween any of the others. That's why she has been a sore disappointment to me. What the Wains must feel, after spending all that good money on her. But they aye put a good face on things, I'll say that for them. They let them be marrit at Victoria Quadrant, to make it look respectable, and there was a letter from Lady Wain this morn, saying what a bonny bride Effie made—-just as though she was."

"They're of a suitable age for each other," said Bartle, while his thoughts painfully assembled to wonder was it because of the difference in their age that Effie had forgotten him and married someone else. But she had loved him since she had been six—how could love with years behind it thin into nothingness at the first breath of parting? If it had been true love, would separation not have acted like lock and bolt?

She had loved him since she had been a baby of six— that was not love but hero worship, a child's bright eyes spinning a halo round her dominie's ordinary head. In his absence, his place had been filled by reality, John MacLintock who had had down on his upper lip before he was fifteen.

"Their ages juggled thegither would no make sense," Rachel said darkly with such emphasis that he knew she was quoting her shepherd husband. "Why could she no wait a year or twa instead of burdening her life with weans before she's out of her teens? And her wha could have made something of her life with all the leaning she's had."

"He is older than she. He is to blame more than she," replied Bartle, levelling out his mind, as though thought by that trite process he would not have to do with anything other than a deadly sameness.

"That's no what Mistress MacLintock will be thinking I'll be bound," retorted Rachel. "She'll be telling her man it has been Effie's doing from start to finish. Effie marrying the saw-manager's son is a better match for her than him marrying Effie, she'll be thinking. Ay, but Effie might have marrit anybody had she only bided an found a good job for herself. Ye're aye reading in the papers about lords and folk like that, when they're old as the world, marrying their nurses and the like."

"You must tell Effie I was asking for her," he said suddenly standing up.

"Ay, that I will," Rachel agreed willingly. "Good-day to ye, Mr. MacDonald. It was reel nice of ye looking in."

\* \* \* \*

He wondered how he would ever reach Tornichon. There seemed little point arriving anywhere now. Instead of life unwinding on a continuous thread, he found himself with useless ends and pieces in his hands. The future when he contemplated it at all enveloped him like a winding-sheet, but there was no dead body with which to enwrap it to get it out of the way.

174

What he was feeling he saw pictured on the landscape around him. How had he ever felt rejoiced by these far-flung uplands or seen anything but monotony and melancholy in these wastes of field, fold and marshland? Everything was rain cold and, instead of green, looked fish grey. It was as though what his grannie called the socking of the tide had passed over it all, leaving it drained of colour and of life. This was not land or ground, this was sediment and grounds found at the bottom, at the foot of everything.

Even when he saw Effie coming along the open road towards the schoolhouse, he did not feel his heart thrust like a knife at his side. He was seared as ground that could only produce rock. The road being so level, all who came along it were outlined against the sky, so that for a few seconds, while they were on its crown, boys running to school bulked like men, while a flock of sheep were haloed where they caught the horizon as though they had merged into one.

Now, before the level road dipped, Effie was rimmed brightly, and he was reminded of how, when he had been herd and lain on his back on the grass, he had seen a flower span and engulf the heavens. She was walking swiftly, but the schoolhouse, because of the flatness of the road, looked as deceptively near as she did, and it took her some time to reach it.

He had caught sight of her out of a side window and stood watching her approach. Once when he could bear it no longer he went into the kitchen and pretended to do something. When he returned to his stance, she was near enough to see her features. He remembered thinking that Lorna Wain was like the berry and Maysie Wain the flower; now as he looked at Effie, he saw she had something neither of them had ever had, as though she had gathered into her slender compass both flower and fruit.

He went outside as she approached the schoolhouse. When he moved down the long unwindowed lobby to reach the door, he heard her light swift footsteps like heartbeats. He stood outside in the middle of the road and when she saw him she stopped dead, as though her heart had stopped beating for all time. He was near enough to see the fineness of her hair that had clung to his hands like silk, but although she was almost as close as touching, he knew a river surged between them, a river they had used to sing about in the barnlike church between Barnfingal and Auchendee, the river mortals were afraid to cross and on whose brink they trembled. He was not afraid, but he knew the river between them was all brink and there was no bridge across.

When she spoke she was not apologetic, placating or gentle. Her words seemed to be pulled from her, like flowers torn up by their roots.

"Why did you never tell me you were my father?" she asked hoarsely.

He stared at her down the road. The miracle was happening as it had happened thousands of years ago when the waters divided and a people had crossed over to the other side on dry land. She thought he was her father: all he had to tell her was that he was nothing of the kind.

"Whoever told you that?" he said incredulously.

She could not speak and he took her to the seat he had made for her. It was against the end of the house, whose stone gable was bare as a stable. The ground rose steeply there but with his long step he was able to include the hummock in one bound. He liked to do that, for the mound had always reminded him of her because it was white with daisy heads, and he would have thought tramping on them was like tramping on her. He had placed his seat here that in the evening they would be able to watch the sun set over the shallow land, making each pool and puddle glint like the scales of a fish, glancing on bogs and filling them full as rivers and lochs with light.

She turned towards him on the wooden seat, pushing her hair behind her ear with the flat of one hand, an unconscious gesture that tore at his heart because it was what a child might do—or a woman bemused with age.

"Why did you not tell me you were my father?" she cried again, as though that were the groove her thoughts had worn and they could not escape from it.

"Whoever told you that I was?" he demanded.

"Lady Ninian of course," she replied, "and Mr. Blair, when I asked him."

He stared at her, his brow so puckered where his fair eyebrows invisibly met that it looked bored.

176

"But what does it matter who told me?" Her voice shivered and splintered in his ears. "What does anything matter except that you are, and you never told me. You let me go on thinking that——" The words choked in her throat and she could go no further.

"Lady Ninian!" he exclaimed at last. "How dare she tell you such a thing."

"Better she tell me than nobody tell me," she cried, beside herself. "Better I know, than I go on thinking my lover and not my father is waiting for me. I did not love you as a daughter loves her parent. Surely you knew that, you must have known that."

How she hated him, how she must always have hated him— Maysie Wain. He saw that now, as he thought back.

"It is an unwise enemy who under-estimates the strength of his opponent," she had said to him that day in his mother's cottage. This was her method of taking revenge on a life-long enemy—to separate from him the girl she knew he loved.

But he would tear up her falsehood and plant in its place the flag of truth. More easily than she had lied, could he now prove to the girl beside him that he was not her father.

In his haste to demolish once and for all what lay between them he turned to Effie, to shatter her with the truth. But even as he looked at her he felt the words he would have said storm together in his mouth and pile themselves, one on top of another, to form a barrier.

He saw the wedding-ring keepered by the insignificant engagement-ring on Effie's finger. The truth was not going to undo her marriage. She would still be John MacLintock's wife after she knew that her one-time dominie was not her father.

If he told her the truth, would there be any chance of even mediocre happiness with the boy who was now her husband? It was not his fault she had married him when she loved another man. Such was the effort to hold back what he longed to tell her that Bartle felt the sweat spring from his body as warm as blood.

"Why did you not return at once to me?" he shouted at her. "Why did you take from her what you should only have taken from me? I was the person, the only person, you should have faced. Why rush into a marriage with a boy you did not love? What sort of wife do you think you will make him who never did you any harm, except care for you as much as he will ever care for anyone?"

"I'll never love anyone as I love you," she said, her gaze intent on his face. "I know I couldn't. It was wicked of me to love you as I did, as I went on loving you even when I knew you were my father. What had I to live for? Could I stop loving you as I had always loved you the moment I knew who you were, even although I knew such love was wickedness? Is love a clock you can put off and on at will? I have not found it so. Was it not fairer to become John's wife than to return to a father you loved as a lover? I would never have married him so quickly if it had not been to help him, and I was glad to help him since I could not love him. The Wains offered him a post in one of their shipping-offices abroad, but only a married man could accept it."

He ground his teeth to keep the groan within himself. The effort seemed to rive him in two: he felt he would never come together again, but always remain disjointed, split, broken.

He should have known what Rachel must know by this time, that Effie had not married because she was going to have a child. She had married John MacLintock "to help him", unaware that Lady Ninian had brought their marriage about.

In the pride of self he had thought himself immune from anything that Maysie Wain could do; he had believed that he had left her with no ammunition to mount any attack. Self-centred in his own way as she was in hers, he had not realized that she would fashion her own weapons.

"I never want to see you again," Effie was saying beside him, "I never need see you again, for we are sailing for Calcutta in October. All that is behind me now, as much behind me as it ever will be." Her eyes widened as she thought of what lay behind her. She looked at him over her peaked shoulder. "You didn't mean to do what you did, did you?" she asked. "You didn't realize what you were doing, did you? You loved me as a father loves a child, and I thought you loved me as a man loves a woman. I should have known, I should have seen, I should have felt, but my caring for you as I did, as I always did from the beginning, must have blinded me. My love for you was older than I was. I have a lifetime now to grow accustomed to do without it."

He hid his face in his hands. He had big, strong-looking hands, but he knew as she looked at him that she suddenly thought how old he was, his broad shoulders bent, his hair so fair it might have been white. He felt old as granite, with his manhood flattened and fossilized, but he had enough surge of life within his veins to wish that she did not think he was old, to agonize over that being her last memory of him.

It tormented him in the days that followed. He felt he could bear anything, thole until doomsday, if only Effie could discover that he was not her father. He strove to reach her with his thoughts, to send them crashing out to her, to roll them like boulders across the space that divided them, but it was more than space that divided them now and he knew he was his own boundary he could not break through.

Sheep were supposed to leave their dead, and graze as far from them as they could. But he could not leave his, for wherever he pastured his dead lay there, making sterile each green field. He realized the reason of this was because he had no dead to inter, whose grave he could keep green with his tears. He was his own dead, and he could not leave himself. Wherever he went he carried with him the weight of his own tomb.

For now he knew why this calamity had befallen him. It had not fallen upon him so much as been brought about by himself. He was harvesting now the sin he had committed all those years ago with Maysie Wain. He had thought that lay behind him but he had been forced to learn that sooner or later what lies behind has to be faced: it could not be shut away as though it had never taken place.

Even the comforts and consolations of religion evaded him. He felt he had done nothing to earn them and that was why his soul received no succour from what had refreshed it in the past. Yet he clung to his religion as the one thing that gave a pattern to his days, a set to his thoughts, as a wanderer might watch from afar the lantern lit to speed other travellers home. There was nothing like home about the country in which he found himself now, a land stripped of everything but roots, with not one familiar landmark or even a milestone in sight.

Father Owen arranged an interview for him with the Abbot of the monastery at Fort Halliam to give classes in higher mathematics. Bartle imagined when the suggestion was made that he would be wanted to instruct the novices, but the priest told him they had their own master and no outsider would be allowed contact with them. The proposal was that during the holidays he should give certain classes to the monk who taught mathematics in the school. Fort Halliam was too far away for Bartle to attend each day, particularly when the classes would have to be fitted in not to disturb the monk's horarium, but Bartle was to interview the Abbot when arrangements for him to stay at the inn or hospice could be made.

It was spring, and when he entered the monastery grounds he saw rings of daffodils growing where the moat used to be and round the great boled trees, with clumps of crocuses at their far-reaching roots. He met some visitors returning from seeing over the church, and held open the gate for them to pass through. Their voices, gusty with talk as voices are after a period of enforced silence, pursued him up the avenue like echoes.

The yellow-green of unfurled leaves fretted against the grey stone of the buildings; and the combination of young leaf against stone lent an unearthliness to the scene, already enhanced by the deepening hour of twilight. He did not know which buildings were the hospice, the monastery itself, the school or unfinished church; he saw movement in none, but he had no feeling from them of deadness or even withdrawal. The evening light glanced from the many windows and as he recalled the voices floating back to him from the gate, he thought it was the world that had withdrawn from this place not it from the world. Despite their seeming emptiness, there was nothing blank about these buildings; instead he was aware of an absorption so eager it was akin to exhilaration.

A bell chimed the three quarters from some hidden tower, it was not a particularly beautiful-sounding bell, but it suddenly supplied the simile he had been seeking. The life lived behind these walls was as enclosed but as vibrant as the inside of a bell. Music would sound totally different in a belfry, where it was rung out, to what it would sound without.

As he approached the door to which the avenue led him, his face lifted to the unseeing windows, he concentrated for the first time on the life lived in a monastery, a life moulded to a required shape within three heavy shells smoothed to the core, strung between heaven and earth, where the terrible act of suspension had the same impact on the individual as the clapper has on a bell.

A monk showed him to the room where he awaited the Abbot. There was little about the room to reveal it was part of a monastery; it might have belonged to anyone whose piety infringed as little on his business-like tendencies as his business-like tendencies infringed on his piety.

The silence of the place eased and settled round Bartle. It was a silence so deep it had no disquietening effect upon him. He felt lapped by it, as though he were inside a water circle, a circle that increased its circumference for as long as he waited——

He was unaware of anyone's presence until he heard movement at the door. It was the Abbot who entered. He was not a tall man and his habit made him appear burlier than he was. If the face to its owner is like the tide-page to a book, then the Abbot's could not be said to speak volumes. As there was plenty of room in his mind, so there appeared plenty of room on his face. He had no gestures and there was an orderliness about his presence that slowed Bartle's thoughts as he looked at him. Here was one who, not torn with travel, was reaching his goal in measured footfalls.

"You are Mr. MacDonald of Tornichon school," he said once the door was shut and he was well inside the room.

"Yes," returned Bartle, continuing to stare at him. "Father, I've come."

# Epilogue

"BARTLE," Father Bernard repeated thoughtfully after the child. "And is that your only Christian name? Then what is your surname?"

"MacLintock," said the boy.

As he wrote it down in the attendance-book, the monk remembered he had been told that the new boy's parents were Protestant but they wanted the child brought up in the Catholic faith. Because he was so young, they preferred to think of him in a Benedictine community rather than at an ordinary boarding-school.

"MacLintock," he repeated, as he blotted the name. "It rings out like a spurred foot, or a horse's hooves on a country road!" He did not add, raising echoes all the way. He shut the flat book and looked down at the child. "Your people live abroad," he stated more than asked.

"Yes, in India," answered the boy, confident enough now to be discursive. "But not my two brothers—they're both at Glasgow University. They're called John and David."

"They must be many years older than you," said the monk, lifting the desk lid to put the book inside. "And where did John and David go to school?"

"At Faal. They stayed with grannie MacLintock, and she stays at Faal."

"John and David and you are fortunate to have a grannie waiting to hear all you have been doing since last she saw you. Is grannie MacLintock the only grannie you have?" but even as he asked the question, he knew the answer.

"Yes. Mummy's-grannie died before I was born. I never knew her, but John and David did. I was born over here, but it is so very long ago I can't remember it, only India."

Down the draughty corridors of time, Effie reached the man who was now Father Bernard as near as she could ever reach one who for long had been walled off from the life of common-day, which meant that she reached him now merely as an echo, a hurry of footfalls on the other side of a door, and then silence.

Rachel had died when Effie was at home with her. She had told her daughter her father was Alfred Wain, and Effie had realized why the dominie she had loved and who had loved her had been unable to deny parenthood when she confronted him as a married woman. She had gone to Tornichon to see him, and heard he had been for years a monk in the monastery at Fort Halliam. She had called her youngest and best beloved child after him and sent him to be brought up as near to him as possible.

"You've a finger off," the boy pushing against his knee was saying. "Mummy's teacher had a finger off too. She says he was the lealest man she ever knew, but he's dead now—long ago. Fancy, he lost his finger when he was just my age, letting a fox out of a trap. How did you lose yours?" His small dark face was avid with interest.

"Surely your mother's teacher was older than you when he tried to let the fox out of the trap," replied the monk. "You're eight, aren't you?"

"Rising nine," said the boy, and added to prove it, "eight and seven months."

"Eight and a bittoch," acceded Father Bernard. "Eight! That's a fine age, a braw age to be! I'll take you down to the refectory now."

As they passed along the broad passage, they moved in and out of the sun striping the cloister wall through the windows with wide bands of light. The child trotting beside him was thinking that Father Bernard's habit made a sound not unlike his ayah's sari at home. He had always liked that sound because it had meant light coming into darkness. Father Bernard of course was enormous compared to Baba. Walking beside him was like walking beside a tower or a pillar. His hands were hidden in his wide sleeves and he must have been thinking of something very far away for the boy had to bump against him to attract his attention.

"There's one striking," he said. "I'm thinking of Matthew," and he squeezed his eyes tight shut to show how hard he was thinking of him.

But Father Bernard's thoughts were not far away: they were as near as thunder to judgment-tied mountains. He was thinking not of Matthew but of his Master, whose words Matthew had stored. And as he remembered them, "Heaven and earth shall pass away, but my words shall not pass away," Father Bernard's eyes were wide open.

WS - #0020 - 140224 - C0 - 229/152/11 - PB - 9781904999775 - Gloss Lamination